Born in London in 19 … the author of over thirty titles, many of … genre. His education was broad … England, Ireland and France … from 1950 worked at va… …urants throughout Europe. It was … …ntinent that influenced the style and s… …it books. The first of these was published in 1961. … wn for the creation of Inspector Piet van der Valk, an … e detective engaged in ordinary crime, political intrigue and international affairs. Freeling is married, has four sons and one daughter and currently resides in France.

BY THE SAME AUTHOR
ALL PUBLISHED BY HOUSE OF STRATUS

The Back of the North Wind
Castang's City
A City Solitary
Cold Iron
Criminal Conversation
Double-Barrel
The Dresden Green
A Dressing of Diamond
A Dwarf Kingdom
Gadget
Gun Before Butter
The King of the Rainy Country
Lady Macbeth
Lake Isle
A Long Silence
Love in Amsterdam
The Night Lords
No Part in Your Death
Not as Far as Velma
One Damn Thing After Another
Over the High Side
The Pretty How Town
Sandcastles
The Seacoast of Bohemia
Strike Out Where Not Applicable
Those in Peril
Tsing Boum
Valparaiso
What Are the Bugles Blowing For?
The Widow
Wolfnight
You Who Know

# This Is the Castle

Nicolas Freeling

HOUSE OF STRATUS

First published in 1968



This edition published in 2001 by House of Stratus, an imprint of Stratus Holdings plc, 24c Old Burlington Street, London, W1X 1RL, UK.

www.houseofstratus.com

Typeset, printed and bound by House of Stratus.

A catalogue record for this book is available from the British Library.

ISBN 1-84232-846-8

# Part One

# One

The alarm went off at six; Dutheil got up at a quarter past, obeying movements long since formalised into a ritual.

The alarm-clock itself, for a start, had to be the right kind. Many had been tried. Modernistic ones with angular shapes and distorted faces, things that made tea if you allowed them to – and poured it all over you, as likely as not, said Dutheil: a man distrustful of machinery and frequently disturbed by uncanny tricks machinery played on him.

Or dear little gold ones with elegant corseted waists and enamelled faces painted in vivid Limoges colours, coming out with grave miniature chimes. All had been discarded crossly after a brief experiment; they didn't let him sleep, or they didn't wake him up, but they were none of them things you could feel confidence in. It had to be the alarm of his childhood, a pale flat-faced thing complacent as a halibut and much less good-looking, which ticked noisily on the painted wooden dresser (one leg missing, a small billet of firewood serving as crutch) with an insistent clack, very like the farmwife's wooden soles on the kitchen flagstones. On Dutheil's bedside table, Louis XVI, mahogany with a marble top surrounded by an ornamental pierced-metal gallery, this alarm-clock was plain eccentric.

Self-consciously so, people might think, even Laure, his wife. Not that she said so; she hadn't, she wouldn't; she never did. He would have said that the clock had character, like old steam locomotives and kitchen stoves, cranky pieces of machinery that recognised and obeyed one hand only. Such clocks were always half an hour slow, however often you sent them to the cleaners; to make the alarm go off at six one had to set it at twenty past seven and nobody else knew the secret. Laure would have been amused, for he was very like a machine that only she knew how to make go.

A ritual. The moment his hand cut off the jangle, which had to be done in two seconds even if one were lying on the wrong shoulder, he would stretch out on his back, sink into billows of luxury, making himself a present of the most pleasurable ten minutes of the day. Poverty – wasn't it Henry de Montherlant speaking? – is forgotten under the bedclothes; admitted, he hadn't been thinking of Dutheil, who was a popular novelist with plenty of money, who lived in a manor house with a formal garden, and an estate, with vines and everything, and a view of the Alps as well as the Jura.

At ten past six the billows stopped, replaced by a pleasant veiled haze; dawn of a new day.

A bright new day – the sky is blue
The storm is gone – the world is new.
This is the Castle of Fountainblue
All this, dear children, belongs to you.

His eye checked that it really was ten past. Sometimes it was only five past, and those were the best days; a sign that he was in form, that the razor was sharp, that he would work well, that for a few hours at least he would not be attacked by any mortal diseases. At a quarter past exactly he threw the bed-clothes back and allowed fresh air to invade his stomach; he detested pyjamas and had to have all the windows open at night, an Anglo-Saxon habit which Laure had thought dangerous and unhealthy when they were first married. She had got used to it.

He dressed; when poor he had been addicted to silk dressing-gowns, for that was something you had when you were rich. Now that he was rich there was no need of such things. He went down through the hall to the kitchen; luncheon in the chateau, and dinner even if there were no guests, was eaten in the formal dining-room, where the Louis XVI mahogany furniture was so raspingly severe that nobody could possibly eat breakfast there. An irritable, queasy-stomached perfectionist, he could only endure the kitchen at breakfast-time, and then he could only endure it if he made the breakfast himself.

It was a nice kitchen with a floor of smooth hexagonal red tiles in the Provençal manner, and it was surrounded by sculleries with flagstones and marble slabs, where food could be kept without recourse to hated frigidaire. The huge range was solid iron; it burned gas – he would have preferred to burn wood but the Spaniards would not stand for it. Always the worst of servants; they ran your life for you. The best he had managed was the wood fire in the big salon, which had a carved stone chimney-piece that appealed to some Spanish instinct. An altar, perhaps, to which they presented offerings with austere, baronial ferocity.

Dutheil ground his coffee by hand, too. He did not have earthenware bowls to pour it into, for that would have been affectation. Blue and white porcelain, and a big-bellied coffeepot. Large plain traditional cups, a pleasure to arrange on the bare table. Spaniards at least liked pine tables, and understood them; the smooth-scrubbed wood smelt beautiful. He poured two cups, slopping one, so that he cursed, and had to rinse it under the tap. He took a cup up to Laure who was asleep but woke at once as she always did. 'Thank you darling.' Smell of warm sleepy female in bed; nice smell but he was now in the mood for bare scrubbed pine tables. 'Morning, darling.' He kissed her forehead; it was all part of the ritual.

Downstairs it continued. He sipped his coffee and took it into the library, where he drew the curtains, undid the Chubb bolts (which set off the burglar alarms but Laure, accustomed to this, switched them off from the head of her bed), opened the French windows, and pushed back the heavy wooden shutters. He finished his first cup standing there on the terrace, looking out to study the day: it was going to be a very nice one, a soft sweet September morning perfect for ripening the grapes, still knee-deep in dew but promising to be hot. He put his cup back on the kitchen table, unbolted the door, and not bothering with a jacket crunched in his slippers across the courtyard. It was gravelled, not paved; he would have preferred it paved but the cost of flags – he wasn't having any cement paving stones – frightened even him. It was one of the long list of things that needed doing before he could feel satisfied with his castle.

He went on across the courtyard, through the gate out into the village. Here everybody was afoot, had been for an hour. Tractors rumbled down the street, paying no attention to him; he did the same thing every morning. In the baker's were three old women; he waited patiently through small talk in *franc-comtois* dialect, soothed by another good morning-smell. The village shops were not impressed by Dutheil, on principle; and had no intention of hurrying to suit him.

'Good morning, cher monsieur,' in exactly the same voice that she had just said 'Au'voir, mame Machin' – a voice he liked because it too was exactly the same every morning. 'What's it going to be?'

'Nice dark brown ones.'

The flour all down the front of his pullover delighted him. Laure, with poppies and cornflowers embroidered on her corn-coloured dressing-gown, was pouring out her second cup of coffee. His daughter Véronique, in black stockings and a tartan skirt (she was just seventeen), was drinking her first, with her portable radio on the table in front of her. The noise it made was never very pleasant but today seemed better than usual; he was relieved. She gave him a perfunctory kiss and he was even more relieved. She wasn't in an impossible mood, then.

'No croissants?'

'They were too hot still, just a bit.'

'Oh well…'

She broke the still handwarm bread, slapped butter on it, dipped it in her coffee and crammed a huge piece in her mouth, Dutheil watching indulgently; child had the digestion of an ostrich. She appeared tousled, but not objectionable; her black strong hair – his hair – looked splendid even combed as it generally was with her fingers. And at least she smelt pleasant – in the last year Véronique, mercifully, had taken again to washing.

'What's it like out?'

'Perfect.'

'Perfect for going to the baker,' tartly. It was a big grievance; the village was twelve kilometres on twisting country roads from the outskirts of the town with its schools. Her brothers, at the university, had progressed to the dignity of a deux-chevaux car, but Véronique had to travel on her little Solex put-put bike and when it was cold or rainy this was a hardship. Girls were no longer forbidden to come to class in ski trousers, but she still had to swallow a lot of bracing fresh air before eight-fifteen in the morning.

'Really perfect. No wind and not yet hot.'

They had a flat in the town two minutes from the lycée. The boys often stayed there; Véronique could never see why she should not be allowed. Dutheil's views on teen-age girls by themselves in flats had been the beginning of many rows.

'Isn't that Ella Fitz?' The radio was making a new, nicer noise.

'It is,' rather condescendingly; 'how did you know though?'

'Well,' a little nettled. 'She was a big star when I was a little tiny boy. I agree that I'm fifty, which to you is Methuselah, but if she has the secret of eternal youth why may I not try too?'

'She takes pains to stay modern, that's the difference.'

The mood was not impossible, no, but it was tetchy and on such a nice morning he could not be bothered; he decided to change this conversation.

'Do you recall that marvellously funny photograph of Marilyn, Laure? – like a baby, naked on the piece of black velvet; rather lovely she did look. Rather a clever fellow – to get her into the right frame of mind, he said, he put Ella Fitz on the gramophone. "Begin the Beguine", I think.'

'I love the bit where she goes up high,' said Laure, buttering bread.

'You've got it all wrong,' said Véronique scathingly. 'Was Artie Shaw – had to be a sexy piece. You might call it sexy, I suppose,' in a snubbing voice. 'Not quite corn but a ham sandwich on rye,' blowing away crumbs and drinking the last of her coffee. 'Take more than that to make me sexy is all I can say, even on black velvet,' picking up her briefcase.

Dutheil, whose famous memory had been caught out in a mistake, was irritated at this infernal knowingness.

'Hark at the expert,' with heavy pettishness. He regretted it the moment it was out of his mouth, but Véronique always did have that maddening trick of making him do things he regretted. She was now, plainly, extremely insulted; that was just too bad. She walked slowly over to the door, buttoning her jacket.

'Balls to you,' she said calmly with her hand on the catch. 'Self-satisfied lecherous old fool that you are.' And slammed the door behind her to give it emphasis. As though it needed any, thought Laure despairingly; that's torn it.

He was too startled for a second to have any reaction. Then he felt wounded at being startled, and indignant at being wounded. Very indignant he pushed his chair back though it was already far too late. The chair made a loud indignant squawk on the tiles and the Solex sputtered outside in the court, in mocking laughter.

'Pay no attention whatever,' said Laure quietly and very quickly, 'I know that it was unforgivable but believe me – pay no attention.'

'But I'm not just saving face, damn it.'

'Don't be wounded – you can't be that easily wounded.'

'Being wounded is not the point. Do I really have to stand here and put up with behaviour like that?'

'You don't have to stand at all; it looks ridiculous,' pointed out Laure, always so damned reasonable. 'She was wounded – she's greatly taken up with her first lover, and is sensitive on the subject.'

'She's always being wounded – I'll show her something before the day is over. She counts on my forgetting everything, on my not having the energy to be bothered – on my forgetting any insolence after half an hour to calm down. On my being preoccupied with work – anything. Well I'm not working, and I don't intend to forget.' He was working himself up.

'I do agree rather,' said Laure vaguely, paying out line. There had been many of these episodes – she felt pretty confident that he would not go on being ruffled. One couldn't go round storing up grievances over a girl at a tiresome age.

'The boys were never like that,' truculently. Oh no? she thought – so much for your famous memory, always so conveniently selective.

'Contradiction, yes, answering back yes – but they kept at least some notion of respect.'

'Aren't you going to call them? I'll get Leonarda moving on the library; she inclines to be lackadaisical recently, I notice.'

'Yes yes; I don't intend to get pushed out of my own kitchen. Pour me some more coffee.'

'Nobody's pushing,' said Laure peacefully. 'It's only a quarter past seven.' It was a flutter before the feathers subsided; only at seven-thirty would an army of Spaniards arrive, wanting the kitchen to themselves. 'Heavenly day it's going to be,' she went on, 'if breakfast was an hour later one could have it on the terrace.'

'And I'd get no work done.' He relented a little; Laure had not been irritating. 'It would be rather nice, wouldn't it – brought by a Negro page-boy, like the first act of "*Rosenkavalier*".'

The thought of the Negro page-boy consoled him, so that he pottered off quite amiably to tell the boys to get out of bed. Notorious over-sleepers the pair of them; now he never had rows with them – why was that exactly? They were amiable and easygoing, they were old enough to have learned some tact, they were too lazy to be aggressive, but this was only part of the answer surely.

Or was it that they were so like Laure? That was part of it, he thought – they were very like her: they had her small wiry build, her clever short hands, her straight fair hair, rather lank, inclining to look dull. They were ordinary... Everyday looks, everyday intelligences the pair of them, middle-of-the-roaders. Neither had any interest in literature, but he found that easier to forgive than their apparent lack of anything spiny, spiky in their characters. They were a vague disappointment to him – they were so irritatingly safe. One could rely on them to pass their examinations and never marry the wrong girl – and that was not like Laure, who had been so particular to marry the most unsuitable man in sight and throw up her whole gleaming career to run after Dutheil, that fly-by-night, that do-nothing-good. She might lack his vagabond streak, but she had always been grateful that it was there!

They took, perhaps, more after Laure's parents; pair of bourgeois, both of them... Yet he was proud that they both did well, following peaceful courses at the university that would lead to vaguely scientific careers, wrapped in a haze of jargon which he could not understand, so that he felt impressed despite himself.

They were asleep in the same room – window open he was glad to see: no sweaty socks here. Odd that they preferred to sleep in one room and work in the other, together at all times, since they were supposed to have loathed one another for twenty years, but there never was any accounting for what one's children did; he sighed, thinking of his adored Véronique.

He punched Daniel, the nearest and eldest, in the ribs.

'Hoy. Hop hop – nearly half past seven; Susanna will be making coffee.'

'Man,' peacefully, 'do that again and I'll break you clean in half.'

'Good, but beware of the cowardly pamphleteer with no muscles but a naughty pencil.'

Jean-Luc now shot very suddenly indeed out of bed. Very gaudy pyjamas – both seemed to be going through a dressy phase just now.

'Oh – Mutti – I was supposed to be in town at eight.'

'You might have told Nique,' amused. 'She'd have called you if only for the lift – she's gone on the bike, in something of a pet.'

'I wouldn't tell that one the time,' said Danny placidly, 'it becomes more insupportable each day.' Both were now looking at him in a way he interpreted correctly as a wish for him to buzz off. You've called us; all right, but don't stand there now being all wide-awake and matey, went the message. We wish for privacy and not conversation; besides we are not interested in Véronique's misdeeds.

Very well. They were polite! They spoke to their father and to the Spaniards with the same Spanish politeness. They showed no interest in his doings, and he doubted whether either had ever read one of his books! Probably thought them hopelessly old-fashioned but were too tactful to say so. He felt grateful for these qualities which were surely unusual at that age. One believed in being outspoken – 'I speak my mind…' – a lot of good that did, to be sure. He had never fussed at them; perhaps this was their way of showing gratitude. He wished he could stop fussing at Nique.

On his way to his bathroom he stopped at Nique's door, which stood, of course, wide open. Window tight shut, the slut; one might have guessed it. Decidedly stuffy – now good, he would respect her privacy just as he would the boys', but in that case why leave the door wide open?

He could supply the answer without trouble – because she was like him. Why else was the door open and why else was there a mess; books, records, and dirty brassieres slung about everywhere? And she looked like him – she even had his big peasant hands of which he was so proud – working hands – and she so mortally ashamed.

Iñez wouldn't touch that room; last time she had tidied it Véronique had made a scene.

'Very well,' Laure said calmly, 'you will simply do it yourself and learn that bad-mannered sluts are rarely appreciated by their families or friends. And you will kindly apologise to Iñez at once.'

Must have been the word 'friends' but it had worked; she had spoken very prettily to Iñez, who forgave all, of course; the Spaniards had a soft spot for Véronique. He felt, indeed, that they took her side against him; absurd, that.

The day had a shadow on it; it would help if he cleaned his teeth, which he did, staring in a raw looking-glass lit by raw horrible strip lighting in the dark little lavatory off the hall. Too much trouble to go upstairs to his own bathroom, which was very belle époque: he glared irritated at the horrid glass, wishing it would suddenly shatter into a thousand fragments. Quite annoyed when it refused to obey his will he stumped off to the library and work. That would fix him up!

# Two

It was certainly going to be a hot day again. At seven in the morning, though, in Paris, the moist grey pallor of the sky seemed unpromising, and the two men in the car, chilled in light summer suits that already had a crumpled look, were in an evil mood towards everything, even one another. Both had the dry tight faces that come from getting up, earlier than accustomed, when liverish from too much whisky and too little fresh air the night before.

The two men had to catch a plane. Nobody who has to catch a plane in the early morning is ever in a good mood; the maddening hurry followed by the aimless hanging-about; the rudeness on the ground and the false geniality in the air; the depressing atmosphere; that awful airline coffee…

Added to all these grievances they were late. Marc Sabatier, who was sixty, did not enjoy being hustled at any time, and Robert Thomassen, the American, was feeling anti-French. Understandable that instead of conversation there were two cross monologues going on, breaking out into muttering every now and then.

As always there were roadworks. They had to make a complicated detour, threading through unheard-of back streets round the Porte d'Italie; the arrows that stood about saying 'Autoroute' and 'Orly' looked even more than usually improbable: had small boys been amusing themselves during the night?

The tyres of the big Citroën hissed on brief bits of asphalt, rumbled on cobblestones, and squealed at corners Mr Sabatier was taking too fast. A maze of red and white metal barrier appeared; the car dodged about in it like a rabbit and plunged into a tunnel plastered with yellow reflectors. Sabatier heaved a deep groan and disregarded several notices telling him to keep within 60 kph. Within a minute they were on the autoroute and breathing suburban fresh air, a yellowish grey haze smelling of chemicals. The Citroën, an expensive model suitable to a prosperous publisher, ran very fast indeed, but all the time gained was lost again at Orly – it always is; crawling about on one's hands and knees, looking for a place to park. Clutching crammed briefcases the two men scurried along the interminable corridor, pursued by the voice of the girl controller, through a nightmare series of loudspeakers. 'Will passengers who have still not presented themselves at the boarding gate please do so without further delay.'

The irritable, now breathless muttering increased as the girl tore their passes rudely in half and pushed them through the door, where they were kindly allowed to stand in a smelly bus, everyone staring with deep dislike. Mr Sabatier was an old hand, leaping very spryly off the bus, sprinting up the metal stairs, saying 'Good morning, good morning' to the stewardess with a false brightness that equalled her own, and bagging the best seats. After an interminable wait, punctuated this time by the noisy unwrapping of sweety-papers, the plane made a shocking din, Paris was gone, and everyone looked, with the always-new astonishment, at blinding-blue sunlight and cool green forest. No more cement-dust; it has all been worth it after all.

'That,' said Sabatier suddenly, pointing, 'is the Castle of Fountainblue – next stop is quite a fair imitation.' Thomassen smiled; he had been hearing about this. The two men were on their way to visit a novelist who lived at the other end of nowhere – they would have a long boring drive in a hired auto after their plane landed, and the prospect had not improved the early-morning irritability. Things might be better when they got there; Sabatier had said, vaguely, that the fellow lived in grandiose style with a horde of servants: it seemed paradoxical in a man with a reputation for living in tightly-wrapped seclusion, avoiding journalists like the pox.

Thomassen was a New York literary journalist, a mixture of Jewish and Norwegian, tall and heavy-boned, about forty-five and looking conventional enough, with horn-rimmed glasses. He had rumply boyish hair that worried him slightly because it was beginning to slip backwards; at fifty he would look a lot more Jewish than he did now.

He was a fairly common type of literary man, who does not make much money from novels, despite rave notices and a big critical reputation, but quite a lot from journalism. Editors wanting a think-piece on Castro's educational policy or social legislation in Chile often thought of Thomassen. More to the point at present was a reputation as an expert on Literary Europe: he had had a Guggenheim grant, had spent two years in Rome, lived a year in Paris, done postgraduate work at Oxford, could whip you out five thousand words on Malraux or Moravia without taking his hat off. This time his mission was quite pleasant, remunerative if boring; a series of exclusive interviews with novelists. Almost a holiday really if it were not for all those bitty little plane-trips.

'Try and get them a bit younger,' said the literary editor, taking the cigar out of his mouth and waving it about (they had had a pleasant little literary lunch and were now getting down to the subject). 'A few obvious locomotives at the start to build circulation, but Simenon as the heir of Balzac – it's all been done rather, hasn't it.' Heavy sigh. 'I'm counting on you to give this series freshness, a vivid quality; let's see.' He put the cigar back in to aid thought, scrabbled about, and came up with a felt-tipped pen, bright red. That's vivid enough, thought Thomassen, reminded of the horrible bottled cherries put in drinks to make them more expensive.

'Perhaps we end up with Russia as a climax, but we start with a Literary Common Market, ha.'

'What's young?'

'I suppose under fifty – under forty if we can find them, but not a lot of geniuses every goddamn literary agent in New York has already turned down,' tilting his chair back and playing with a rubber band. 'What's that phrase? – saw it in somebody's catalogue the other week – "Unreadable and for me that always does sort of spoil a book". Intellectual and popular together – Lawrence Durrell but not of course English-speaking.' Very well, very well, it had all gone on rather, but they had picked five or six. Since coming to Europe he had done a dozen and this one would be the last; the editor had liked it. They would perhaps be called 'Conversations with...', and the series might last three months.

It had been Sabatier who had suggested Dutheil. Sabatier was a friend; he had even published one of Thomassen's books. He himself had been against, at first. Dutheil seemed to him a bit cheap, a bit second-rate. Not perhaps slick, but decidedly over-popular, he would have thought. And wasn't he a bit old?

'Fifty.'

'I'll see what my editor thinks.' Dutheil was certainly highly thought of in America.. The editor had been oddly enthusiastic.

'Yes yes, by all means – don't interrupt me please, I'm talking to Paris – sorry, what was I saying? – yes, excellent.'

'Not a bit Greene-and-water?'

'No no, my boy – where is it he lives, Switzerland?'

'Somewhere that direction.'

'Jump on that plane.'

He had gone back to Sabatier and had gradually become interested. There weren't that many interesting ones under fifty... The crackly tissue-paper young women who ran publishers' press services had showered him with so many self-important young men. When he thought of that frightful pretty boy of twenty-four...

'He's not exactly easy,' said Sabatier, taking a large drink of whisky. 'Got precious little use for journalists.'

'That'll be a change.'

'In fact you'll only get in at all if I push you in,' rearranging the flower in his buttonhole, now wilting a little.

'Mm?' a scrap ruffled. Who was going to turn down a three-thousand-word feature, exclusive to the biggest circulation in literary America?

'Neurotic about privacy, that's why. Never comes near Paris, gives no interviews – make rather a catch for you.'

'Not sure I want it that badly.'

'I'm a friend of his,' said Sabatier, paying no attention. 'I stay there sometimes – rather nice. If I say simply that I'm coming for a couple of days – I have some business to talk over with him – and that I'm bringing you, making no mystery about it, I think he'd be pleased if anything. You make a refreshing change from the type of total clot that pelts about asking writers whether they like their eggs boiled soft or hard. A couple here have been eaten alive by Dutheil in the past – rampants.'

'Rampants?'

'No, of course, in English it means the opposite – here it means servility; creeping basely upon your stomach in the presence of huge sales. Dutheil doesn't have any vanity. You'd amuse him, I think, and that way you'll get a lot out of him. Really he's intensely open and trusting, spontaneous to the extent of being childish. Realising that he wraps himself in these idiot barriers of equally childish cunning. The initial impression is of someone with crafty slit eyes peering out through an arrow-slot in the tower, whereas really it is a small boy with its head under a blanket. I'll get my girl to ring his secretary.'

There was apparently no impediment to Monsieur Sabatier popping down for a day or two and bringing an American friend; Thomassen found himself curious.

The plane arrived about nine, when Marcus discovered that his stupid girl had forgotten to ring the car-hire company. He was unperturbed, insisting on going into the town anyway, installing himself in the best hotel, and making a monstrous fuss about bacon and eggs, a Parisian eccentricity received with resignation.

'When I travel I do so in Anglo-Saxon style. Why have I not a chauffeur with a wicker picnic basket? I wish to wash, get uncrumpled, eat breakfast, and read the paper in comfort after jouncing in the infernal flying-machine; my equilibrium is disturbed and I must recover tranquillity of soul. This is a pleasant town – do you know it? – no? – we'll have a little stroll to settle our digestion while those wretched people find us a reasonable car; they offer me a resplendent choice of tin cans and I've told them to go away and meditate upon their sins.'

Thomassen, with a sober Norwegian streak in him somewhere, felt that this time-wasting was immoral.

'I thought we had a good way to go still.'

'So we have. Over hills too; all bends and kinks, ghastly – this is the far frontier, my boy. Dutheil likes to believe that the railway age has not yet arrived; sweaty and dishevelled guests tumbling in on top of him wouldn't be the thing at all. Arrive in a carriage, or possibly a sleigh, in mid-afternoon.'

'Afternoon!' Thomassen was aghast.

'In the morning he works, and sees nobody. We're not invited to lunch; he won't have anyone at lunchtime, which is sacred. We aim at appearing about three o'clock, fresh and disposed.'

'With our copper-engraved ivory calling-cards.'

'Get out of this habit of bustling about,' said Sabatier indulgently. 'I know a good place for lunch about half way.'

'I feel,' stopping to look at some distant Alps, 'that I'm on my way to Berchtesgaden to call on Hitler.' Sabatier found this a tremendous joke.

'Ha – we'll tell him that. Just so, but this is his countryside, his house, his life – he's not pretentious; on the contrary you'll find him engagingly simple, but you have to do this job on his terms. You're not paying three thousand dollars for a half-hour interview. You're a guest. You stay the night – two. Not three; the guest is fish; stinks on the third day. You'll get nothing whatever in a hurry. Take it easy, the house is delightful, the food excellent, we've perfect weather, and the wife is an exquisite hostess.'

'Ah. What is she like? – tell me.'

'Intelligent, attractive; delicious woman. Bill please,' to a hovering waiter. 'What?… Oh, it's ready at last is it? A lot of bloody papers to sign, I've no doubt. Stuff and nonsense, they know me well, I've had autos from them a dozen times. Yes? – where was I? Sweet Laure, yes, very bright but lacks all imagination. Pity, she's his slave, she thinks of nothing else. She sacrificed herself absolutely, you know, she knows it, and she doesn't care. Something rather splendid about her. You think I'm being indiscreet and you're gloating,' arranging himself in the hired Citroën, a cheaper model than his own, and touching the nylon upholstery with deep distaste. 'It doesn't matter my telling you – you can't print any of it.'

'Who else will I find there?'

'The secretary – dear Nora – she's his slave too, in quite a different way, but totally devoted. He sleeps with her occasionally in a detached sort of fashion.'

'How does one tell the fashion?' laughing.

'Oh he told me, in one of his expansive moments,' placidly. 'Then let's see; there are children, two or three, around twenty, that kind of age, students, you know; quite normal, not at all reduced to quivering wrecks. Then there is a horde of Spanish servants, most efficient and delicious – one is wonderfully looked after, you'll see. Leave a dirty shirt on the floor and you find it again in half an hour, washed by hand and ironed.

'Let's see then – there might be a friend or two – the Court Doctor, probably. The local man, but he has a sort of confidential position – comes to dinner every week. Dutheil likes to keep an eye on his health – he's a seigneur in his funny little way. Oh, I give you one very useful tip – don't be seduced into playing croquet. That, you'll find, is proof absolute that I'm on your side and really working for you – I've known bright dynamic young men led away sobbing after being inveigled into playing croquet.'

'You trying to make me nervous or something? Fine countryside, this, in an arid way.'

'Where he lives is rather magnificent. The house is on a kind of spur, cocked up with a fertile valley, thirty kilometres or so, between them and the mountains. Vines on their own slope, farming ground at the bottom, corn, fruit, everything. Woods, fields, and mountains all round. The view from the terrace is staggering – ever seen the Pyrenees from the esplanade at Pau?' Thomassen, who lived in the low thirties between Third and Lexington on Manhattan's east side, with a panoramic view of the power station, was a tiny bit awed despite himself.

'What is this place, a bloody castle?'

'No no, I was joking about that. There is a kind of manor house, bits of which really are Renaissance, but greatly hacked about and restored. All the jokes about Fontainebleau do have a base in fact because here too bits have been knocked down and more bits added every fifty years since the seventeenth century – there were even farm buildings tacked on. Architecturally a mess – not the kind of place the Beaux Arts would get excited about. It was practically falling down and he got it cheap – put fortunes into it since. Mind, there are lots of fine furniture and pictures, and it is a historic house.'

It was getting very hot in the dry plateau country; just as well after all, thought Thomassen, that they had plenty of time. Not a day for hustling. Late September it might be but the sun was spilling thick and golden over everything, almost greasy but not quite – like very good olive oil… There were smells of thyme and rosemary; autumn hay would soon be lifted and the autumn crocus would stand in the fields and it would be chestnut time and mushroom time, but it seemed still high summer. The men were covered in powdery white dust and Thomassen soon felt Norwegian blood coming out strongly. Despite clothes bought for a New York summer he felt dishevelled and sweaty, and was grateful when Sabatier said, 'See what I mean?' in not too offensively teaching a voice, and stopped for drinks and a wash.

'We start to climb now, and it'll be cooler.'

'Can't say I'll be sorry – my shirt is sticking.'

'Remember what I told you – maids will wash it – Spanish women!' with approval. 'Did you bring another suit, by the way? It's just that he likes one to be a bit dressed at dinner time – the only really formal moment there is, in that house, but there it is.'

Thomassen glanced at the publisher with a scrap of amusement. He might not be awed – but he was properly broken in and trained! Not used to being awed himself he was not used to awed publishers either – what was there about this Dutheil that had everyone so horizontal? Just another popular novelist. The road started to wind upwards in shoelace bends, and his spirits rose with it. This was better, at least, than being stuck in Paris, on a day like this.

# Three

From eight onwards the library was his, for work. Eight exactly; the strictest rule in the house was that Leonarda, the downstairs maid, should have this room dusted, polished, and aired by one minute to eight, and not leave any brooms behind, either. Laure, admirable housekeeper, saw to it that there should be fresh flowers every morning – dahlias today, dewy and pleasantly smelling of moist earth, making him feel well looked-after, expensively served: it was expensive, damned expensive – no use expecting him to have guilt feelings about it. It was comforting to feel, this morning, well on top of one's work; he felt in fact today like a schoolboy at the beginning of the holidays. A manuscript had been sent to Marcus a fortnight ago, but, much more important, a new manuscript had been finished yesterday. It was all raw and green still, but it had been put on the shelf to ripen like a cheese. In three months, perhaps, it could be tasted, to see how it was getting on. He had always two or three books at varying stages of readiness, draining as he called it, losing over six months at least ten per cent of their weight as he went over them very slowly, with a cigar and a felt-tipped pen.

Now perhaps he could enjoy a few days' peace. Nique was back at school, thank heaven, and the boys tranquil after three weeks sailing just before the university faculties reopened. Hm, he wouldn't get a few days' peace; he had never seen such a thing in his life. Had anyone? Would there even be one day's peace? He didn't believe it; it was a thing one measured by the gramme, like saffron in the rice. Minutes, seconds – he had known occasions (generally over the drinks, alone with Laure, after work was finished and just before lunch) when he had spoilt it, fragile as it was, by counting the number of seconds, imbecile that he was.

Just like saffron. What was it? – stamens or pistils or something biological of the sort. Pinch the fragile stuff in one's fingers and it became a dust, and the flavour went out of it while you watched.

Never mind. At any second something would come trampling in – a person, a book, a pain, a fear – harassing his skull, heavy-footed, but meanwhile here was a day, and a fine new one. It might perfectly well be his last; make the most of it. Today's thought: live as though you will die tomorrow; print it on a calendar. He opened the French windows, which Leonarda always shut, damn the bitch. The terrace got no morning sun; he walked to the corner of the house and down the steps, which did. Happiness today, perhaps, was looking at trees, leaving footprints in dense, gossamer-decorated grass. Yesterday it had meant much the same thing but yesterday was another matter altogether; today his socks were getting wet.

'Figaro,' he bawled, climbing back on to the terrace. Face filled with disapproval, tightly corked, sealed, and labelled, the Spanish majordomo appeared. 'Bring me those brown shoes, not those veldtschoen things, the light ones – you know which I mean. Hell; do I have to get them myself – the ones that need mending – as you very well know.' The end of this phrase was spoken silently, though he was not really afraid of Figaro. He was not going to stay in the library; he was going out, and snapping at Figaro was on account of feeling guilty. It was sinful self-indulgence. Rather like buying a thick bar of chocolate, with whole hazelnuts as well as raisins, and eating it all alone, yes, every scrap.

There was nothing wicked about a walk, of course; one had to walk. It was just the taking of a walk already at eight in the morning, which was the desperate hour, the hour at which the day's work stood or fell – my, what a mixed metaphor. Working one burnt the nerve cells, and walking replenished them; a simple matter. Seriously – unless he walked, daily, he got horrible miseries, in his liver, his spinal column, an arm, a knee. He didn't know where it would be, but it would be painful as well as a worry about arterial sclerosis or something. Going for a walk already is indecent, and that is why Figaro is making such faces – what a time the imbecile is taking, with those shoes.

There were three kinds of walk. The first, and most frequent, was a working walk – but it was not a walk at all strictly speaking. It was a polar-bear, a nervous pacing about when he did not know what was going to happen on the next page. In wet weather, on the terrace, the length of the stone balustrade with the ornamental urns. (These had always contained geraniums, which he had recently decided were corny. He had had them replaced by spiky fleshly agaves, but was not at all sure this was a success. So far he had been obstinate in keeping them because everybody else detested them; perhaps he might keep just one, say the one on which he had carved his initials and the date. So exceptionally childish, said Laure crossly. Yes, but necessary.) At these times a little stand-up desk was brought out – like Charles Dickens giving a reading – with an exercise book and three or four coloured ballpoint pens. If it was moderately dry, the desk stood on the gravel of the box walk, in the formal garden (carried out by Figaro).

The formal garden, with yews, cypresses. and stiff flower-borders, was at the bottom of the lawn to give a good perspective from the house, and terraced into severe horizontal steps. The lawn, beginning at the terrace, flowed down to the line of clipped box, and out at either side, flooding out like a sea to the trees. It was anything but horizontal, and was full, with a carefully artificial naturalness, of bumps and hollows, which was one reason why he was unbeatable at croquet. Half way down, at one side, was an absurd little hut of wood with the bark left on. It was an idiot thing, a blot indeed on the view, but there was nowhere else to keep the deckchairs as well as the croquet things…

He did not pace about on the lawn, of course; the constant polar-bearing would wear the grass out. In a morning he might walk up and down fifty times, on the terrace or on the box walk; that was what he had bought them for... To walk up and down on, the knife sliding over his fingers; under, over... it was the one thing he did not lose and never had, because it had quite literally never in his life been out of his reach; it lived in a special inside pocket.

Children often have these fetishes, over which the psychiatrist nods wisely, but Dutheil was more interested in adults who had one, and when he met such persons his eye became a tiny crumb of glass, exactly like Long John Silver. He did not play with his all the time, but only when working. It was a tiny African dagger, from somewhere on the West Coast, a narrow leaf of bluish steel set in a wooden handle that was sewn into tight-wrapped leather ending in a heart-shaped knob. The leather sheath had a strap with a clasp that fitted over the haft and pinned it into place. So fine was the workmanship that the whole thing seemed one piece; so well made was it that forty years intensive playing had not frayed it, nor ever would.

The thing was not much more than the length of his hand, a big hand like a mechanical grab; he had been terribly self-conscious in adolescence about his great raw paws. He had admired his mother's hands, Van Dyck hands in lace cuffs; he had been nineteen before coming across a Picasso drawing of Igor Stravinsky playing the piano, or his hands, rather...they had comforted him. He could not play the piano, himself, but he was pretty hot with a ballpoint pen or a croquet mallet. The fetish, this morning, sat in his pocket as it always did, but he gave it no thought; he wasn't working, this morning.

The second walk was different altogether; it was the Tour of the Domain, and went down to the river. The Seigneur quite often carried a little rifle on this walk, to pop at pigeons and things. He liked to feel his feet buried in his soil, so hardly won, so completely unsubdued.

Beyond the garden were fields and trees, all his. They sloped down to the bottom of the valley where the river lay ravelled and twisted, piling itself up with drift against sunken willow snags, getting in its own way with sandflats and gravel-bars – a nice little river, one of the hundred odd fed by the snows of the hills, flooding turbulently every spring into the tussocky pockets of marsh yellow with kingcups. It flowed shallow and talkative over stone, turbid and narrowed in earth – there was one place he knew where you could go in clean out of your depth.

On his ground the loops of the river enclosed a tangle of willow, alder, and evergreen oaks. It was a playground: a pity that the children were too old to play with it. He played with it himself, and had spent, sometimes, marvellous hot still hours with Véronique; not for some time now, he thought wistfully. There was a swimming-hole, and tree-houses; a decrepit canoe and a waterlogged punt; there were secret paths and lairs; there was even an outcrop of the hill, a rocky mossy bit full of feathery poison-green fern, with a cave. He knew where to find orchises, horsetails, kingfishers, and herons, and how not to stumble suddenly knee-deep in the boggy bits. Nobody else ever came near the place, for the far bank, which was not his, was muddy and soggy, alive with mosquitoes and dragonflies, choked with scrub. The river meadow beyond was full of marsh grass, not much use even for pasture, and the farmer did not even bother ditching it for drainage. Only occasionally in autumn might he come squelching down in his rubber boots with a dog to shoot a few ducks; the river bank was alive with game and Dutheil had often got hares and pheasants there; ducks were a lot harder to shoot, and without a dog harder still to retrieve. If one lay up in the tree-house one might see the otter, and at twilight, if you didn't mind being eaten alive by the mosquitoes, you might see the enormous ghostly shape of the grand-duke, the terrifying and magnificent owl.

The third walk, which he had decided now to take, was a serious affair, for exercise, up the hill instead of down it. The view from the terrace, not even half way up the ridge, was merely spectacular, whereas that from the top of the Whaleback was quite simply beautiful, magnificent as the grand-duke, cruel and noble. One looked across the valley to the hills (so-called; they went up to two thousand metres) but twenty kilometres beyond were the mountains, marching ever higher as they curved away southward. Three ranges, distinguishable in certain kinds of weather, which he had special names for. Violets dim – he had never looked to see whether he had the quotation right; he wasn't writing it down or anything...

The nearest was the blue range, colour of the eyes of unfaithful husbands. Always visible save in mist or rain-cloud, and from its look one judged the weather. Second was the smoke range, nearly always visible from the Whaleback but more rarely from the terrace. These mountains were the violets dim, sweeter than the lids of Juno's eyes. Farthest was the high range, of snow and ice; the pearl range, very high, always visible but clear only on special days. Cytherea's breath...

Today one could see two; the third was wrapped in the shimmering haze. Above was a huge bare bright sky – it was tough, hard autumn weather, the sun a hammer at midday and already burning off the whiteness which brought the thermometer down to three or four degrees at dawn here so close to the hills. Another week and the whiteness would be no longer dew but frost.

There was a wind up on the Whaleback. There always was; today it was the slow northeaster that reminded him of the story in Kipling; the wind that meant that Thor was about. He stopped at the top, puffing just a bit; his terrace lay perhaps two hundred metres above the river bottom but most of the climb was in steps. Going up was more gradual and more steady, levelling off four hundred metres above the plain. The village lay below him, red and grey, lichened, mottled, patched here and there with newer redder roof-tile. The opened book, spine uppermost, of the Romanesque church, thirteenth century. The little needle spire of greenish slates, rounded and tightly overlapped – that was the Reformed Church, showing how near they were to the Swiss border. Dutheil was fond of both, but never went near either save in an occasional, furtive way; he was deeply frightened of churches, which might reach out and grab you.

Beyond the village rose the steep-pitched slates of a Renaissance roof – the 'chateau' – his house. A rhyme came into his head – some children's book? – something Véronique had had, that he used to read for her. A bright new day, the storm is gone…

The storm is gone – he had it – the world is new.

> This is the castle of Fountainblue
> All this, dear children, belongs to you.

Of course – Ludwig Bemelmans had written it for Madeleine and Pepito, when they woke in the caravan of the gipsies, in the Forest of Fontainebleau.

On one side of the house massive walls enclosed the kitchen garden and the orchard; on the other his vines marched in orderly rows up the hillside. The formal garden, and the wilderness, were masked by the house itself; the eye ran on down to the fields in the valley bottom, and the pollarded willows showed the idle serpentines of the river.

From up here one could count forty villages, said the locals; he didn't count them and never had. Spreading over the flanks of the Whaleback were the best fields of the region; vines on the lower, steeper slopes where the road went down in switchbacks between the copper-turning foliage. Corn, maize, tobacco on the upper levels. He liked it up here, by that absurd pigeon-house tower he was fond of. It was exercise, of course, his three kilometres up and three down insisted upon by Gilbert Royan, his doctor, so approved of, so necessary – but he liked walking; he would, he was sure, be in a bath-chair in a few years and he wanted to get the most out of walking now. (He had planned the bath-chair long since, a curly one of wicker-work, shape of a seventeenth-century Dutch sleigh. One would skim like a swan, steering with a slanting, ornate iron bar. How would one skim? He was damned if he would be towed by a perspiring protesting Figaro – perhaps a rather old pony, such as drew the children in Victorian fiction in what was called the governess-cart, whatever that was. Or goats? Perhaps a donkey!)

He was not, however, going to be enslaved to exercise as though he were some damn footballer. He came here for purification. Wasn't it Kipling, again – a writer he admired – who had spoken about a webbed and inward-turning eye? Better phrase than neurasthenia, that idiot word; so typical of modern medicine to conceal its ignorance behind phony and pretentious Greek.

It was not only the eye – there was a blindness and a deafness, combined with a migraine, that miserably acute over-sensitivity to light and sound. Sometimes a paralysis – how terrified he used to get, before he understood it, finding he could not move a wrist to write with, or that he could scarcely drag one leg forward to set in front of the other. He was used to it now, as he was used to the boodie-man, the Balrog – well-known figure admirably drawn by James Thurber, who is just about to grab the innocent bourgeois stumping along – his wife is just saying, irritably, 'You and your premonitions...'

Sometimes it was a frenzied irritability, a general attack by Itchy Powder – brought on invariably by trifles, such as the wrong salt at table – whoever had heard of eating fine salt with boiled beef. Or the two pencils – both used, both broken, and neither re-sharpened. One had to remember what the little doctor says to Marlow, in *Heart of Darkness*. 'In the tropics the most important thing to remember is at all costs to avoid letting yourself get upset.' A writer, ha, lives permanently in the tropics.

Sometimes it was violence; he was capable of it, alas, and had known himself glad when shaken by rage that he was so scrupulous about always keeping the rifle unloaded. Once – though that was long ago, when they were poor, in the Whitehawk days – he had hit Laure, really hard, slapped her spinning. She had crouched there silently while he stood paralysed by terror. She had packed her case, strapped it to her bicycle and wheeled it out before finding it had a flat tyre and starting to cry, out loud, in tearing sobs, finding she could not go, knowing she could not go, knowing she could not go anyway, would never go. Nowadays he had taught himself a lucidity that prevented real violence. What was it – a sense of proportion, or a sense of the ridiculous, a kind of deflation of swollen vanity? It was called sanity but who knew what sanity was composed of? He didn't, Gilbert didn't, it was good and sure that psychiatrists didn't, with their lunatic urge to explain everything.

The little doctor… Everything to a writer was larger, more coloured – and more dangerous. The tropics: life here is cheaper than a box of matches. Incident became catastrophe; the mosquito bite that became blackwater, the thumb-scratch that would be general septicaemia in three days. Accident became crime. You let a gun off at a scuffle in the bush – that marauding baboon again, perhaps even a leopard – and found you had killed a villager who was recapturing a strayed chicken.

He had slapped Laure, a real one, crack, along the jaw and temple; stop her infernal yap. An explosion; she had gone staggering and sat on the floor – it had cut off the flow, all right. Cut off the flow – he stood paralysed at seeing not the crying girl on her knees but a tumbled bespattered heap: blood flowed, not words.

She had accused him in her cold logician's voice of all his little dishonesties and mean infidelities, his stony selfishness, everything that bit into her, crunched and ate her. And he knew it all to be true; that was why he had flared in sudden untenable anger. Dangerous when one lives in the tropics. He had felt his neck swelling. And if he had had his fetish, his little dagger, in his hand? Or a gun? He would have cut her down, blown her in half, anything to keep that dreadful voice stilled.

And his ever-ready, ever-willing imagination provided him with a weapon at once. They were in the bicycle shed; he had been chopping firewood – the little axe was under his hand. He had killed his wife and massacred his own life. She was dead, so fatally easily. The police would now come, and listen patiently, bovine and intelligent within their trained distortions, while he spluttered the ludicrous explanations.

'But I am a writer – I live in the tropics – life is precarious, here. I would never wittingly kill her; I love her – can't you understand? – I killed her because I love her.' It was not their concern to understand; it did not interest them. McNaughten Rule; did he distinguish between right and wrong? Clearly: very well then, no more to be said, is there?

'But that has nothing to do with it – oh, why can't you understand?' Not interested; tell the judge. The judge – god…'

For ten seconds he stood shaking, teeth clenched on the hand that had hit Laure; ten seconds in which to recite the whole of *The Ballad of Reading Gaol*. There is no chapel on the day on which they hang a man. The chaplain's mouth is far too dry, and his face… Laure got up and stood unsteadily.

'I'm leaving you. You might have killed me. You hated me so much that you would have killed me.'

He had gone on standing, hardly listening, knowing she was not dead. But it had been so real; he saw still with dreadful lucidity the squalid year before him, waiting for the Assize Court, waiting in Reading Gaol for the quiet, polite little man with the tiny suitcase who would come one morning. The Governor came, too. What did he say? In France they didn't tell you the day; they woke you bluntly – and was that not more humane? – saying 'This is the time to show courage – now, today, this minute' and then gave you a glass of rum.

'You have been a model prisoner, my man, and given no trouble. I am sorry it has to end like this.'

Poor Governor – his mouth is far too dry. To be able to spit while walking to the machine – that is what proves courage, say the hard boys: try it. Laure had gone to pack her suitcase before he had cleared his bemused head and known she was alive. Just your silly, treacherous, childish imagination. Writer? – don't make me sick… A writer learns to discipline it.

Learn to discipline your mind. The important thing, in the tropics, is to keep calm at all costs.

The cure to every ill was the ridge of the Whaleback, especially the tower that stood at the top in a patch of weedy ground marked '*Terrain Militaire*', in all seasons and times, when the sky was wrapped in scarves and hazes of every colour, and he examined the flowers growing round the concrete bunkers; from the Hitler time, buried now in clumps of elder, hawthorn, beautiful nettles – like André Gide he loved nettles. Those exquisite elder flowers, charms of white and green and cream. Kipling again – the charm was to take of earth as much as either hand could clutch – how did it go? Was it not for that, that he had bought the chateau?

And the others – the poppies, the eglantine… Kipling, mind, could be awful; in his rhetorical vein he ranted like Hugo. Violets from the undercliff, wet with Channel spray – *qué*, violets! He had lived there, he knew the path between Black Rock and Rottingdean as well as Kipling had. Violets, indeed!

About the poppies he knew a better poem. 'Mine in my cap is safe. Just a little white with the dust'. They grew and blew all about the tower, a fine example of between-wars French military thinking; an inflamed octagonal of purple brick hung about with ornate bartizans – one would swear it dated from 1870 but for the carefully incised date, proudly saying Nineteen Thirty-Seven… It was amusing to see planes fly over; one looked at the tower, and back at the plane, the slim silver dart, proudly modern, quite as out of date as the tower really. A big four-engined thing was lumbering across the sky at this minute – good grief, antediluvian, though it had been the last word ten years ago. Pile of junk – his contempt for planes was equalled only by his hatred of cars; christ, the horseless carriage, could there be a more nineteenth-century notion than that?

The land was more stable. Down the slope a peasant woman was doing something on her hands and knees, with a white handkerchief over her hair, a Chardin – a Breughel, come to that. He turned slowly to look east. Haze and dust hid the valley where it broadened, where the city stood over towards Switzerland and the cathedral reared up and pointed a finger towards God – damned uncomfortable sight; he hated the east; neither fair wind nor good marriage. No, his eye had to point south towards Rome; this was Roman country. He did not like Celtic countries, all pixies and hobgoblins, wild hunts and headless horsemen. His was a weathered land, smooth, rubbed, very heavy and very light, like a Louis XIV commode.

The absurd tower was an anchor. He was frightened of God, of that awful finger in the east searching him out and pinning him down. One had to have a philosophy, if only to serve as a cement – and what did he have? – the world spun, faster and faster; the centrifugal force was colossal and one had to cling to anchors. Everything burst and flew apart in fragments, whirling in specks of pathetic dust like a plane, a fashion, or a popular novel. Marvellous communications we have; get Hawaii on the television by satellite but we've no contact at all, we are utterly isolated, as far apart as an American President and a Vietnamese peasant. Is that why sex is so important to us? – it is about the only form of real communication we have left…

The birds were making an infernal racket. He did not care for birds; to the lark in the clear air he preferred the silent sparrow-hawk. The Americans called a silly woman a birdbrain; how right they were. The stupid way they flew, the idiot noise they called song – and was there anything to equal the self-satisfaction of a hen – of course, a pheasant. The vulgar gluttony of a thrush? – sure; a seagull. To make a pie of four-and-twenty blackbirds – such a good idea – had not, obviously, always been an idea that upset the English: feeling sorry for birds was, very likely, a consequence of the Industrial Revolution, like putting petticoats on sofa legs. Much refreshed by this notion, and wishing he had a gun (there was a strutting thrush, just the type that takes a bite from every cherry), Dutheil began walking back down the hill.

# Four

My life, thought Laure, rooting in the dirty-laundry basket to make sure that Dutheil was still wearing summer shirts all day, is in essential exactly what it was twenty-three years ago. Then I was poor; now I am rich: I see no real difference. Doubtless it will be the same twenty-three years from now: let's see – god will be seventy-three, I'll be sixty-seven, a meagre but active granny. Need to be active – there'll be nobody else to push him in his famous bath-chair. I'm the type that goes thin rather than thick, and I won't have a discontented mouth. He goes around thinking all the while he'll die tomorrow, whereas I know perfectly well I'll still have him around when he's eighty, thinking up new places to live, unable to find his fetish because unable to remember what jacket he was wearing, worrying terribly about his virility because he can only manage to sleep with me twice a week.

This made her smile, so that Susanna, Figaro's wife and the 'camerista', looked cross and suspicious. As inquisitive a biddy as stepped, she could not abide other people thinking and not to know what about. Her name, of course, was not Susanna, but even Figaro called her so, having entered joyfully into his adopted character. She was a squat bun-faced personage given to thinking that dignity should be equated with working very slowly; and plainly, the position of camerista was one of great dignity. Not just laundry queen, not just sewing-woman, not just Laure's personal maid, not – quite – housekeeper: yes, it needed a good deal of dignity. The absurdity was that without understanding the joke in the least, for neither Mozart nor Beaumarchais, predictably, entered into her scheme of things, being 'Susanna' played a large role in her life, putting Dutheil, who detested her, into stitches. She referred to him as 'Señor Conde', and addressed him as such to his face. Laure often thought of telling her that he was supposed to have designs upon her virtue; it would make for an amusing situation surely.

One had to scoot Susanna along a great deal. The other two Spanish women, divided roughly into upstairs and downstairs, did all the housework, and 'Il Cuocco' (god's phony Italian!) lorded it in the kitchen, so that slowcoach had really nothing to do at all but wash, iron, and mend, all of which, indeed, she did very well if only one had enough patience. Dutheil hadn't; Laure had. That was one lesson she really had learnt in twenty-five years, although he was not by any means the first tiresome character she had learned to grapple with; her own dear mamma…

Laure did not complain about being rich, nor about this preposterous house, nor about the ghastliness of running about after servants. She had equipped herself with the necessary tools; for instance, since after eight years here and three in Lausanne Susanna could not speak a word of French, she had had to learn to talk a slow, careful, accurate Spanish, excellent on technical things like buttonholes. Abstract conversation would have been something else again, but as Dutheil (who pretended to know no Spanish, the crafty little boy) pointed out, abstract conversation is not part of the opera. Mister Gigadibs the literary man illustrated with a tag from his old Browning. 'What's the Latin name for parsley?' he declaimed gleefully. 'What's the Spanish for Swine's Snout?'

The two women were going over Count Almaviva's winter clothes. Because the weather was very hot it might suddenly go very chilly; then there would be a great to-do. He was convinced that he had hardly any clothes, that he was totally uninterested, but that since it was almost impossible to find anything wearable you must watch anything you have like a hawk, or the women will give it away to the sally army. He never, he said, spent a penny unless in painfully replacing what literally fell in shreds, and was never comfortable anyway except in properly faded corduroy trousers. This was all the 'bare truth', except that Laure knew that there is no falser face than that worn by that tiresome naked woman – oh go and get dressed, do.

The thing was to find the right combination, not only for temperature but for direction of the wind, humidity of the air, activity engaged upon… There were much-darned pullovers (you can't get anything like that nowadays) worn to just the right degree of thinness, there were cotton training-suit days, there were pyjama days – as though he were Almayer or something, said Laure crossly. They all had to be handy, instantaneous, or everything would be all over the floor and Figaro, Susanna, and Laure would all find their heads ringing.

Twenty-three years ago it had been just the same. A coat just right for walking, and a coat just right for going to work on the bike; a loden raincoat that had belonged to Laure's father before the war, and had been kept because 'such good material' despite moth-holes, and, happily, inherited. (It had turned up recently in the summerhouse, where the most peculiar things gathered.) Nothing changed, thought Laure. Nowadays he no longer slept with chambermaids; he slept with Nora instead; comes to much the same thing. She used to worry terribly about the chambermaids, and she had worried very much about Nora. That at least was a step forward; Nora was a good exchange for chambermaids. One could not imagine a more scrupulous person. But Laure could not be sure that there was much real advance. True, the complicated machine grew and grew and grew, becoming ever more decorative and sophisticated – but the castle, now? It was propped up by floods of money and an army of servants, but it seemed to her identical in essence with their first flat: the huge, slightly slummy Regency house – their living-room had had three French windows and no furniture; typical Dutheil.

Laure was the daughter of teachers, from a dynasty of teachers, and had been brought up with one central idea: that she too was being prepared for the noblest of professions. Self-sacrifice. 'In Which We Serve.' The acrid smell of ink and chalk that permeated one's clothes permeated the character too with a certain acridity, which she learned was the smell of nobility. An ideal; for this the hours of piano practice, art appreciation, trying to see why bad reproductions of Raphael should not bore one paralysed, endless blackboard work in a deserted classroom during summer holidays, while less privileged children played under the shadow of the plane trees. Hours of cooking and sewing, with Montaigne's *Essay on Vanity* while the sauce thickened slowly, and Benjamin Constant's pages marked with scraps of coloured thread. What a perfect little prig she had been, thought Laure. When at the university the dawning sensation of being a prig led her into a series of violent reactions, fits of mild religious and political mania that first flabbergasted and then revolted her poor parents; each painful little struggle seemed to them one more wounding betrayal of all they had ever stood for. When – it seemed the one chance of escape from the rigid mould of which she had acquired a neurotic dread – she flung her cap finally over the windmill and married a penniless rootless boy – a barman! – they washed their hands of her. Ingratitude personified; so much sacrifice, so much effort, so many ideals set at nought by this inhuman girl – very well; as you make your bed so shall you lie upon it.

Laure was grateful now – for the lessons in patience, perseverance, and civic-mindedness. One clung to the path chosen, and that despite obscurantist clerics, inbred alcoholic peasants, a feeble government, and the growth of communism in urban slums. A challenge. She had seen straight away that the stuff in this odd, abrupt young man added up to something more than a barman. Right; she was not going to shrink after setting her shoulder to the wheel. It had not been with a romantic eye that she saw him, although Brighton (she had been sent for the summer to learn English) after Poitiers seemed like a big bunch of grapes straight off the vine, after years of grocers' raisins tasting of the paper bag. Still very much of a prig, she had seen the matter as a question of chemistry, and back at the university, hating Poitiers as never before, she grappled with reassembling the molecules in the right order.

It had been no more than a pleasure, at first, to meet someone who spoke French, someone who, it appeared, was vaguely French, who lay on the beach on his stomach reading *La Chartreuse de Parme* – and this was welcome after three weeks of speaking English with a Roedean accent. And in Brighton, being a barman seemed less of a profession reeking of brimstone than it would in Poitiers...

Of course, at first there was a delicious sensation of consorting with the criminal class. A barman! – at home she would have recognised such a kilometre off and given it a very wide berth, trained by injunctions ringing daily in her head since the age of four. In Brighton it seemed so much less wicked, somehow.

Not a bad life, he explained. Much better than a waiter's. You were more independent and customers, even the rude ones, were rarely rude to a barman – drink seemed to have a status higher, mysteriously, than food, and was accorded a sort of respect. He was left much to himself. He was underpaid, but he made it up with tips and sandwiches. Laure, hot on social inequality, wanted to know more, and learned about the hotel business. (Those were the years when everyone was underpaid, but they were also the palmy years before the invasion of accountants; all hotel workers had rope enough to run a barter system of materials and little privileges; there was a healthy amount of squeeze on both the hotel and its customers.) Missionary instinct coming out strong, Laure worried about its being unhealthy, about catching tuberculosis, about...about... No no, he said; pale and thin he might be, but he made the most of his time off in the fresh air, he went for long walks. She soon discovered, indeed, how oddly tough he was under the apparent fragility.

Good days, those. Laure remembered their wedding – they had had lobster for supper, a masterpiece of the barter system; he was on good terms with cooks. Laure, frugally brought up, had never had lobster before. He knew how to cook it, too.

'It is a female lobster – see there, there inside, that is the coral – that goes in the sauce; I'm going to make you a Newburg. Look, I've cognac, and I bought some cream – people don't know how to do it, they think you smash the shell up and make a phony Américaine but that's not classic; Adrien, the sous-chef, showed me. Just a bit of white wine; that was easy; I got it out of the dining-room.' She loved it, but she had drunk Pernod for the first time in her life the same day… How sick she had been – and how gentle he had been…

He used to come home at night, when she had already been in bed for hours; bringing home things for supper – a piece of pâté, a slice of smoked salmon in a lettuce leaf: the pleasure of eating in bed at eleven-thirty at night! Her mother would have condemned such goings-on out of hand: contrary to hygiene, honesty, health, and eventual happiness, and Laure did not give a hang. She waded straight in, to knit him together, to give him a purpose; the ideas about chemistry, organic or inorganic, soon went overboard.

She remembered the stove she had finally found to heat that glacial great room, found at a scrap-metal dealer's, for a pound. She got it up the stairs alone after giving the man half-a-crown to bring it on a barrow. He had been horrified.

'Why didn't you wait till I was home, to help you?' Even then, six weeks married, she had known better than that! He would have broken the stove and the banisters in one climax of released nervous tension. Laure smiled again to herself, so that Susanna, worrying away among the flannelly cowboy shirts, got glummer and more suspicious than ever.

# Five

Doctor Gilbert Royan lived in a house with no view, past the Protestant church and next door (so handy) to the little cemetery. It was just outside the village, where the road along the flank of the Whaleback was hollowed between high banks, and bordered by poplars which made, it was true, a pleasant avenue besides providing much-needed drainage, but in autumn and winter it was a dreary spot. The house, known since always as 'the doctor's house', dated from about eighteen-fifty; it was square and ugly, plastered a vile brownish shade. The wooden shutters were losing their last hard curled scraps of a paint that had once been cream-coloured, and the garden, totally neglected, was full of rank laurel, not just gloomy but downright sinister. Dutheil spoke of this house as 'La Maison des Turpitudes' or 'Villa Ballets-Roses'. The gate, devoured by rust, creaked horribly, or would have if anyone had thought of shutting it. On a patch of damp gravel stood Doctor Royan's two filthy deux-chevaux cars. He cared no more about all this than he did about the view.

'A preoccupation with objects,' he teased Dutheil, 'is the sign of a vulgar and shallow mind, I'm afraid.'

Inside was sombre, but warm, dry, and surprisingly comfortable; he was a good doctor with a large practice. He was sitting in his consulting-room, which had mushroom-coloured walls and dark-olive leather mattressing on the soundproofed doors. There were the usual tomes of medical science which nobody ever looked at, and there was some gay Marseille faience. For some years there had hung a pillowcase, with 'Look, just let me do the worrying' painted on it in mercurochrome, but he had got tired of the joke and banished it to the waiting-room lavatory.

Doctor Royan had had breakfast and gone out early; had indeed visited four bedsides out of hours. If one didn't make an early start one never finished, but especially today; he was going out to dinner in the Dutheil mansion, didn't want any evening interruptions, and was polishing off possible panics in advance. He had trained himself years ago to do with five hours' sleep, but at strategic intervals through the day he believed in fifteen minutes' total relaxation and he was having one of these now at nine o'clock before letting the morning sickies crowd in.

He was a type of doctor, in physical appearance, one sees often; a bald man with a pink cushioned look; face like an expensive doll's behind – Dutheil speaking. He had small sharp eyes of a dim nasty green colour ('pus-coloured eyes') and almost non-existent fair eyelashes. Short, stubby arms and legs – he had the thick column of energy, the big head of steam one needs to be a general-medicine doctor in a country practice. If you're short of animal vitality, he said, become a pill-roller. He had a great deal, including a Bourbon taste for food, drink, and his wife. She had the build for the job too; known to Dutheil as 'Strapping Steffi' she had robust country good looks and a figure that looked overblown in a frock but perfect in a white overall. Marvellously calm on the telephone and a placid nurse, she was a good doctor's assistant. She loathed Dutheil.

'I'd rather read a woman's magazine at home than listen to him talking,' she said, and offered no further explanation.

Royan was Dutheil's age – the two men were friends. By the local bourgeoisie he was thought of as too brusque – not to say rude. 'Horribly casual – but he does give one confidence.' 'A nasty jeering manner.' It depended on whom one was listening to. More plainly he was a good doctor but disliked being called for a liver-attack after eating too much mayonnaise. The villagers got on better with him; he was rapid, brutal, hurt you but cured you.

He was meditating this morning on the familiar theme of Servitudes and Grandeurs. Nora, Dutheil's secretary, had rung him up yesterday and asked him as usual if he were free to come to dinner next day. Strapping Steffi was amiable enough about this, and it could generally be managed, nor was it embarrassing – she knew her talents weren't suited to a house like that and sensibly refused to be bored. It did not matter greatly – despite formalities, Dutheil did not worry if there was not an exact balance of men and women. But he was not thinking about his own servitudes; more about Dutheil's. Over the years the man had lived here Gilbert had found himself becoming, subtly, Court Physician. The man never appeared in the waiting-room, a thing he thought of, probably quite rightly, as making you far iller than you were already. Nor did he phone in a panic to summon one to an imminent deathbed – or only rarely. Instead, from the start, invitations both formal and casual had multiplied. Drop in for a quick drink after your round. Come to dinner on Thursday; I'm expecting interesting guests – a professor from the faculty; we might achieve conversation.

Sometimes there were peremptory phone calls. 'I expect you on the terrace in five minutes – there's going to be a remarkable sunset.' Cunning ones. 'Now you're plainly tired and this will do you a lot of good – a nice game of croquet.' Loaded ones. 'I have unearthed a biochemist, whatever that is. You can come and help find out whether he's really as illiterate as he seems.' Medical gambits were quite often proffered over a drink, sometimes as downright consultations. 'I can't quite decide whether it's my inner ear or my middle ear that's giving me trouble.' More often they were provocations. 'I've been reading; Kipling and his doctor who was a big What, Sir Something, went about capturing hens and listening to their digestive noises. Remarkable; the man was not even competent to diagnose a stomach ulcer. To find out what was wrong with him the poor old bugger had to go to a French doctor. But we are now grateful for incompetence – we might, otherwise, not have some remarkable stories about pain.'

Dutheil didn't have any stomach ulcers. Robust physiology and nothing organically the matter at all.

'Thanks to my understanding of medicine,' he said with his own bland conceit. 'I eat well, I drink well, I fast, and drink tisane. Like Voltaire, who lived to be a thousand. An orderly quiet life. But one must have interests. One must make demands on the mind and everything else will stretch itself to keep pace.'

'Quite so,' said Royan patiently, giving the black croquet ball a resounding thump and for a wonder capturing Dutheil's red, 'but that is all the flattest banality. Simply character, and a coincidence Pascal died at thirty.'

'Because he was determined to be ill. Now Elizabeth had no use for physicians – so sensible of her. Turned on her cushions and died in dignity. Whereas Louis – who certainly was not inferior in force of character – allowed himself to be terrorised by the ineffable Fagon who had butchered his entire colossal family – why? Monks all lived to be a hundred when people scarcely got past thirty. The only advance technology gives us is dentistry – the diseases are all the invention of infernal quacks like you.'

If his arterial tension was good (attributed to eating rye bread, growing one's own potatoes, and walking uphill) the fellow's nervous tension ('For which there exists no unit of measurement', triumphant, as though he had won a point) was frightful; he put as much effort into striking a match as most people did into an hour's work. No wonder he had those terrifying collapses, crawling upstairs on his hands and knees. No wonder that 'Three hours is the maximum that I can support Paris'. It was not always easy to treat these nervous famines; the man refused pills.

'Pity,' said Gilbert, 'that neither Laure nor Nora has any talent as a masseuse. Why shouldn't we arrange for Figaro to have some training? – he's like you; got the right kind of hands.'

'I refuse to be messed about by men,' snapped god: that was that.

'Why not have a swimming-bath installed?' on another occasion. 'That idiotic ballroom's running to waste as it stands. Or below the terrace – it would be expensive but you're rolling in the cabbage.' It was received poorly.

'What, like Jolly Jack Kennedy? – swimming up and down giving interviews to reporters – à la bonne heure. Next thing I'd be dictating to Nora while doing the daily dozen – why don't we have a gymnasium while I'm at it?'

But the man was amusing; Gilbert was always pleased to go. He had dinner at the castle every two or three weeks, bringing his bag, knowing that there would be a casual request to 'look at me' in the library after dinner. And ten days rarely passed without Gilbert's dropping in for what Figaro called 'Cocktails' at seven o'clock. The two men had become sufficiently friendly to disregard each other for half an hour, before some damn coat-trailing idea got launched at him from nowhere.

A good writer? Royan had no idea; he never read books. Secretly he suspected that he might be a mediocre writer. But quick, full of interest and talent and vitality; maybe he was good; Gilbert was no judge of that. He was unexpected – soft as butter and tough as an old belt, tender towards crapulous people and ruthless towards anything good. It showed sometimes in peculiar ways, the unforgivingness towards something very good. He recalled the first time he had noticed it, in what seemed something of little moment.

They were sitting in the hall, watching sport on television; Dutheil was fussy, of course, about television.

'Object has no earthly value except if it's showing you something actually happening. What do they get? Politicians, squalid catastrophes, abject trivialities – or sport. I refuse – except for sport. There is an occasional flicker of art.'

It had been the winter sports at Innsbruck; the men slaloming and Guy Perillat making his second run. Dutheil was vastly excited and even Royan magnetised.

'This is what all those boring Greek sculptors wanted – Myron, Scopas, all that Discobolos crap. Look – perfection of style and essence of combat.'

'He's going to win, damn it,' squeaked Gilbert.

'Of course he's going to win, but who cares about that? He's attacking all the laws of dynamics – look at that; razor's edge. He's conquering life – immortality, lasting fifty-seven seconds.'

What happened? Is one not forgiven for achieving immortality? It lasted fifty-six seconds – Perillat, losing his concentration in the last metres, hooked a ski. It is a terrible thing to see so good a skier thrown in a heap of boneless rags into loose dirty snow at the feet of jubilant peasants – far worse than to see a gold medal won by what Dutheil called 'unheard-of nonentities'.

Royan slapped his glass down, breaking the stem, which gave some faint and gloomy relief but no satisfaction.

'I could weep.' He was disconcerted to see Dutheil sitting perfectly still, lips pinched together and eyes like an angry kitten.

'He didn't want to win,' in a flat, even voice.

'He's always been an unlucky skier,' in a come-now way.

'Afraid to win. Fall like that – fall on purpose.' The tone was so bitter that Royan was a little shocked.

'It's not all that important.'

'You think I care about a putty medal dipped in gold paint?' with a controlled ferocity and cruelty that was disturbing. 'He made something perfect and he threw it away.'

Fifteen minutes up. Servitudes of a rural doctor, thought Gilbert getting up to let in the first sicky; I pay too much heed to the biggest and brightest butterfly in my district. Dutheil is not that fascinating a personage. He is a frightened and vulnerable man who goes to extraordinary lengths to fortify himself against a hostile world, and the castle is – deliberately? – a colossal expense, so that he has to turn out huge numbers of probably rather catchpenny books to meet it. He does it; under what compulsion? At what price? Recently he had found the fellow in that comic library of his, snorting with laughter over his latest reviews, and had decided to be a bit astringent.

'Yours is the kingdom, I see; the power and the glory of the book page.'

'So I learn,' sniggering.

'And what about the kingdom that is not of this world?' A mild joke; he had been disconcerted by Dutheil going white and staring at him.

'Shut up, will you.'

Half way through the morning a phone call asked him to come out and look at another important local figure – in fact a far more 'important' person than Dutheil; – a man known throughout the country and with a reputation even throughout Europe, whose words carried real weight. The local deputy, and the figurehead of a fairly important political group. Good speaker, excellent debater, fine mind – always in the paper, frequently on television – able, very able. He too had nervous diseases despite a physique of pure aluminium; skin trouble that gave him a patchy look, a tendency towards asthma that worried him horribly, troubles with his bile duct: he rode himself far too hard and was a sight more difficult to treat than the flexible obedient Dutheil. Royan liked the man very much, though he did not care greatly for the politician, who had too ready a smile, too ready a reply to every damn thing. He could not stand the wife, a locomotive – pure poison in his opinion, killing her husband by bringing him into conflict with genuine hopes and undoubted ideals. Sad that in comparison to Dutheil there seemed to be an awful heap of servitudes, and precious few grandeurs.

# Six

His legs were leaden before he reached the bottom of the slope; he found the village street toilsome work. He could do with a stick. It would make him look old. Possibly, but he was old, terrifyingly old, even if he was sometimes very young, capable of skipping or climbing a tree.

Nobody in the village paid him more than a glance; very polite but then so was he. He didn't appear in any Rolls-Royce, but on foot or even on a bicycle, and in much the same clothes as they wore. He pottered about, without airs, doing no harm to anyone. He suspected that if he took to a stick like some damn bourgeois rentmaster they wouldn't like it: yes, he valued their good opinion. He might start playing the fool with a stick, pointing it at people – only a step from that to talking about 'my folk'!

What did they think about him? Nothing at all, he guessed; it was quite a corrective to vanity. That he was crackers in a harmless way, but possessed some alchemy for producing gold in the laboratory, like Nicolas Flamel. Fellow writes books – what could that convey to them? A book was the catalogue of the Manufacture des Armes et Cycles in St Etienne – a gold-mine of beehives and mole-traps, gadgets for stringing fence-wire or reloading your used cartridges; a marvellous book, distillation of three hundred years of rural lore, and he only wished his own sold as well. In the country there was only one other book and that was the gentleman from Roubaix with the mail-order clothes. Anything else was something to regard with the deepest distrust. Still, he put the evil eye on nobody, and he hoped that reassured them, believers that they were in books being things that made your brain go Plouf – were they so very far wrong?

He felt old now, as he toiled in at the gate, which wasn't a gate. For eight years now he had intended to replace that farmyard door by something tall and austere in hammered iron; there were so many things. It would do no good anyway – the gates would still stand open all day: no warfare of his would stop the courtyard looking slummy. He stopped in the middle of the yard – court was altogether too rich an expression – feeling dissatisfied as he always did; the garden side might not be too bad but here nothing seemed to alter the mouldy tumbledown impression. The 'big L' to his front and right was patchwork; the Renaissance house buried under solid rural underpinning. Not shoddy – that was just the trouble. Reliable village workmen had made such a good job of turning a seventeenth-century court into a nineteenth-century farmyard that even the Dutheil millions were daunted. The Beaux Arts authorities had laughed humiliatingly; a total ruin would have more artistic worth than this! He had compromised. The entrance was still fine, and the fountain had not suffered too badly even with chickens drinking out of it, and if hay had been stored in the ballroom and cows stabled in the carriage-house that was just too bad; he wouldn't give any balls.

At the left he had modernised the 'little L'. The ugly range of stone with its meanly frowning windows now made quite pleasant houses for Spaniards, and indeed they kept it spotless. He couldn't object to Figaro's band of brats playing in the yard any more than he could to the Figaro granny. Nor to the interminable washing and the incessant shrill gossip. But damn it; he wasn't putting up with toffee papers – place was getting to look like a municipal camping-ground. Not a man to be seen, of course – but there came Leonarda out of the scullery door, struggling with a dustbin. Oh well, no man was helping her either; catch a Spaniard demeaning himself by carrying a dustbin!

'Leonarda, the children must be taught respect for their surroundings – lolly papers in the fountain is downright disgusting and what's all that straw blowing about?'

'They got it for the American pigs.' None of them called him Sir or Mister or anything. They said You; for two pesetas they would have said Man.

'What American pigs?' What was an American pig anyway?

'The children's pigs.' Her nose made a startlingly good imitation of a small animal eating dandelion leaves. Ah – yes.

'Indian pigs – no.' Writer, concerned for accuracy. 'Guinea-pigs.'

'That's right.' Gales of laughter at her mistake. Mm, there was evidently no way of attacking a child's guinea-pig.

'They must be told to get it all away. I help you with your dustbin, and you are responsible for seeing all that muck cleaned up. Fair enough?'

'Fair enough,' said Leonarda, who was getting something for nothing, which no peasant would complain about.

The dustbin had a squalid reek, as the freshest vegetable trimmings acquire, by a detestable chemistry, the moment they are mixed in a bucket.

'What's this?'

'For pigman,' innocently. Aha. Leonarda and her husband, that horrible Cuocco, making money. He saw none of it, of course; they made money on everything but only by closing his eyes to it was he able to suppress the keeping of chickens in the courtyard – pigs, very likely! Servants were outrageously spoilt. Rent free, vegetables and fruit free, wine free, electricity free: what didn't they get? They were scrupulous about ten cents found in his trouser pocket but they loved the idea of making the pigman pay them for his kitchen refuse!

It rankled sometimes. He had been a servant himself, and remembered it well, but these weren't servants – they were his equals in all but name: did that give them the right to play with him? They didn't play with Laure who made them, bluntly, buy their own meat. Though he bellowed at them frequently, as he did at the children or, come to that, at Nora, even at Laure, they took no notice. Still, there was one thing he had arranged craftily. The orchard, the kitchen-garden, the flowers, and the vines came under Kieffer, the overseer, who was Swiss and who detested Spaniards, and to show his superiority over them was forced to maintain a frenzied honesty: the war between Spain and Switzerland afforded Dutheil keen pleasure.

He was tired, his legs were wooden, his face sagged. And here of course came Nora out of her office – her name really was Nora; Nora Noël, improbable as it sounded. She was Belgian, a large, fair, plainish woman given to dressing in an oddly ornate way, on account of which the boys had nicknamed her 'Passementerie'.

'Later, Nora, later; I'm very tired.' He turned sternly back to Leonarda.

'You tell Madame Figaro from me that if I see any more toffee papers I'll come myself with a stick and whack all the children one by one – yes and you too.' This notion of course enchanted her; more gales of laughter. He helped her bring the dustbin to the gate – as though that would help; the pigman would still drive his filthy truck into the courtyard.

His world, over which he was skipper next to God! Nora, who would not dream of answering back, had gone straight back to her rabbit hutch with the utmost meekness. He got the same unquestioning obedience from Figaro, so named because in his estimation the entire Dutheil empire would stagger without his guiding hand: crumble and collapse in a matter of minutes. (One had grown so accustomed to this constant menace of disintegration as to have sometimes an uneasy feeling that it really was true.)

Figaro in the Lausanne days had been a tremendous joke, puffed with importance at dinner parties, humiliated by being valet-chauffeur – Laure had had to tell him that Dutheil was too nervous and absent to make a really safe driver. Later he had become reconciled to the menial duties of valet by his conviction that he knew every fold of Dutheil's mind as well as those in the clothes… Figaro was now also head-mechanic (in pre-Figaro days Laure had been both plumber and electrician but she saw no need to tell him that).

In Lausanne Susanna had completed the menage but for the castle Iñez and Leonarda had been added. Both had husbands, for whom jobs had had to be created – by Parkinson's Law they had all made themselves indispensable. One was the carpenter; he really was, by great good fortune, an able workman and in addition he did painting, plastering, upholstery, and generally stopped the castle from falling down. The other had been much more troublesome – a damn worthless do-nothing: a great expert, according to himself, on melons. They had very nearly been forced to grow melons; mercifully he did know enough to point out that this would certainly be a fiasco. One of Dutheil's major, memorable achievements was to have turned him into a passable cook. (Laure had done this really but it had been his idea.) Elementary psychology, what; to turn the idle clochard into something useful one had to give him a domain, and status the equal of the others. 'Il Cuocco' was a success on the whole; unexpectedly gifted, a great deal better than eating Leonarda's horrible cooking, with him hanging about with his hands in his pockets, heaving great sighs and hankering after melons. What a shocking alliteration, thought Dutheil; one noticed such things automatically: professional deformation.

All this – 'the staff' as Nora called it – was an expensive luxury, as she fairly frequently pointed out. But to the castle it was quite indispensable.

# SEVEN

Nora detested housekeeping: nothing imaginable could be more boring. At the beginning (for Nora belonged to pre-Figaro days of unreliable daily women) she had dreaded coming in of a morning for fear Laure might shove a duster in her hand and say 'Nora be a love and help me get this room straight before Monsieur finishes shaving'. Perhaps this detestation was rooted in her childhood – the sooty streets, and all the house so shining bright; lace curtains offensively starched, pleated like altar-boys' surplices; brass gleaming gold (rusty iron, polished brass, and coaldust was the Belgian flag); linoleum that one might only approach shuffling on felt soles, called 'skates'; woodwork shining and glowing like, like...like what? At a loss to say how bright, one day when Dutheil asked her, she had said 'Bright... bright' lamely. 'Freshly oiled bodies of sunburnt Cretan virgins?' lavishly helpful. 'It doesn't sound very Belgian,' said Nora timidly; she knew she lacked humour – she couldn't help herself. No, he agreed gravely, it didn't. 'You know what my mother used to say? Nobody is ever going to write their name with a finger on my sideboard.' 'How the devil would you do that?' 'In the dust,' not at all sure whether she was being laughed at.

Childhood – starched check apron, with insufficient pocket for ever-wet hanky (spare hanky, dry, tucked in the elastic of one's knickers). Pleated serge skirt, starched white cotton petticoat, navy-blue knickers, always horrible; when old and faded, the crutch bleached to grey, the elastic got slack and they had to be perpetually hitched up under the armpits of little girls with no hips and a bulging stomach. When new they smelt fearful – the whole shop smelt fearful; there was nothing worse than the smell of shops where thin women, faded by artificial light, sold materials to red-faced, sniffing, peering economical suspicious mums, though the child liked the big wooden ball into which the bill was screwed with money. Click, they pulled a string with a handle, and gravely it rolled along a sweet tramway, rolling, rolling towards an impressive glass cage very far away, where they kept money, like a bank.

When new the knickers were sheer armour-plate, bitterly scratchy, leaving fierce red marks on meagre blue thighs. On Sundays there were white frilly ones, starched like the petticoat, equally odious and one was forbidden to play. Only the children of the poor wore weekday knickers on Sundays.

They dictated, it seemed, the whole life and certainly the conduct of little girls.

'Mama, what's a sin?'

'It's a sin to let the boys see your knickers.' This was a hit at Corinne, Nora's greatest friend of the moment, and much disapproved-of; not only were hers black, as though she were in mourning for someone ('her innocence' said Maman, darkly, incomprehensibly), but she was suspected of playing Father-and-Mother, in the coalshed.

It had taken Nora years to get rid of the habit of hitching her pyjama trousers up as far as her armpits; as for the knickers she greeted the arrival of fine weather with joy, because then she need not wear any. Who would know? Dutheil – which hardly mattered, said Nora fatalistically.

Knitted black stockings, square-toed black shoes, scuffed but solid (only the children of the poor wore sabots). Hairy hand-knittted grey cardigan; black sateen overall. Flannelette camisole and cotton underbodice against the winters of Artois that punished disobedient little girls with bronchitis. Soot black; coaldust black, greasy shoe-black, offensive shiny slippery stove-black. Sky was black, nearly.

Soul was black – very nearly. How Nora envied the children of the poor. Even the neglected, *les petits crapuleux*, with perpetually runny noses and – supreme liberty – no knickers. In winter they had strange yellowish knitted things of peculiar shape and holes invariably in embarrassing places, and they displayed the lack of both underclothes and hanky with a superb unconcern. The boys played with them. The boys played with Corinne. Why did the boys not play with Nora? True, she was utterly forbidden to play with them, but nobody forbade them to offer. She played with her doll, slapping it without any real satisfaction therefrom, sitting on the scrubbed-daily pavement and devoutly hoping the boys could see her knickers, but worried, because if they could, so could God.

'*Sage*,' said her mother. '*Mais sournoise*.' Nora knew it was not unfair, but could not work out how to be the one without the other. Good, but sly. Because she was good – and more, perhaps, because her father worked 'in the office' – she was sent to the Sisters of the Visitation; she had to be good, because she knew it was a tremendous sacrifice. The Sisters were the Best; Liège or Brussels could show no better.

Nora knew algebra and trigonometry, and history-down-to-1918 (King Leopold II might have been a dubious character – 'we have no right to judge, my dear children' – but King Albert was indisputably a saint); Nora waved her flag and screamed for beloved Astrid with a fervour outdone by none. Nora knew Maeterlinck and Verhaeren, and Huysmans (only the 'afterwards' bits). Nora knew geography and botany and embroidery.

It was not a university education. That was not something you got when you lived in the Rue de la Croix and your father was a stock clerk. She could not understand how Laure, who had been given such inestimable privileges, could have flung them away. Now Nora would no more have done a thing like that than…than…forgotten to wash, say, undoubtedly the most important thing there was. Not only for Maman, to whom not washing was the first, essential condition of being children-of-the-poor, but also for the Sisters, who made cutting remarks on the subject and opened windows in

January, regardless of the malicious Bronchitis-imp lurking without. Sisters, it was whispered, had to wash in ice-water, which was perhaps why they were at once so sensitive and so ruthless on the subject. It was indeed, agreed Nora, very nasty to sit next to '*les jumelles*' who, too plainly, '*se négligeaient*'.

In the Rue de la Croix there was no bathroom, and of course no bidet; one put a heavy china basin (embellished with improbable burnt-sienna peonies) on the floor, set to work on one's hunkers, and woe woe if the lino got splashed. If your fan was scrubbed so was your soul – or well on the way. The curé might be a bit unsound on this basic point, but even he would agree to the close co-relation…

Nora waited till she was twenty-one before coming to her decision, as simple as Laure's but much more deliberate. Never again would she put stove-blacking on anything, and never again would she endure the stink of the soapy water in which clothes have been boiled. For all these years she had been *sage*, even if *sournoise*. All these years she had obediently lugged the lumping schoolbag with the piano music, the clean napkin, the bread-and-jam '*goûter*' (and the damp sponge in a smelly oilcloth bag), the white cotton gloves and the embroidery. All these years which seemed to resume themselves in Mother Mary Charles-Borromeo telling in an odour of eau de Javel and little girls' *pipi* all about Saint John of the Cross, that disheartening personage. What she was going to do had at least the merit of not being sage, that most negative of virtues. Neither was it sly. She was going to get out. What, wasn't an education something that supposedly got you a husband, even if the boys had preferred to play with Corinne?

She had no clear idea where she wanted to go – anywhere, confusedly – anywhere that wasn't the Rue de la Croix, anywhere the ground had a different colour, a different smell. She did it: snip. It was absurdly easy; a ticket to Liège and the next train south, which happened to be going to Geneva. One's education came in handy straight away, on the platform there in Liège station; she knew all about Geneva. Her English and her German were very fair; she would enroll in a secretarial course, learn shorthand-typing – there would, she was quite confident, be jobs for a girl who could spell accurately in three languages. There you were; away from the eau de Javel one found plenty of reasons for being grateful to the Sisters.

Nora, humble, conscientious and painstaking, had no trouble. People approved of her – and learned quietly to trust her. She had convent virtues – she would have made quite a good nun, she thought sometimes, with a faint tinge of humour. Poor and chaste, but very disobedient. To be shut up with the stove-blacking and the eau de Javel – never, as long as there were fields and flowers – no. But scrupulously honest, and scrupulously virgin.

She worked for a man in Geneva who himself ran a secretarial agency. He had a good eye for a girl; within five minutes of her walking in to ask for a job she had been hired as his assistant. Well – secretary, but after a few months of his finding this treasure among his raw material… It was pleasant work: a tall modern building, an airy office, an interesting job, generous pay, a reasonable employer. It surprised and angered her when she found herself so ready to do something disloyal…

She noticed as time went by that he left more and more responsibility in her hands, while he popped out more and more for 'a haircut'. She liked it at first; she screwed her courage up to ask for a rise – and got it, without demur; plainly he valued her. It seemed ideal; troops of English and Swedish girls on their voyage of discovery passed through her office, where she gave the right touch, she hoped, that would help them; she felt sympathy. Some were hussies, brazen sluts, even downright whores – much good might that do them. Their clothes were sophisticated and generally, she thought, very unsuitable; they pretended great worldly wisdom but brassy or timid, prim or whory, they were all in search of romance, she noticed; hm, she hoped they found it. Romance – yes, she knew about it – had she not herself…? Nowadays, she thought vaguely, she was in search of a more complicated satisfaction; she didn't quite know, but she didn't want to be a nun.

It was a routine assignment, and she had no idea it would lead to disloyalty. Her employer came in with a memorandum. The city of

Geneva runs largely on expensive unnecessary paperwork, he was prosperous, and a thick golden stream of commission chinked on his desk – he had the habit, since Nora had grown indispensable, of going out to long lunches by the lakeside, manicured and smelling gorgeous, driving an Oldsmobile cabriolet of undeniable 'standing'. 'Do a bit of mental work on this, will you?' The casual assumption that her lunch-hour needed a bit of mental work to round it out... It irritated her; she knew the kind of work he did over lunch!

One of his hand-written scribbles. 'Personal secretary – novelist (successful). No literary work as such but close liaison, confidential files, etc. Afternoons, frequent evenings. Lausanne. We are asked to find twelve possible suits who should write hand-written letter (far too many, send him six). Essential: bilingual French-English, tact, discretion. Will handle visitors, journalists, business. Pay nothing startling but prestige work – job rates a B.' Jobs, in the code, were rated A to E. A was rare and flossy, going with lunches-overlooking-the-lake, B was diplomat or senior civil servant, international Advisory-Level stuff; it seemed high for a mere novelist, a bird of which Nora had less experience; what made her curious all of a sudden? Romance? She was far too hard-headed to be taken in by that; novelist indeed! Now why was she curious? – now really; she couldn't see herself being seduced by something with a beard. She went on being curious and it annoyed her, like grit in one's shoe; oh, well – easy to get rid of it. It had come on the telephone; would be on tape.

Dutheil's voice on the recorder was not seductive. She scarcely knew his name; she was no great novel-reader. There was a wife, children, all kinds of snags. When Monsieur Macaigne found out he would be furious – she would be black-listed: adieu the comfortable life, It was going out on a branch carrying a saw; now why, why?

She played quite fair. Eight suitable girls were found: Nora's letter, in her clear convent writing, made nine.

She got a telegram two days later, asking her to come to Lausanne over the weekend, and a week later Monsieur Macaigne was looking at her with the mournful eyes she had seen used on many girls to turn them to jelly; on her it had a bracing effect.

'Who would have thought it of you? Stabbing me in the back like that – I'll never trust a woman again.' She did not point out that the woman who trusted him was slightly misguided too.

She had not hesitated. She guessed that he chose her because she was not particularly seductive, unlikely to be a trouble, a distraction, or unreliable; when he did seduce her she was strangely unsurprised, as though she had always known it would be so – Nora Noël would never make a good nun. This, flatly, was her life's work. She was a cornerstone of the castle, naturally, but she had already been a cornerstone in Lausanne. She had her own small 'flat' in the little L: an office and a room, all done for her by a Spanish maid, who brought her meals on a tray, unless she was having dinner in the house, a thing Dutheil liked when there were guests, so that it happened three or four times a week. Still humble, patient, and anxious to save other people pain, Nora got on perfectly with all the Spaniards. Even with Kieffer – Nora knew how to handle the Swiss. An overseer – it was just the same as the lawyer, the accountant, the bank manager, all of whom ate out of her hand. She even got on well with Laure; as for Dutheil she had never had trouble. Strangely, she even respected him in a way she had never respected Monsieur Macaigne, had never respected her mother, try as she might. And respect, she had learned from the Sisters, was at the root of things. She even respected herself, even if she lived in sin. Sin was a thing one had to live with. Dutheil was the only man she had ever slept with. She knew him well; he could be abominable sometimes but he was so anxious, so frightened, so ridden and ground down by sin. She worried about sin but he sweated blood. He did not go to church but she knew how he was tortured by his duties and obligations. After all these years she had got a bit vague about Saint John of the Cross, but she sometimes thought there must be a resemblance. He was intensely religious, she thought, on the whole. The Sisters might not have seen it but they did not have the experience she did.

# EIGHT

Dutheil went to the library, his favourite room, where he felt happiest. It was of course a beautiful room, next to the salon; it had no boiseries but was panelled, a grave room, high-ceilinged, nearly a cube. It was the library though few books were kept there; it was his working room, and if he became self-satisfied its gravity and severity were the first antidote taken. The furniture was simple, upright – his table and chair were genuine Louis XIII, in the house since always and the best thing there. Everything else, he was painfully aware, including himself, was second-rate. Like the pictures – he would have none here, though they hung in the salon, the dining-room, the hall, on the stairs, and in the first-floor 'gallery' – the pride of the house. The museum in the town had been abominably crafty about those pictures; after years of looking at them he knew that they were neither good nor bad, simply rather dull; a lamentable defeat it had been.

When he first saw the castle he had been impressed, but it was in a filthy state; it was hearing of the picture collection that had tilted the balance. The lawyers – and Laure – had been unanimous in turning it down. Sieve of the Danaides, said the lawyers, rightly (Laure said nothing; she had just looked – but Laure was always right, damn her. Why didn't she make a mistake once in a while? Beside Laure he seemed so childish…). He had been obstinate; the pictures were a great investment. Could one get them back? – that was the thing. They were in the city museum, having been confiscated at the Revolution, handed back at the Restoration, given again under a sort of complicated loan-bequest; hm, said lawyers, the thing seemed possible. He had seen them in dim municipal gloom, with impressive gilt frames; splendid stuff. Chevaliers, companions-in-arms of Francois Premier – must be Clouet. Florid and stupid war-horses of two centuries later in cuirasses and blue satin – Drouais; Nattier…! Flemish, Italian, Spanish delights, looted no doubt during campaigns with Turenne, Luxembourg, Saxe; he was on fire. It was oddly – suspiciously, with hindsight – easy to get them back; after he had become the proud possessor of the whole collection (it cost money) the city curator became warmer, almost talkative.

'We hung on to them to stop them disintegrating, really, though I'm afraid most need cleaning badly. Oh they're all good schools – schools well represented here already, however. We couldn't get rid of them – that is to say they were never really ours,' hurriedly. 'Delighted they should go home where they belong – this cupola must have given someone the collecting passion in the eighteenth century.' Too late Dutheil had realised that if a revolutionary confiscation was of any real worth you didn't get it back from the state that easily.

He had been plagued then by art quacks, buttering him up, seeing easy 'restoration' money. The Rubens – it was a real Rubens, but he found how little Rubens could be worth when he offered it secretly to Sotheby's and found them singularly lukewarm. Or the Zurbarán, which would be wonderful under all that varnish; he had given in, and the result was so new-looking that the reek of emotional piety was like rancid oil, and he had given the beastly thing to Figaro to hang on his bedroom wall and encourage philoprogenitive instincts.

Worst of all had been that monstrous Italian thing stuffed full of classical draperies.

'Now that,' said the most buttery of the art experts, 'is really very very good, but been all over-painted under Madame de Maintenon

– prudish, you know; all the nudes were abolished. They should all be naked.'

'You mean there's tit in colossal quantities under all those curtains?'

'I can take it all off for you.'

Whetted he had agreed. Cost a fortune and was now more unappetising than ever. His head ringing with art he had shown the pack of houseflies the door. At least the boiseries and the floors were genuine, and even repaired by a Spanish odd-job man looked noble, honest, true. Best thing in the house was the light, green and silver and gold, flowing in through the tall windows and raising him up to the high hills.

The bookcases were full of stuff he never read – who wanted the Complete Works of Voltaire, in rather mouldy calf? Who, came to that, wanted the Montaigne? But at least it was first-rate, perfect, a showpiece; green morocco and arms of Gaston d'Orléans, it had captured him, lying in wait in the Rue Jacob for him coming back from a bibulous lunch at La Pérouse with Marcus after a book had stayed at the top of the library lists for the third month running – he was accustomed to that, now.

He had hated the thing ever since – a thing like that, which you were afraid to read or even handle, wasn't a book. Like Uncle Penstemon's hat, every time you touched it you took a shilling off its value.

He had a few articles of this sort; sheet-anchors. Things, things much too good and much too valuable. Pretty, certainly, but only bloody objects when all was said. A counterbalance to the grandiose trashery of the castle. A silver sugar-sifter, signed Paul de Lamerie and dated 1730. A Sèvres cup and saucer, kings' blue, that had belonged to Marigny, so that Madame de Pompadour had certainly drunk from it. No good to him, unless he could drink from it too, and it was so christ-forsaken valuable he didn't dare.

Sheet-anchors... 'If anything happens to me Laure has the Montaigne' (and the Sèvres, the sugar-sifter, the little tiny Renoir with the explanatory letter from Jean, the autograph draft by

Talleyrand dated from Erfurt, the Stendhal scribble of an abandoned chapter for *Lucien Leuwen...*).

Books were all over the house, of course; cloth covers behind glass in the gunroom; paper covers, musty and good-smelling, on open shelves in a butler's pantry place obscurely called the West Room, up to the ceiling, in company of a weird mahogany stepladder and a bulbous horsehair couch, both offensively early-Third-Republic ('You know, this stepladder was once climbed by Jules Ferry to get a good view of the Lycée Janson-de-Sailly').

Here in the library were the Good Leather Editions. Walter Scott and Victor Hugo, strong stuff; dark meat – he smacked his lips whenever he looked at it. 'When I am rich I shall have the Complete Works of Balzac in leather' – he had to laugh; how many such fantasies had not been planned in the Brighton days before he was married, on interminable solitary walks up the Race Hill or Hollingbury. Virtually all the fantasies had been realised; the castle was there, real and tangible, simply stuffed with art and literature – of course nobody touched the complete-Balzac-in-leather, though Figaro admired it intensely. If he wanted to read *Père Goriot* he had a copy in the west room, whose paper had gone tobacco-brown, whose cover had been missing for twenty years. Bought on a second-hand stall when he was nineteen – *that* was worth money. 'Ernest Flammarion, 26 Rue Racine. Imprimerie française H. Mathon, Wiesbaden (Allemagne Occupée).'

A devil of a lot of art and all trash. Most from long before his day, of course. Who had admired the silver-mounted arquebuses in the gun-room, terribly gothic, like nasty Nuremburg torture-toys next to his lovely simple little .22 from Walther in Ulm? Or the rococo silver coffee-pot, Figaro's joy – pastry-cook's art. Silk carpets and tapestries, uniforms and cocked hats, nineteenth-century prints of the Railway Age, and a suit of armour on the stairs. Trash, stuff to entrance a ten-year-old. Mind, it had entranced him, and he would still not part with a scrap of it, the more obstinately because Spaniards complained about the dusting.

He was proud too of his cunning. If they got burglars (a secret terror) they would be flummoxed by all the art, wading about in stuff brought by the lorry-load and emptied into those awful baskets at Hotel Drouot. They would never find the little Renoir, reeling about intoxicated by Meissoniers.

He opened the Louis XIV commode where he kept materials – dozens of pens and notebooks, like a stationer's; he loved stationers'. For birthdays people gave him art: his family gave him notebooks bought from the Prisunic. In lower drawers were his *cahiers* and manuscripts – he had no great hopes of these. Such things were bought sometimes for colossal sums by universities in Texas, but he had left instructions that they were to be kept for twenty years at least after his death and only sold by Laure if in want. Nothing deader than a dead author; his sales would dry up instantly and the castle would go down like a pack of cards. Nor did he believe it would rise again with a Reputation, in twenty years or thirty. Stendhal had a safe bet hoping for a reader in nineteen-thirty, but the world went faster nowadays; books are eaten for breakfast, like cornflakes. The reprint houses had gone through three centuries of literature in ten years. Just to show what a soap-bubble it was!

Quite right – everything was. These lousy objects; he often felt like making Talleyrand's letter into a spill and lighting a cigar with it. His reputation. His life more than anything – so absurdly fragile. He took great care about crossing the road and getting into aeroplanes, and he asked himself every day whether he had still six months to live. This was not a vulgar hypochondria, for attacks of which he simply rang up Gilbert Royan. Surely life was no more than a preparation for death, and that needed daily thought. How – no one had or would put it better or briefer – to be absolute for death.

Dying did not alarm Dutheil; he was a coward, but not that kind. Not even dying a dirty death, screaming. Others had done it. In a crisis he was always lucid and could tell himself that he would do all right in the pinch. I have a few drops after all of the right blood, he thought jeeringly. Stendhal blood; Julien, anxious to 'prove it to himself', Fabrice at Waterloo, understanding nothing but that 'this is a battle; I am present' – or Lucien at Nancy with his lancer regiment: 'They despise me; very well, let us look for a good duel'... No no, death did not alarm Dutheil. It was the 'And then?' *Et ensuite...?*

One could say – he did say, often – that there wasn't anything at all. What ailed him? – a hangover from childhood, nothing more; a black-clad father-figure with a cane, who pursued him. What was Christmas? – a propaganda device to take the public mind off the price of patent cough-mixtures. A seasonal 'taking up slack in the economy' as the jargon had it... And what was it that performed an annual resurrection at Easter anyway – Christ the Redeemer, or the great god Pan? Or was that all the crudest undergraduate claptrap? He didn't know for sure; he had never been an undergraduate. It seemed to him that there was a gap in his life that had thrown him permanently out of rhythm, that he had passed from child to adult without a pause. All Hamilton-Smith's fault.

His greatest nostalgia was for student years, the years he had never had. To have been a neophyte, passing examinations and ordeals, to study philosophy and theology, to step forward finally a Templar, a Knight of Saint John. To have been trained... All Hamilton-Smith's fault; he had turned aside, seduced by the witch Kundry, and had fallen into lecheries and fornications from which he had never escaped. What would break the evil spell?

It was not fair. Every people was ruled by its priesthood, whether that happened to be the Temple or the École Normale – but the training, the formation, was indispensable. He had nothing; he was just a little scribbling writer poking about with a stick among the ruins of civilisation. No idea of history, of philosophy.

A church terrified him. He could not blame Hamilton-Smith for that; it was himself he could not forgive. That horrible steeple, sticking out like a finger above the invisible town, menacing him.

'I am here. I am waiting for you.'

'No,' he wanted to yell. So childish.

One would have to take one's chance like anybody else. Meanwhile what would remain among the shattered fragments of castle, for Laure? He sighed like Cardinal Mazarin to think that 'one would have to leave all this behind'. Let us see. He took a notebook and started to make a list. He loved lists.

He traced, indeed, his writer's instinct to a passion for lists. As a child he had drawn houses – caves, huts, forts, – castles… For each he had made a careful list; the necessities. Every child did, of course, but how many were as punctiliously exact as his? The hours spent brooding over the 'Manufrance' and 'Army & Navy Stores' catalogues! He saw every item vividly, and nothing would suit but to find a corresponding illustration of which he would make a careful drawing in the list, with all technical details. Dutheil sat at his desk contented. Without realising he had just attained one of those rare moments of happiness.

# NINE

The two travellers, having plenty of time, stopped for a lavish lunch. They had found a nice restaurant in a village which the road bypassed, so that traffic in the sinuous main street behaved in a leisurely rustic way, stopping for a chat in the middle of the road. The dining-room was large, airy, with the windows all open on to a terrace and vines curling in over the sills. One of those folklore villages; waitresses in *franc-comtois* costume, locals at the bar talking patois with the owner, and a menu full of peculiar local things that one saw nowhere else, like *ombré chevalier.*

'What are you fancying for a start?' Sabatier was saying expansively.

'I was just thinking about crayfish tails.'

'Oh no, not those boring old crayfish tails – we must certainly eat these peculiar things; get ourselves in the right frame of mind – now this *ombré* thing is a fish found in the mountain lakes.'

'Do we need a special frame of mind?'

'You do,' threateningly. Thomassen could not be bothered; he decided to think this over after lunch. There were more pleasant preoccupations for the moment.

'I'm all for this lake fish – or what's this other thing? – sounds like potted chamois but that's not possible, surely?'

One eats and drinks well in this region, and both of them punished the goodies, making up for the hot dusty journey. Sabatier, noticed the American, with amusement, was becoming steadily jauntier and more dashing. The decidedly cross and dishevelled figure complaining about that nasty aeroplane of a few hours earlier had recomposed into a familiar spectacle of the sixth arrondissement, an unchanging and historic object, something like one of the literary bishops, perhaps, who survey the horrible Place Saint Sulpice from their niches in the preposterous fountain.

His was a very aristocratic publishing house, strategically placed opposite the Senate on the dreary side of the Luxembourg. Not perhaps as aristocratic as the houses so rarefied that they never publish anything at all, but properly antique; poky, confused, and happily out of date. Sabatier presided in the pokiest, dimmest, most panelled office; the kind of place reached by turning awkward corners in pitchblack passages, stumbling over odd steps, lurching into the women's lavatory.

It was then a salutary shock-treatment for the visitor to find him presiding over destiny and four telephones, all streamlined and vigorous, a symphony of pearl-grey in the hair and suit, and rose in the complexion and the buttonhole. Dynamic but still able to read in a pleasant, anachronistic way. He had now, Thomassen could see, reached the ruminative stage, aureoled by the peace of mind that comes only from good digestion of provincial food. The moment was propitious.

'Now why a special frame of mind?' inquired Thomassen.

'Eh?' He was turning over cigars in a distrustful way. 'I'm sure this has never seen Cuba but oh well – clip it for me, would you? What? – oh, the frame of mind? Have you ever read any of his books?'

'Of course. Hell, what do you think I'm doing here? Looking for the *Chartreuse de Parme*?'

'Yes of course,' vaguely. 'Effortless reading, hm – picturesque, colourful – Chile, Turkey – I particularly like the one about the Minister for Foreign Affairs.'

'Find that one rather boring myself. I prefer the one about the general.'

'A bit Greeney?'

'What would happen if the two came face to face?' suggested Thomassen, laughing in an unbuttoned after-lunch sort of way. 'Perhaps in a godforsaken corrugated-iron shack in the middle of Paraguay? Imagine them shouting crossly at each other, "That general's name; I saw him first." '

Sabatier was now enjoying a thoroughly babyish cigar-ritual, crackling it, blowing in it, lubricating it, turning it round and round while kitchen matches crept discreetly closer. Thomassen watched, impressed in spite of himself at the legerdemain. Big virtuoso. Finally he was actually smoking the thing.

'Except,' said Sabatier, taking it out to make sure it was burning evenly, 'poor old Dutheil, he's like this cigar, probably never been near Cuba. Be terrified to set foot in Paraguay, I feel quite sure – ants and snakes and things, and no mineral water. You'd find him playing croquet in his garden, as you'll shortly discover. He never goes away – or rather he makes peculiar sorties into places like Prague but he never travels – loathes cars, refuses to set foot in planes, says trains have become vulgar; you don't know who you might be sharing the first class with, nowadays.'

'You mean you don't believe he ever was in South America?' becoming interested.

'Can't swear to it. He refuses utterly to give any details.'

'I suppose it might be possible,' said Thomassen, wondering about it. 'Conrad wasn't either, come to that.'

'Aha. Now maybe you're getting warm.'

'Really? You see a resemblance? Surely not.'

'No no, of course not, not as a writer; utterly dissimilar. As a man, a bit. That's what you're here for. Forget about the writer – see that better back in Connecticut. But the man, perhaps? Neurotic pessimist aristocrat – effects of ironic despair and no faith in human nature – oh yes, certainly.'

'I thought he was very proud of being prole – me the manual worker.'

'So he is,' peacefully. 'Comic, complex object, poor old bugger.'

'Why poor old? Rich as hell and ten years younger than you are.

'Aha. But I don't spend all day worrying about dying tomorrow morning.'

'Moralist with ulcers.'

'Yes indeed and fussing himself sick whether he really believes in God or whether it's just his liver. Fascinated and appalled at the idea that there might be a divine providence shaping his ends – he's like a Jew that's never been circumcised.'

Thomassen felt too contented, and on the whole too well fed, to be able to worry about Dutheil. He would see for himself soon enough.

'Have I told you the story of the Jew that had never been circumcised?'

'No,' said Sabatier, who was in a royal humour now because his cigar tasted nice – came from Cuba after all. 'You can tell me in the car. Not that we're in a hurry; I have a pleasant feeling of leisure. Nothing ever happens in that house; the only telephone is in the secretary's office.' They had about thirty kilometres to go, which would be spent in an aftertaste of kirsch and cigar. A bit of ribaldry will go nicely with that, thought Marcus; this fellow tells good Jewish stories – like all New York Jews he has to draw attention to the fact.

# Ten

Dutheil was still sitting at his little list – was it a book, in embryo? Journalists always asked you about books, what influenced you or some such claptrap. What would you say to such innocents who asked what book you would like to have signed?

Such cock; it was generally bad books that left indelible memories – a phrase, a flash. One distinguished little between good and bad books – in it all went. You read everything and you never knew what influenced you – look at him, stuck with an earthly kingdom after being intoxicated by Sir George Sitwell!

The door opened and Figaro appeared, blue-chinned importance.

'Get out,' said Dutheil, not even raising his eyes. Well-trained, the fellow disappeared like an eel under a rock.

'Figaro,' he bellowed just in time. Resurface at once on small neat feet, with his false humility.

'Do you know the watchword given by the emperor Antoninus on his deathbed?' Mystified, too tactful to show it – waiting politely.

'Aequanimitas.'

Aha. He thought about this for a while, till a happy crafty smile appeared.

'Very very good. That is us.' He whisked off appeased – Spaniards loved phrases and this one was a mine of folksy sayings – probably made them up as he went along. What was the one about the old woman, who did not want to die, because 'she was still learning all the time'? That's me. I've got everything that I put on the list, and now I've got it I'm no longer interested – a characteristic of children, that.

A bad feeling, not working. When at work he respected himself; others respected him. Even Kieffer understood a craftsman. He could put his hand out without saying what he wanted – there it was. He need not clutter his mind with irrelevance – for all the administration Laure was there.

When not working, things went wrong. Then he was a bourgeois, a parasite. He resented it, and it was at such times that he lost confidence, clinging to Laure's skirt. It fidgeted him to be in the house and not feel her there at arm's length. He felt it right now, hating it, and had to go off in search of her, passing Iñez on the stairs, furiously certain that she was grinning in a knowing way – all the servants knew how he could not bear having Laure out of his sight. But it was genuine, an eating misery, like a jealousy, as though he was hoping to catch her with a lover and only in pain allay his suffering.

Damn, am I not entitled to a holiday? I could pack a bag, go to Rhodes, to Prague, to Stockholm. I prefer to stay at home. Have I not that right?

Laure was in her bedroom, anxiously examining her little table.

'What are you doing?'

'I think that when you brought my coffee the saucer was wet.'

Hell, he was in the wrong again. A ring on a piece of good furniture, fussing Laure – he had only wanted to sit a minute in her company, on the balcony perhaps, in the sunlight. He had wanted to talk to her about Véronique; it was worrying him. And now she could think of nothing but her table. Oh throw it away; I'll buy you another. She kissed his eyebrow distractedly.

'What have you been doing?'

'I made a large walk.' Now why in English did one say I took a long walk – it sounded like medicine!

'Well, why don't you make another large walk? I've rather a lot to do.' And off she went – in search of Bernardo: emergency first-aid to the damn table!

Left on the balcony he leaned his elbows on the railing and lit a cigarette. A gardener was digging a border, a man of sixty odd, light and wiry, silver-haired with the little 'tonsure' of baldness at the back. He drove his spade in and stopped to look at the house – neither tired nor lazy: just that it was a beautiful day. Seeing Dutheil he gave a little flip of his hand, one craftsman to another; that cheered him up. Why should a novel not start with a gardener? What had been Chesterton's definition – ordinary things done by unordinary people? The man was so tanned that even at this range his eyes were bright delphinium blue. He had a reddish checked shirt and a new overall; detestable purplish shade, like the blue in French flags, which isn't blue. He spat on his hand; the spade was beautifully polished by skin and earth. A craftsman, as good as Dutheil, who would by the end of the day have created beauty. Damn that table. Now the house would be in an uproar; Figaro looking reproachful and Bernardo looking wounded and all the women with told-you-so expressions. He was an egoist, clumsy and inconsiderate; very well, he would go out till lunch; maybe he would even be late for lunch just to pester them. He could make a scene – but all the servants would know it was guilt at making a ring on a Louis Quinze table. He gave the thing a kick; discreetly, not hard enough to do it any damage, and went into his dressing-room to sweeten himself by changing and leaving clothes on the floor. That would pay Iñez out for looking at him on the stairs! and since he had a bad reputation for untidiness it would be put down not to injured vanity but just to chronic vice.

In the gunroom he took the little Walther, his favourite, a rifle that balanced like a fencing sabre with a willing sweetness, an exquisite thing, with a plaited leather sling that smelt good, and a beautifully shaped walnut butt. He pulled it through and put a dozen cartridges in his pocket; might get a shot at something if only a lousy blackbird.

On the terrace he turned; lot of fuss going on, surely. Not just the table – maybe there were guests coming. Nobody told him – he didn't count! Or had the weather made Laure decide to have a turn-out? Windows were all wide and the women hurtling about like jets – even Susanna urging everyone else on with loud bullfighting noises. Laure spoke admirable Spanish; he himself spoke enough, crude South American. He understood everything but did not let it be known; it might have stopped servants conversing as though he were not there, under the illusion that he was far too stupid to understand, a thing which suited him splendidly. The other day; he had been having a siesta, and Figaro and Susanna had met in the hall.

'Asleep?'

'Asleep. Too much lunch.'

'Too much lunch and tumbling Nora!'

'Silly old fool.'

He shouldered the Walther and ran lightly out down the steps on to the lawn, past that rustic summerhouse – idiot affair, sort of wattle-and-straw roof, as though a plaster Astérix-and-Obélix lived there!

He had to give some thought to what he was going to do about Véronique.

# Part Two

# One

Some nineteenth-century notable had thought up the Wilderness in the early days of the romantic movement. Perhaps an émigré who had spent years in England, and had learned how to embellish a country property in the taste of the day from an early version of Sir George Sitwell… At least he had had enough sense to leave the formal garden alone, but the trees he had planted beyond in a naturalist scatter, enshrining a folly in the shape of a fake classical temple, spoilt the perspective. A hundred years later the willows, the copper beeches, the Lebanon cedars had grown into splendid patterns and Dutheil would not have dreamed of cutting them. He liked the Wilderness too; a low-lying sunny glade with bamboo clumps. Doubtless chinoiseries and grottoes had been planned, but the fall of Charles X, the growing threat of a republic, and Louis-Philippe with his umbrella, so disagreeable a spectacle to a good legitimist, had disturbed the projects, and the first whiff of Bonapartist gunpowder in 1850 had been enough for the chatelain to drop everything and make an abject bolt for the Swiss border.

The twentieth century had added the greensmearing shrubberies; laurel and rhododendron running wild; the air of overgrown neglect was attractive and Dutheil would not let Kieffer mess about with it.

Véronique – she could not be allowed to get away with this. All very well to go on about the tempestuous psychology of the adolescent girl. Servants humiliated him, Laure humiliated him –

the girl would think she could ride rough-shod over the whole garden if things were allowed to stand. A shock treatment – just to show her that he wasn't standing for such behaviour any longer. Something short and sharp; none of these bourgeois punishments like withdrawal of affection: that would only drive the girl into further rebellion, perhaps even into running away. She was not too old for a thrashing. It sounded easier than it was, but having got that far he decided not to let unpleasant notions spoil what was left of the morning. He climbed the high bank out into the field; pollarded willows at the bottom marked the line of the river and at the far end, where the road ran down from the village into the valley, chestnut trees masked the high stone wall that protected him from the gaze of tourists, in the summer.

It was too early, and much too dry for mushrooms; the open ground showed cracks. But the chestnut trees were at their best, leaves beginning to turn, ripe fruit falling – toc, landing at his feet and bursting open – the perfection of that… Human beings would ruin that by picking it up, so he picked it up. Dark glossiness, polished like the stock of the Walther, so soon to dull and dry. Creamy roughness like a Brie cheese would darken miserably – corruption lying in wait for chestnuts, for cheese, for Dutheil. Whimsy hit him. Did God pick up a chestnut, breathe on it, and toss it where it would grow into a sapling? Would it be one, in ten thousand chestnuts? What about writers? They lay littered and sterile everywhere; how many became saplings, and how many became trees as thick and tall as Dutheil? Who had picked him up, breathed on him and tossed him in the compost heap? Did a writer even have a seed to germinate at all, or was he just an ill-tuned radio, picking up blurry fragments of words and music that floated in the invisible air?

Terrible, terrible whimsy, stuff he had put in early books till dear old Claude, his first publisher, had looked at him, pushing his glasses up on his forehead, a mild blue gaze somehow saddened and dumbfounded at such bad writing, murmuring, 'Peel it, my boy, peel it.' Old Claude read Kipling; he was that generation. He had told Dutheil to go and read him too, to learn to 'peel it'. Well, he had. If ever there was a writer to be jealous of! Damn fellow – once he had really learned his trade he had never needed to do anything as crudely long-winded as writing a novel…Poor old Dutheil, such a successful writer, who had to have the thing padded up to the ears with rubbish, sixty thousand words long. Had he any real talent at all? Frightened of most things, he was most frightened of all at his own success.

One thing at least had been spared him – the really big seller. Technically all his books were sellers – anything that goes to thirty thousand copies is a seller – but he meant a really big one. Sitting watching the telegrams come in – that was war. He had known writers who thought they were tough melting in the candle-grease of their own vanity amid the bright flames of publicity. It had been one of his incomparable strokes of luck, to have neither had nor needed a thing that sold a million. Like Nostromo, he had grown rich slowly. And like Nostromo he looked fixedly at his fingers as though imagining that the silver had left stains.

I am eaten by fear to a shell, he thought furiously. Fear of drying up, fear of being a rich phony, of becoming self-satisfied. I feel fear each time a child leaves the house, and each time Laure is out of my sight. And God, the bogyman, worst of all.

He walked across the field resolutely, away from chestnuts. The English called a worn-out joke a chestnut; they were dead right!

He unslung the little rifle; he had seen a squirrel but he was kindly disposed towards squirrels. He might see a duck, though, or a pigeon – which he would very likely miss. He always carried a rifle, never a shotgun; he preferred missing things, really. When he hit it, whatever it was, it would be properly killed, and he could feel triumph, and did. A hen pheasant rose under his nose and clattered away stupidly; there you were – easiest shot in the world, but not with a rifle. No regrets; beastly thing anyway – not even good to eat.

He had to shoot things every now and then to keep the Spaniards in order; they never believed him capable of anything. Did it matter what they thought? – did he have to cringe to the good opinion of the servants? Apparently he did, since he found it salutary to throw a rabbit on the kitchen table from time to time.

A bum popular novelist. Not that he would have wished to be an intellectual; he was sorry for intellectuals, and contemptuous as a rule; they were such a bore. They didn't believe in sin, and the delicate balance of their sensibilities suffered, so that they went about worrying lest shooting a rabbit turn out to be an immoral act. He believed in sin all right, and was the robuster for it; if it weren't for his belief in sin – and reparation – they'd have him in the bin in no time at all!

If he were going to shoot anything he'd better do a bit of stalking – not that one ever got far stalking pigeons, those intellectual hypocrites of the bird world, looking so dovey and quakerish, the crafty bastards. A duck, now, – it was innocent and you could shoot it. All notion of shooting a duck, however, was dispelled by planes. Mirages – true to their name stealing like shadows in upon him, very slow, almost lazy, at treetop height exactly as though planning his assassination. He gazed at them rapt. As they passed the noise shattered all the rural meditation that had been going on, leaving him open-mouthed and dizzy. All the ducks took off at once in hot competition, determined to go even faster and make even more noise, thundering away insanely pleased with themselves so that he had to laugh, quite forgetting that he had wanted to shoot one. The planes came over again, high now in the bright blue air and still climbing; as he watched the outside one shook loose and in sheer gaiety rolled in a liquid right-left-right movement that filled him with happiness; one forgot fear when even a plane lost its rigidity of terror and played. Other people did not like planes but other people did not taste with his tongue…

Figaro would be keeping a watch through the windows, no doubt, and would shortly announce that Monsieur was safely on the home stretch. Laure had told him once of hearing Figaro say, in tones of indulgent irony, 'Monsieur has gone for a walk, to tell himself stories…' He wished he had shot a duck, and got his trousers sopping wet retrieving it, as he generally did. He could have thrown his trousers at Susanna, standing lordly and indifferent in his underpants amid Spanish squawks, banged his shoes down on Figaro's stupid toes and waited for the lazy bugger to pick them up.

He had a great deal of sympathy for Count Almaviva, beset by those stinkers who run rings round him while he stands there, taking his wig off to scratch his head in a puzzled way, regretting his good nature in abolishing his *droit de seigneur* over these awful giggling chits, longing to get his riding boots on and take a really good run at that fiendish little bastard of a Cherubino's slim tempting behind. *Se vuol ballare, Signor Contino* – yes he damn well did.

Figaro, of course, was not the first person to think him a very soft chocolate. Others had thought the same, had bitten wolfishly, had been nearly cut in two by the razor blade sunk deep but upright in all the pink goo.

# Two

The smirker met him in the hall and he gave himself away at once.

'Where is Madame?'

'In the Salon.' Gelatine-coated smile.

'Take my gun, Figaro, and put it away – it doesn't need cleaning; I didn't get a shot. Planes frightened the birds away.' Why make an excuse? Was it anything to do with a majordomo if he had had fifty shots, yes and missed with every blasted one of them?

'I'm tired,' sitting heavily. 'Help me off with my shoes. there's a good chap.' Another mistake. Never say you are tired. Since you have done no work, how can you possibly be tired? Opposite him was a large Empire looking-glass, rather nice, with a gilt classical urn perched on top, nobody would ever know why. He stared at himself bleakly. Odd; one has a tooth out – one's swollen face must look like a potato. One is tired – one's face must be falling to pieces with fatigue. Look in the glass, and be quite indignant at looking so placidly normal.

'I have no vanity,' he was fond of saying, knowing it to be quite untrue, yet convinced that in some praiseworthy if obscure way it might yet turn out to be exact. When asked whether the castle were not a form of vanity he looked benign.

'I make money – you're not going to tell me there's something indecent about that? You would perhaps prefer me to invest it on the Bourse – prop up a social order of which I am thoroughly ashamed?

Buy house property and be a rent-master? Bury it in a Swiss vault, in dread of Communists coming to take it away?'

'A vulgar display of wealth...'

'This is a historic house of some beauty; it stood empty and falling to pieces. A children's holiday colony wouldn't look at it. I care for it, I bring the countryside to life. I pay colossal, staggering taxes. I get no subsidy. I conserve tradition and historical interest – your objections are those of a puritanical prig.'

He was tall and bony – his mythical English blood, perhaps. A round French head – his funny little head like a pot, as Laure said with affection. Coarse dark hair – rusty and scrubby compared to Véronique's. Pale and rather watery blue eyes. Small well-shaped ears – but who looked at men's ears? He did, but he knew nobody else. Bony nose, tending to aquiline. If he had had more chin he might have had a look of the Prince de Condé; as things were, he suspected, it was more a cross between Lord Peter Wimsey and the milkmaid: a thought that gave little pleasure, besides being unfair to both his parents. At fifty a small stomach had begun to put pressure on his trouser buttons. Still, he walked, he rode a bicycle: sports... Heights gave him vertigo, sea made him sick, skis flew away from him, little balls moved six inches to one side just before he hit them. At his English school everyone had called him 'Useless'. He hadn't shaken off that goddam school even now. He was frightened of England – he might meet Mrs Hamilton-Smith in the street. What would he do if she suddenly accosted him? He would stare rudely with horrible pale eyes, saying, 'I have no recollection whatsoever' – but he preferred not to take the risk.

Young Woodley had been on the whole a stupid and unsympathetic child; he did, however, have a small, sneaking fellow-feeling for him.

He was still sitting in his socks when Susanna came sailing by upon some idle and pretentious errand and threw him a glance; contempt for parasites. It stung him; he found his slippers with his toes, stood up with some difficulty, and went into the salon – empty; where on earth had Laure got to? He pottered into the library and stared unhappily at Sir Walter Scott. If he lived – always that – then he would dig into the foxed, marvellous-smelling pages of *Peveril of the Peak*. After the children had gone away, after getting rid of frightful Spaniards, castle, Passementerie. A retired literary gentleman. Two plates, two cups, two spoons; a little house with dark trees, a tiny orchard and a tiny terrace, crooked rooms, and a pump in the back. Ten years? – if he had that much writing left in him. Before he could settle down to the long peaceful draughts of Sir Walter there was a long way to go. Véronique… and he was so tired; would he ever reach it?

There were Laure's steps, at last, in the salon.

# Three

Laure was getting ice-blocks for the sacred half-hour before lunch, the moment he was happiest, bless him, when working at least. When not working – well, happier than at other moments. Where could he be? – sulking somewhere because she was late. Still, he had been roaming about the whole morning in the fresh air, which should have done him good. And she couldn't help being late; she had been in the kitchen, having heard from Nora that guests were expected. Nora had told him, of course; he had forgotten to pass on the message, which certainly meant he would say indignantly that he knew nothing about it.

Good psychology to be a minute late sometimes; devoted wife was one thing, and doormat was another. Marcus was coming; all right. Bringing a journalist – that might be a bore, with god so jumpy and touchy right now: tired after a book, and that annoying behaviour of Nique's. Laure very nearly sighed. She would make strong soothing drinks, and would allow him to fall into total silence while he read the paper. Spaniards didn't understand drinks, he said. After twenty years she reckoned she had a fair idea but one never knew for certain.

There he was; he slumped wordlessly, a warning to keep her mouth shut, and picked up the paper. There was silence for six or seven minutes.

'Hasn't Nora brought the post yet?'

'She's sorting it – he's taken to being late again. His new scheme is to go through the whole village before going back for ours.'

'Surely Nora can ask him to get ours first.'

'So she has, but he won't. He has a mortal terror of appearing servile – you know how it is; don't complain to me.'

'Ridiculous – post belongs at breakfast.'

'Lovely – all stained with porridge and bacon fat. But you know it would only interrupt your morning. Anything in the paper?'

This was classic; a remark that had to be made.

'Nothing whatever; squalor. The French Prime Minister was applauded at Cahors, the English Prime Minister was booed at Shepton Mallet, the German – let's see – aha, at Braunschweig of all places – mm, turbulent troublemakers were removed by the forces of order – do I have to go on? There's still America, Russia, and China.' Good, he was feeling better. She was well accustomed to all this; a bland male preference for women who could not read. They pretended they liked intellectual wives, which was sheer hypocrisy. They liked the kind of woman who says vaguely, 'What is going on in China?' just as she is settling her bedclothes and putting the light out.

He always said there was nothing in the paper, which did not stop him reading every inch with concentration. He would say he knew nothing about China and cared less, but let Gilbert raise a point, even if it were the balance-of-payments, or the trotters at Vincennes racetrack…

As to Diverse Happenings, they were holy writ. One never knew when 'Jealousy Drama at Nanterre' might turn into a novel.

She had to read the paper furtively, pretending later to have been doing something feminine like painting her toenails. Her mission in life was to preside over literary pregnancies and parturitions; she was used to this idea but still sometimes felt remorse and rage for her obliterated life. Not that she felt sorrow for her interrupted career; she had understood the problem after reading the biography of Joseph Conrad, a writer Dutheil had no use for. Jessie! – that was the wife for a writer, frankly and placidly unintellectual, but with enormous nervous resources. One had to be very tough; Laure sipped her drink, leaned forward as though at the fortune-teller's, and flipped idly through the pack of cards that made up the rat years, so-called from a phrase of Dutheil's. 'Running about Europe like rats with brown-paper parcels.' The irony of it was that the castle which she loathed, had in a sense been bought specially for her, so that she had to be grateful! His way of 'making up for the rat years'; a typical Dutheil gesture, carried through with panache, even courage, despite staggering a little. Complaining about everything else, he never complained about this appalling handicap he had set himself; Laure was touched by this.

She did her best. She saw to it that Figaro – how she hated the pair of them – did not make life too insupportable; there was a lot to see to – a strain, but she could be as tough as Jessie. She could never be ill, for instance, however ill she felt – he would instantly become far iller; if she got a headache he went down with migraine... She shuffled the cards together, tapped the edges straight, put them away neatly, and had a good swig at her Campari.

Dutheil was observing her quietly behind the paper he was pretending to read; ha, she thought he sat there poring over every word: very innocent. He loved that innocence in her. She was a jewel – a neurotic jewel to be sure; writers' wives could be nothing else. Carrie Kipling was a classic case, a textbook illustration to the wives-neurosis. Laure was that bottled-up and sealed-in kind too, with the characteristic need to busy herself with everything, worry about everything, shield him from everything. He couldn't complain, in view of the swarms of time-wasting irritations he did need to be protected from, but one felt annoyance sometimes at being so resolutely wrapped in cotton wool. Worrying about Nora, about Véronique – now if she could just realise that her intenseness and over-anxiety had the worst effect on that admittedly tiresome girl. With the boys she was perfect, always had been, but boys knew how to handle Mama, understanding her; a girl couldn't.

Perhaps the most wonderful thing about Laure was her quick readiness. No matter what happened she was there under arms, punctual to the second. *'Bereitsein ist alles.'* And she did it easily, naturally, without advertisement or self-praise; she was simply ready. The example he remembered, always, was at the time after his first novel when he had rashly given up his job. Pennies were stretched as taut and thin as bread-and-scrape; all Laure's ingenuity going into new ways of cooking mince-loaf. And he had done something quite typical – spent the rent money in a junk-shop!

The two vases were a pair, real Sèvres, apple-green. The myth come true in fact: something of genuine value in a junk-shop. No antiquary had noticed them – must have been buried among the chamber-pots in an auction-lot of Victorian bric-à-brac.

He had no shortage of excuses; they were without chip or crack, they were worth twenty times the price, and they were the first objects of beauty he and Laure had ever possessed. That was the trouble – having got them one couldn't bear to sell them; it would have been an evil omen for the novel, a bad-luck bird. Had he known that those two vases would stand in a dozen squalid lodgings, would be bundled into many ratty brown-paper parcels, but that they would save his life, that if he sold them he would never become a writer?

Laure had. He had sat with his head in his hands, agonising over the few pounds that had stood between him and the Labour Exchange and were now gone.

'Don't be panicpot.' Her phrase; said gently, not to wound or humiliate.

'Does it help, not to be panicpot? Will it alter anything? Will it put the money back?'

'Just leave it to me.'

He found her sewing that evening, doing something to a black skirt, Some scraps of white material had been made into tiny aprons, starched and ironed. The two Sèvres vases, washed like the baby in lukewarm soapy water, stood gleaming on either side of a cheap alarm-clock...

'Polish my shoes, would you?' she said casually.

'What's all this?'

'Oh I found a job. I'm a waitress.' How had she known that the humiliation of going back for a job as a barman would be a crippling mutilating wound?

'But you've no training – no experience.'

'Nonsense; there's nothing to it.'

'But you're pregnant.' She had been carrying their second child for three months…

She twisted his ear, gently.

'Panicpot. All waitresses have stomachs that stick out. You'll have to look after the child a little, but that needn't stop you working. The Labour Exchange would.'

He had been in a great flap of course, very stupidly; trust Laure to look after herself. The other waitresses in a noisy, vulgar restaurant full of businessmen had taken her under their wing at once – married women, maternal and kind-hearted, in the same straits as her did he know it – always behind in their never-never payments. The 'Whitehawk Girls' showed her how to carry soup and hold a spoon-and-fork, and concealed her ignorance from the manager. Of course the head waiter noticed her mistakes the first day but a terrified quaking Dutheil had totally misjudged his mentality; Laure was clean, quick, and willing, and the Whitehawk Girls, however kind-hearted, were not. They arrived late with dirty aprons, dropped the silver they had dodged cleaning, had laddered stockings and no pencil, and talked all day behind the screen; Laure was a head waiter's happy dream.

Cooks liked her and gave her cold meat; so familiar and nostalgic to Dutheil, the pieces of ham tasting of a paper napkin…

Even the customers noticed; the very first week she brought home six pounds nine and fourpence, counting it on the bed. She kept it up for four months before her stomach became outrageous and the manager got scruples. He had done nothing but polish her shoes daily; the battle was won and his novel written.

He could still remember the names of all the Whitehawk Girls, about whom she told fascinating stories as she undressed; she had never met anybody like them before! Doreen who was always having new perms, June whose husband played the trumpet, Rose and Iris the sisters who spent their money on a colossal weekend roast and a rousing Saturday-night pub-crawl. Mrs Reynolds the cashier and race-horse expert, and Arthur the head waiter, who was even more of a panicpot than he was.

Nicest moment of the day, this, astringent like lemon juice. Lemon the gleam of sun on lemonwood and rosewood, the big map-table and Laure's secretaire. He was pumped dangerously low but now the blood was flowing back, and the nervous influx. He would be starting again soon, but he was not in form yet. I am like a pole-vaulter, he told himself, who knows he can do five metres. Just sharpen him up and he will do five ten, five twenty. A bit of nervous influx and I will do you a jump of five twenty.

Laure glanced sideways from the now-discarded paper. What a look of innocence! – a baby asleep in the cot. Forgotten all about Véronique. Good; in five minutes Figaro would appear bowing lavishly, to announce lunch with theatrical glitter, and after lunch Nora would bring the mail, pruned and weeded, thorns thoughtfully clipped away.

He is like today's weather, hot enough for one to believe it still summer. He has warmth all right; people bask in it, real and undeceiving. There is wind too; you don't notice it here on the slope but up on the Whaleback there is the rustling dry northeaster. If there was cloud you'd see that winter was coming. Sun can go in, disconcertingly sudden, and so with him. But while it is out – why, a perfect day and the grapes ripening, and wind enough to put wine into the lazy air.

The grapes will be ready in a week; if we get some rain to swell them it should be a good vintage. We will all help pick, Figaro and Susanna providing the usual comedy. It happened every year; Figaro enjoyed being out on the hillside – reminded him, he would announce sentimentally, of his boyhood, and indeed it was the one surefire occasion for him to forget his frightful dignity and start clowning with the big basket on his back. Susanna, that monument to sloth, would be one long snivel of woes; oh her lumbago, oh the nasty straw hat, oh the bitter humiliation and fatigue of manual labour, oh how she did wish she were not greedy and did not feel such compulsion to eat the nasty grapes: oh the collywobbles she would get and the dreadful diarrhoea – but it's good for one, Madame, really – wonderful clean-out.

'What are you grinning at?' he asked, not crossly.

'Susanna.'

'Don't remind me of that ghastly female. What's for dinner?'

'Fish.'

Fish; he crossed his hands on his stomach and smiled beatifically: loved fish. Her sins, Laure saw thankfully, were forgiven her.

The door opened and the boys came in, neat and washed. They were expert at handling him.

'Sorry to be late. Awful lot of traffic coming out of the town – weather's too good.'

'You're not late,' genially; 'sit down and have a drink.'

'I'll tell Figaro to give us another five minutes,' said Laure, getting up. Servants – if they announced dinner and you did not appear on the dot they became most petulant, as though you had insulted Spain. Better though, perhaps, than when she had cooked the dinner. He used to pour drinks out and then get furious when she did not have time to come and sit down. And if she did sit down, to accommodate his nervous system, three minutes later there would be a frightful scene, on account of no chopped parsley…

# FOUR

Lunch en famille was generally agreeable; he had an old-fashioned belief that the table was sacred – French peasant blood coming out there, remarked the boys in private. There must be a certain ritual, a solemnity. No guests, no interruptions, above all no servants. Children had never been allowed to complain; they must finish what was on their plate, sit up straight, eat in a civilised fashion, and learn conversation. Dutheil at 'dinner', in fact, was exactly like a governess, a resemblance increased by a fondness for speaking English at meals. At his terrible school – scarifying threat to the boys when small: 'If you don't learn to behave I'll send you to an English boarding-school' – he seemed to have picked up a peculiar turn of phrase, gushing and florid. 'May I beg you to pass the bread', or 'Do me the kindness of picking up your table napkin', generally culminating in a peppery, 'I implore you to stop that uncivilised fidget.' Once old enough to analyse this peculiar behaviour Daniel and Jean-Luc agreed that on the whole they rather liked it; Father, insupportable in so many ways, was at dinner generally tranquil and polite. He did not talk much and he did listen a good deal, respect for children being a tenet.

'Tell me something of what you have been doing', followed by careful attention not over-punctuated by 'Wipe your mouth before you drink' or 'That is a vulgar expression.' He asked their opinions, and listened without snubbing.

What seemed to work with the boys failed with Véronique. But which came first, the failure or her revolt against 'dinner'? She had sniggered, but it was not all her fault, Laure said; he was intensely proud of the daughter who resembled him, was stricter with her and spoilt her more. He had been the first to snub.

'Not the remark I should have expected, from you at least.'

Approval, instead of being downright, had a hazily sentimental, indulgent tone.

'Women should be decorative. I don't care for that frock; I'll buy you another' (at the age of ten).

Contrasted with a ferocious 'I see no need for you to be dowdy', the attitude was confusing. Laure, trying to take the edge off these remarks, got snubbed herself for her pains. Perhaps it was because Véronique was less intelligent than the boys, a thing that might rankle?

Today he was placid. He liked meals, and dinner most of all; he loved fish and had a tremendous appetite from all that fresh air. No book to nag him, and no Figaro. At suppertime, called dinner-in-the-evening when there were guests, there was an elaborate meal and a butler to hand things, fill glasses, and hover. Too Spanish to be truly obsequious, but self-important… But at midday Dutheil would have no guests. It had to be a family meal. Dishes were put on the table and left there, with the butler outside the door from that moment. He would serve everyone himself, he said, and did, a bit pompously.

'A great mistake to push the fat to the side of your plate. You make the meat dry and tasteless.' Laure had not read Osbert Sitwell's memoirs (one of his favourite bedside books) or she might have recognised Sir George in this kind of remark.

'You've been rather mean with the butter, Father.'

'I'll pass it to you if you ask me to; there's no shortage.' None of them, bar himself, really liked fish very much. Laure indeed rather disliked it but knew that there was nothing he detested more than people criticising a dish he was enjoying.

'All the bones in this are on my plate, damn it.'

'One needs a salad plate; I'm always telling him but the bastard pays no heed.'

'You've got a salad plate.'

'Damn it, I've salad on it.'

'Is fennel in season? Or does Il Cuocco pick it and dry it?'

'Figaro does, I expect – he's always out there gloating over the garlic.'

Etymological discussions are endemic in writers' households, especially at meals, so that several pages of the big Littré have greasy fingerprints.

'Why is it called a wolf? – seems an emotional name. Surely it's a bass?'

'The fishermen say it's a cunning animal, difficult to catch.'

'A fish is not an animal.'

'That's the purest pedantry – it's a beast.'

'An animal is warm-blooded – a fish is a reptile.'

'Don't be a damned fool; a crocodile is warm-blooded. A beast is something neither human nor vegetable. A reptile is something uneatable.'

'What about turtle soup?'

'A small child is a beast. Proof is that it's neither masculine nor feminine. *Das Kind*,' triumphantly.

'Somebody talk about another subject,' said Dutheil in a slightly ominous tone.

'We were in the bookshop – that terrible woman was there, Father – the one who hates your books and goes about hiding them.'

'Extraordinary person that,' cheered up by mention of this eccentric female, who did indeed make war on him, pushing his books to the back of the shelf till masked by other titles – nobody could make out why. 'Have we anybody to supper?'

'Nora mentioned Marcus,' said Laure, breaking it by degrees to him, 'some question too of an American coming with him – some journalist.'

'Mm.' It seemed to have been swallowed without too much strain.

'Be here this afternoon as far as Nora understood a rather vague message. Were you going out?'

'No. What's for supper?'

'I was thinking of pigeon vol-au-vent – Marcus does love it so.

'Are they staying?'

'I told Iñez to get two rooms ready.'

Coffee was waiting in the salon, with a pile of personal letters. After coffee he went over to the office, to dictate answers, and sign the business mail as well as contracts, cheques, and complimentary copies. Boring chore but Nora always had the slipway well greased. Passementerie – thank heaven for small mercies, she wore jumpers and skirts at work and it was at night that the chichi frocks that gave her her nickname appeared. He put up with them; Nora was part of life and almost part of the family. She wasn't unattractive either, despite irregular features and her undecided brown hair, which it would never have occurred to her to have tinted – for which he was grateful. When animated, indeed, she looked pretty, taking on an enthusiastic glow which illuminated her, suppressing the sallow look.

She and Laure make a good job of living with each other; both women at times had made a hearty meal of jealousy, chewing up the gristly bits and swallowing with an air of indifferent gaiety.

As for him, he had made various efforts to get rid of her, half-convinced and poorly organised; one would be stuck, said the boys with loud affected sighs, with Passementerie to the end of one's days.

They were indispensable to one another? – it was hardly that simple: too many questions remained unanswered – and unasked – between them. Even the boys liked and valued her, secretly; the show of detesting Nora was an affectation. Even the nicknames... For years she had been known as 'Faithful Truedog' – later, when in adolescence they discovered what after all was an open secret (Polichinelle's secret...yes, that was in character), they called her 'La Belle Dame Sans Merci'. Nowadays, probably they understood the 'mystification' side of Nora better than he did.

He did not understand. Sometimes, for a book, he used situations of characteristics familiar to her; she never made a comment. Never were there conspiratorial or reproachful looks, never a hint of 'We're in this together'. Really he knew no more about her than on the first day she came to him in Lausanne. Had she a family, friends, a life outside that of the castle? Once she had packed and left, and reappeared twenty-four hours later without a word spoken on either side. She took a month off every year – but so did he. Days off she never took – in the mornings she went to the town sometimes, to buy clothes or whatnot, and occasionally she went out in the evening when there were no guests – where? The theatre, a cinema, a concert? Nobody knew. She read a great deal, including all his own books, she never made mistakes in her spelling or grammar: well educated and informed – the perfect secretary.

Was she in love with him? Of course, said Laure shrugging coldly. How could she be anything else, said the boys with guffaws. He had no idea. Had Hamilton-Smith been 'in love' – with him? Nora was like that; a phenomenon. Why did they follow him around, what had he done to get his life madly complicated by dotty women for whom he felt obscurely responsible? But he had learned not to ask such silly questions; it was like asking 'What is a novel?' Characters, a catastrophe, said Mauriac laconically; how right he was. One dealt in characters and one tried to understand the catastrophes.

Nora belonged to the System, following its obscure rules and accepting its exigencies. I cannot say that I desire her, thought Dutheil crossing the courtyard – aha, at least the toffee papers had been picked up – then why? To reassure myself – and her?

It had always followed an exact, precise pattern. There was no need of words. She got an intense, almost a grim look, as though this were a problem, needing concentration; why did she not sigh? – mutter? – even whisper? – even just look pleased…? And why do everything in exactly the same order; taking, for instance, her pants off and hiding them under a pile of paperwork, before taking off her skirt?

Not particularly often – every four, five, six weeks. He did not know when it would happen; he had tried to relate it to incidents – the day, the day before, that week? – no: nothing recognisable. And it wasn't as though she were seductive! Colourless – a poor word: pasteurised, perhaps. The Flanders Mare…it had been one of the first nicknames; it was thought funny that she came from Valenciennes or Armentières; nobody knew where. What did she do, afterwards? Go to Confession, punish herself, make resolutions? She stayed the same. She did not say 'You are wicked', 'I am wicked', or laugh, or cry. Yet she did not lack humour, and would laugh in great guffaws at anything absurd, a dotty letter from a reader, for instance. Sometimes after a trivial slip, a letter mislaid or a date passed unnoticed, she would cry. He felt sorry but had no way of showing it; nor would she thank him.

'You're tired, Nora – no point in overdoing it. We'll go on with this tomorrow.'

He saw to it that she got a rise regularly – she made out cheques which he signed with the other monthly bills, altering the figure every year on the thirtieth of June. He gave her a generous Christmas present, as did Laure. Nobody knew when her birthday was.

# FIVE

Today he came bouncing into the office in a noisy, important way, like a large dog.

'Well well well. Lot of work?'

'Not an awful lot,' placidly.

'What's all this about Marcus?' as though whatever it was, it must be her fault.

'You're not going to pretend now I didn't tell you!'

'Well if you say you did I'm sure you did,' generously not blaming her for his inattention. 'I dare say I wasn't listening.'

'A letter arrived yesterday,' patient, 'saying he knew you were idle and that he thought of slipping down. Confirmed in the evening by a phone message – since you agreed when I asked you. You even said you'd tell Laure.'

'Sorry, I'd no idea. Driving down, is he?'

'Be here any time, I should say.'

'Oh… Well, that will be nice, I dare say.' He needed something to wake him up. It had been a tranquil day, apart from Nique…

'I'm sorry to break in on all the unbuttoned negligence' – she had these slightly leaden sarcasms sometimes – 'but Marcus is bringing an influential journalist from New York, and emphasised that he thought this of value to you.'

'Oh God.'

'There isn't any Oh God about it. Serious – and exclusive. Man's been told what to expect – no tapes or anything.'

'Got to worry about my bleeding image now,' pitying himself. 'Very well, let's have the letter file while we're still left in peace.'

He ought to feel grateful, but he hated it. Laure had sacrificed her university degree and her whole future, so carefully mapped by Mama the history professor of the lycée – where? – Laval, Alençon, somewhere like that. How furious Mama had been; after all, the quiet scheming and thrusting had culminated in a baccalaureate with a mention. Obstinate, stupid girl; why, she had almost been asked to prepare École Normale. All wasted…

Nora had sacrificed heaven knew what – youth, freshness, marriage and children. He felt an obscure resentment; his attention kept wandering from the letters and he realised that his mind was running down a familiar and unpleasant groove. Two women had given him their whole lives and by what right? It was a weary extra load. Had he not enough already to answer for? The career, the stable home, the talent, the children. Even the castle. Not much to set in the credit column. Some honest hard work… If there was a day of reckoning, and if a lot of ashes got dumped into the debit scale; ashes of two women and could one be sure there were only two? Might there not be a few kilos of cinders of Rosemary Hamilton-Smith?

Everything had turned false, and he had travelled on forged papers, from the moment his mother had decided that a country-town education was not good enough, and that to do her credit he must go to England, to a Boarding-School. Eminent intellectual religious order, famous for scholarships to Oxford, and he was a bright boy… At seventeen he was a pale, clear-skinned child, gauche but mercifully free of spots. He had no idea of being gauche, for he thought himself intensely enfranchised; he was indeed a figurehead and for all the wrong reasons. They would have slung him out years before, surely, had it not been for the possibility of the Scholarship. A black sheep, a casebook of what happened if you didn't join the Scouts. The Prefect of Discipline would give him no office; was he not an underminer, an anarchist? The Prefect of Studies would give him little lectures in his room (that smelt of celibate moral theology, the worst smell he knew; an unaired ecclesiastical cleanliness. In this sanctum fourteen-year-olds got given an ecclesiastical version of the Facts of Life). The lectures were about the sacrifices his mother made, and about reduced fees, and Repaying.

They would not give him authority. He was a suspected smoker, suspected masturbator, suspected shaky on the Retreat and the Five Glorious Mysteries – all right! He would satisfy them! He became as cranky and solitary as they could wish, and was even busy with a first novel in study periods. (Mutti, that was a novel; auto-erotic fantasies in glutinous detail.)

He knew nothing about Mrs Hamilton-Smith, in whom he was not interested anyhow; not a suitable target for his brand of erotic fantasy, which went in for nubile fifteen-year-olds, genre Constant Nymphery. One had seen her vaguely, of course, flitting about; thin anaemic-looking blonde thing. One knew that she had some job – nursing was it? – housekeeper? – dietitian? – concerned with the Juniors: wretched fledgelings these, torn from their mothers' laps at nine years old. Really, these English. They lived in a separate building, minuscule snivellers of whom the most homosexual child of seventeen could not possibly take any notice. One had heard, too, vaguely, that Hamsmith had had Misfortunes: been left a widow or something.

Early summer. He had got his School Certificate the year before, with ludicrous ease, and in another month he would sit for his scholarship examination. Just now they were doing athletics, misbegotten long-jumps and things, that he was useless at but anyway despised openly. The flannelled fools and the muddied oafs – what a pity that one had not then read Kipling, not known that useful wounding line. What happened to him was quite by accident; he was sitting on the grass, supported by his flat hands stretched behind him, when someone trod on him heavily; a flannelled fool, wearing spiked running shoes. He leapt up with a yell. Blood spurted in a little dribbling fountain, covering his fingers, and people came crowding round.

'Sir: Sir.' Sir arrived, summoned by gabble.

'I swear I've never seen a clumsier idiot than you. How in heaven's name – here, let me look – it could only happen to you, of course. I suppose you'd better cut along up to Matron.'

Thumb pressed stickily over blood he scuttled off – cheap price for getting out of Athletics.

Matron, fat flour-faced personage who bustled everywhere forcing Syrup of Figs down unhappy little boys, was not to be found in the usual haunts. He stood about uncertainly; the hand was pierced deeply and throbbed now in a swoony nasty way. He came upon a young nervous ecclesiastic.

'What are you doing there?... But you must get this seen to. What can we do? – Matron's not here; she had to go to Town.' So was always called the local metropolis, one of those market-cross places with a cottage hospital, thirty-five pubs, a fleapit cinema, and a bus every two hours. Matron suffered from phlebitis or bursitis or some such obscure malady, and went off for treatments now and again.

'I tell you what; you slip over smartly to Junior School and find Mrs Hamilton-Smith. She's a nurse; she'll know what to do.' One never walked, or even ran, in this kind of place. One nipped, whipped, or even (among younger, cricket-playing ushers) flipped...

Five minutes later his hand was being bathed by something gentle, quiet, and disturbingly female (Matron was none of these things) in a bathroom where there was a face-powdery intimate sort of smell, not at all ecclesiastical. He had always been susceptible to smells. London stank of chips, Munich of plastics, Marseille of pizza: all as a consequence were insupportable.

He had acquired prestige from reading *Madame Bovary* in the holidays (not as sexy as one had been led to believe) but he had never heard of Stendhal. So he did not know how the young tutor resolves to touch Madame de Renal before ten o'clock strikes. But he did have a notion how Julien must have felt. Hair was brushing his cheek. He supposed she was about thirty, but the week before, strangely enough, he had been reading Shaw and had changed his ideas about constant-nymph age-groups. A little essay about Shaw's views on Jeanne d'Arc – pretty unsound Moral Theology. Boring, so he had read illicit Shaw instead, frowned-on stuff about Mrs Warren's Profession. Dreary most of it, but there was a little play about Napoleon. Now Napoleon was God – he had read *L'Aiglon* in the holidays – and this Shaw twerp had no business putting his clay-streaked peasant paws anywhere near Napoleon, but the Celtic charm had got him a bit.

'And what age is she?'

'Just the right age, Sire.'

'Ah – seventeen or thirty?'

Bit of an eye-opener. A dim sort of sweet madness took him, and it was Bernard Shaw's fault. The thought would make him laugh in later years – to have missed Stendhal, and been led astray by Shaw. In a clumsy little thrust of the head he kissed her hair. Her reaction was not unlike Madame de Renal's. After all, nine-year-olds and ecclesiastics – she had forgotten how boys are with feminine flesh. She made a startled little movement, seemed about to say something, found herself at a loss for the right word, and said instead, 'Keep still, or you'll start it bleeding again.' She took a good deal of time and trouble winding him in a very long bandage, round and over and back again; he trembled in a burny shivery way. Nervous reaction from pain; slight shock: she had some training as a nurse.

Finally he was disposed in a black silk sling.

'Now don't bump it or run with it, and you must go with it to Matron before Lights Out.' It was a hot day, and there was a flushed shiny look about her face. As she adjusted the sling, bending over him, he noticed that under the starched white overall, very belted and chilling, there was an uncrackly pinkish undergarment.

At Lights Out he noticed three or four dressing-gowned figures seeming unusually gleeful as they left the Dispensary.

'Syrup of Figs is laid up, joy-oh-joy.'

Inside, Mrs Hamilton-Smith was applying calamine lotion to the scarlet shoulders of a freckled type with a coppernob, who had taken his Athletics too seriously, swaggering about in his little cotton undervest, and scorched his bloody stupid self. She looked up, and became a little flustered.

'Oh – how is it?'

'Sort of throbbing – the bandage is awfully tight.'

'Swollen, is it? Painful?'

'Well, yes, rather.'

'Oh. Matron's got to stay in hospital for a week. She's too much on her feet – she's been told to rest… I don't know… I'll just look.' The hand was impressively swollen, purplish. She took his temperature.

'Mm, not exactly high, but a bit up – quite a lot up. That's natural, I think. I don't think it's infected, but it is rather mauled. Have you had anti-tetanus injections?'

'Huh?'

'You know – Doctor Simpson comes round and gives you a prick.'

'Yes – this spring.'

'Yes, well perhaps you'd better stay in the infirmary, for tonight anyhow.'

He went through to the infirmary, a kind of dormitory holding twenty beds next door, with Matron's quarters at the far end. The only occupant was a fragile child with hay fever or something, who looked at him with listless dislike and went back to a book. In the dispensary he could hear the trinkle of the telephone.

'Oh – Father Superior; Junior Matron here. I was just thinking – there's little Thorpe with his asthma – he's liable to wake up at night when he gets these spells. You know about Matron – yes, awkward – had I better perhaps – yes, I was thinking so too. Yes I see and had I better tell Father Reynolds? Yes – no, only the boy who hurt his hand with a running shoe. A senior – isn't he that French boy? No, I don't think so, but I'm keeping him just in case, and if need be the van can run him in to Doctor Simpson in the morning. Yes, Father, very well.'

Odd, how distinct his memory was – of every word…

She came in to where he was standing waiting.

'Slip quick into bed. I'll give you an aspirin, and an extra pillow. I'll be staying in Matron's room – er – if you hear little Thorpe in the night – er – if I don't hear, erm, don't hesitate to call me.' He would not ordinarily have chosen the bed next to Grendel's Lair, but the idea of her sleeping there was suddenly painful and somehow precious. He felt lucky – he who was so accustomed to feeling the opposite.

Little Thorpe (he was perhaps fifteen) did get restless in the night. Dutheil woke up to alarming whoopy-coughy noises and shot out of bed, jarring his hand, which was somehow a good omen. He did not dare go in the lair, but knocked timidly – she was out at once. Pale-green pyjamas, a constant nymph with tousled hair on a warm summery night.

'You did quite right.' Another remark to which he was unaccustomed! He got into bed, there were whispers and clinks. A dim form was suddenly near him, heart-thumping. 'Are you comfortable?' She gave him some water; his hand contrived to touch a bare forearm. Hair with that odd smell was again near by. 'Sleep well.' Before he fell asleep he knew not only how Julien managed to touch Madame de Renal but how he managed to climb the ladder, to Mathilde de la Mole's window.

And he went on feeling lucky. He was quite well next day; fever gone, no sign of infection, though the hand was painful. He was excused Mass, and got breakfast in the infirmary, quite lordly and somehow better than usual. He got up for class, where the black sling conveyed prestige.

'Right hand too – no writing! Will Ralph let you off the essay?'

'You're little use to me,' said Father Nickleby irritably. 'You'd better study elsewhere. I can't have you here, disturbing the others. Can't have you wandering about, either.' It was a Latin unseen morning, too. 'I found you deplorably weak in history, last week – you'd better take your books to the infirmary, and see about acquiring some basic notion of Hampden's political thought.' She wasn't there, but recent presence was a perceptible burnished-iris shadow.

How it happened – or rather how it lurched from one hideous and delicious insanity to another – he did not know; nor (with benefit of hindsight), quite certainly, did she. A June heatwave, noble and splendid rarity, had something to do with it. Later, when he happened much amused upon *Young Woodley* he was sure that it hadn't been like that anyway, with uproarious sniggers. Except perhaps when the boy speaks her name – Laura (Laura!) and it was 'as though he laid his hand on her bare breasts': rather an emotional simile, remarked Dutheil critically, but, on the whole, justified. Even now, the snigger was needed to carry off the remembrance with a high hand; it was so difficult to achieve detachment. It was nothing to snigger about, to be sure; just an adolescent love-affair, but a rather lovely one, that had done him nothing but good, he said defiantly.

It had unfolded with staggering suddenness, and the remembrance had characteristics of delirium. At once very blurred and very vivid, extremely real and extremely impossible. He had understood nothing at the time, and had afterwards been sure that it had never happened, but had been no more than the sexy feverish little dreams of a schoolboy in hot weather, suffering from a small but painful hand injury and being cared for by a moderately pretty and very ordinary young woman. Surely she must have been very banal and colourless – a schoolboy sees absolutely anything as Helen of Troy at that age. Heightened, moreover, by a heatwave and a slight temperature. She had done nothing, absolutely nothing, but behave with a gentleness to which he was unaccustomed.

But it wasn't so. However easy it might be to dismiss the whole thing as a dream it had happened; it was real. The picture might be distorted, but it was burning sharp. Even lukewarm water burns, on scorched unhealed skin.

He had kissed her, and she had not stopped him. Clumsily he touched her arm, her hair. With the rough insolence that hides adolescent timidity he pushed his hand between the large white slippery buttons of her starchy overall – all the while she was changing the dressing and rewinding the bandage he had touched her in a dry burning muddle of rage, fear, need, and the wish to cry. After she had twice pulled his sad little oyster of a paw away from where it clung he did cry, in tearing sobs, his whole body painfully crisped. She had not spoken; she held him, cuddled him, fondled the paw in her hands, held it tightly, and suddenly, as though it were all she could think of to stop him crying, pressed it back against a small soft breast inside a modest cotton brassière.

It must have been next day that they broke through this clumsy fumbling; surely it could not have been the same night. The amazing sweet insanity had run over the skin of both of them and possessed them, very rapidly. He did not know how long the babe-in-the-wood stage lasted before an aggressive masculinity took over. He knew that the heatwave had gone on the whole time. Four days? Seven?

The first time that he did touch her bare breast (in a very Woodleyish way) a small stupefied voice said 'Don't...you can't do that... I'm responsible...responsible.' Twenty-four hours, at least, after that it must have been when he slid into Grendel's lair in a summery hazy twilight, the pestilent asthmatic little Thorpe well asleep (had she secretly given him a sleeping pill?) and found her staring out of the window – the room not smelling of Grendel – at the gathering summer nightfall. She turned round and stood limp while he unbuttoned the overall; she had underclothes on but she made no effort to stop him taking them off. Indeed she helped him with a hook and eye he might have torn, like a good conscientious housewife.

Certainly, he calculated, it was the morning after that when he came into the dispensary to have his hand dressed – a polite fiction, by this time... It was after breakfast at the end of break, with bells shrilling and a noisy clatter quietening in a breath to the hum of class. She had polished off the morning crop of small boys' ailments, and was mopping the glass table, screwing up jars in a smell of Dettol and sulphur ointment. She gave a laugh of shy bravado when he discovered that with reckless impertinence she had been standing there for half an hour between a dozen broken-voiced brats in early puberty with nothing on under her overall. This sudden leap of the needle on the insanitygraph sent him in a scrawl of ink straight off the chart. Beaufort marks gusts; what, Dutheil tried to remember, is the one that marks tremors?

Brazenly she kept him in the infirmary. Who was going to look under those impressive bandages to see that there were three perfectly healed bluish spots and some slight bruising that was perhaps more sensitive than the rest of his skin, if that indeed were possible? How sensitive can a hand become?

He could not be sure, but thought that it was two days later when the whole episode ended with a suddenness that had, he supposed, that at least to commend it. He was having a bath in the middle of a molten June afternoon, the whole school drowsing on playing-fields and dreaming of ice-cream. A deserted building – even the little Thorpe had been sent to take a sedate walk in the nice fresh air.

The bathroom was opposite the lair, which was now their lair. Had someone noticed that he had not taken a nice walk? Had the little Thorpe, with that sharp adolescent quickness, been less unobservant than he should have been?

Giggling slightly she came to help wash him. It was cool in the bathroom but she complained of the discomfort of the hot starched overall.

'Take it off then.' She did, still self-conscious enough to giggle about this.

'Come in the bath.' Was it astonishing that she did not hesitate before this enormity? No – he thought of these things, but only because he had more imagination. No little girl playing Mother-and-Father in the coalshed could have been more malleable.

They were drying one another with whispers made resonant by the bath, and had heard no noise at all, felt no draught, but the door had opened. They turned, dumb and blinking like calves, finding it difficult to realise that it was indeed the Prefect of Discipline standing there, hands tucked in the side slits of a black summer soutane – a thin sateen-like material with a nasty tendency to crease and shine where sat upon.

He said nothing; he just stood there.

She snatched a towel and bolted instinctively back across the passage into the lair, banging the door in a panic; the priest had stood aside politely to let her pass. The boy, not knowing what to do, tried to get very absorbed in drying moisture between his toes, cramped into a stoop he did not know how to get out of. Unfair really; a bathroom is the ideal place for killing people. There just isn't anywhere they are more defenceless. An unwavering ecclesiastical eye went on looking; the voice at last spoke.

'You will come to my office, dressed, combed, tidied, in – exactly twenty minutes' time, which will be five to four.'

He found a still figure sitting prefectorially before a bare desk.

'You will spend the night in the infirmary. Father Lawton, who received this afternoon a painful blow on the knee from a cricket ball, will also be spending the night there. By tomorrow I shall have telegraphed to your mother, railway tickets will be bought, and your clothes will be packed. By that time I shall have thought over the words I will wish to say to you – you may return now to the infirmary.'

It was utterly silent, deserted; a brooding summer stillness inhabited by a wasp looking for the way out. After ten minutes' vertigo he summoned the courage to look in the lair. Nobody was there. It was perfectly tidy and quite empty. Rosemary might never have existed.

He hadn't cared, at the time. Light-hearted – yes, not just light-headed, joyous – he had jumped on the train, tasting already the pleasure of the night boat from Southampton to Saint Malo, waking up in the lock gates with Breton voices shouting and echoing in this French bathroom. A missed scholarship does not worry a seventeen-year-old any more than a missed girl. Both wounds were only felt long after. His mother was quiet, reasonable, kind. Odd, really, he thought much later, during the war years in uniform. Funny thing that a boy can be deprived of a university education when he has six weeks' school to go, just like that. He thought he understood. The ecclesiastic had not been angry, nor shocked, surely. Had he simply been unable to forgive them for exposing him to the charming sight of a boy and a woman playing together, naked in a bathroom?

He knew that Rosemary must have been tumbled out with as little ceremony as he. Like any good bourgeois sacking the kitchen-maid without a reference, much shocked to find her pregnant, the old boy must have dusted his hands in satisfied knowledge that he has made a clean job of the Lord's Work today.

Dutheil the adult had sometimes wondered what could have happened to Hamilton-Smith. One did not have much to go on. She could not have been terribly bright, and she was certainly very vulnerable. He would not be at all surprised to know that she hadn't lasted long. He could see a vision of a rather distrait and badly dressed young woman working a draughty bit of pavement on the wrong side of Oxford Street, apathetically paying her two-pound fines, getting killed in the stupidest way by a bomb-splinter. He had no notion whether this was a sentimental piece of fiction or the opposite.

# Six

'Come and have a game of croquet,' pushing the last signed cheque back across the desk.

'Very well,' unexpectedly pliable. 'Give you zest; put you in form for journalists.'

Was sleeping with Nora an exorcism, he wondered while getting the croquet things out of the summerhouse? Like those little bottles with a glass stalk attached to the cap, and an acetous sort of liquid that one smeared on an ink stain – aha, an eradicator it was called.

These journalists – tiresome old man Marcus was. He did such things from time to time; a reprisal perhaps against a writer who never came to Paris, never signed press copies and never appeared on television. He allowed Marcus to inflict interviewers occasionally – he interviewed them, without their realising, which amused him, but after the last one he had been furious – Marcus had better produce something better this time, or he would be cross.

A literary livewire, that last one, making his reputation author by author, the way one eats artichokes. Bit of a pocket Napoleon, bouncy and youthful, natty check suit and a lot of dynamism – detestable boy; Paris was full of them, nibbling away like guinea-pigs, determined to be subtle and have insight and generally increase their snotty little standing. Scene-stealer the laddie had been, and unctuously polite, and courageously rude... Ha, he had been lured into croquet and had his little literary buttocks scorched to carbon.

How absurd can I get? What's this; being all vulnerable again? He determined to be polite to this one: American, hm…

He chose the blue and black balls, just to fox Nora; he always played the red and yellow, which 'recognised his hand'. He was promptly punished for this arrogance – some imp of malice was sitting on the blue ball, wagging a didactic finger, telling him that interviewers must be received with simplicity, humility; not just courtesy. He realised at once that he was going to be slapped down in a typical Nora way, with simplicity, with humility; damn you Nora, you virtuous bitch.

She was a firm unimaginative croquet player, easy to beat as a rule, nice and predictable, and this time she had him in her pocket from the first stroke; his blue ball behaving most annoyingly… He judged the slope well; it followed a ripe seductive curve, and then stopped two centimetres short. The grass was dry, fast, and slippery – he had allowed for this; it was most unfair. Nora's red hit him a brisk crack.

She played the stake too timidly, staying lodged against it, but hope rose in vain; she nuzzled up to the blue ball as a preface to clouting it in a most evil-minded female way, so that he went twenty metres before rolling another ten downhill, and then she managed to lodge herself in the hoop; even if one did get her with the black ball one would be unable to help putting her through. One didn't even get that far; he played the black limply, and it trickled, ignominious, back down the slope: easy target. She got it, of course, her yellow ball carrying his comfortably along, getting a soft shot at the stake, and actually having the cheek to go on carrying him past three hoops in a row before she finally lost her nerve at a beastly narrow angle and settled for ruining him, with a simply frightful kick into the rosebushes.

She leaned on her mallet grinning, while he pretended to study the situation, though he could see at once there wasn't a damn thing to be done. A raid was out of the question. It would miss, and she had two balls to make hay and havoc with while he sat there in the corner with the dunce's hat on: thank you.

No, plainly one had to stay well out of reach. Calm single strokes to get the blue back up the plateau, without risk, in two. The black must traverse all along the line of rosebushes, long grass or no long grass, and then go right across the middle. And by that time she would be all the way round, puffed with her own cleverness, and he would torpedo her, capturing both balls together, with any luck at all. Hm, the torpedo was probably a myth; it so plainly was not his day for succeeding a torpedo. There; his blue ball kicked on a hummock at the lip of the plateau and instead of running on smoothly skidded and went fatally over, rolling spinelessly down right into her path; all the yellow ball had to do was to clear one quite easy hoop to clonk him afresh. She would tap her red back to help in the slaughter – but his apprehension was lifted by a noisy hilarious effect inside the house; the guests had come. Ah well; saved him a few more humiliations.

'I surrender,' he said magnanimously.

Nora was surprised. Not like him to give up just because there were guests; on the contrary, guests were generally bidden come quick to admire the Master being Unbuttoned. And she knew that a good croquet player is never more dangerous than when sitting in black ignominy and thick jungle. She had been quite resigned to the torpedo, to getting banged when almost home and then having to stand impotent while he played all four balls round the whole lawn in a single break, her poor red and yellow with their trousers, so to speak, round their ankles.

She wasn't going to be triumphant though. One beat him at croquet by accident. The only person who might perhaps not was Véronique, as slaughterous a player as her dear papa but unhappily getting a lot less practice.

Inside, Laure was getting kissed by Marcus, in that ritual way he had: toc-toc on both hands, toc-toc on both cheeks, toc-toc finally on both temples, this last toc-toc real, two loud explosive sounds like the acetylene cartridges that the farmer puts among the vines in autumn, to frighten the birds off.

Very cap-à-pie, Laure noticed when she could stand away and got her breath back: strenuous business, getting kissed. Not at all marked by dusty hours over shoe-lace roads, though she suspected a good many stops for little rests. Radiant in a summer suit with an extraordinary double-breasted waistcoat of some tropical material. He rather went in for cummerbunds and things, dressy old man. Marvellously spry too, with sources of unsuspected energy at midnight just as everyone began to get cross and foggy – oh well; a handy talent doubtless for a publisher.

He was taller and thinner than Dutheil. His distinguished stoop seemed to have increased unless it was fatigue – he had always that air of being just-back-from-Longchamps, of wonderful grey hats and show-off huge binoculars. His long hands had beautiful almond-shaped nails, his hair was evenly silver, and he had a rather precious tie – hortensia-colour. Dutheil, now arriving upon the scene from the garden, had comments on the shirt – trust him to notice that at once – very very exquisite, needle-thin celestial blue and lilac stripes. He must too, of course, point out at once that the Legion of Honour cord in the buttonhole clashed with the tie.

Laure liked Marcus, while none too sure whether she approved of him. He had turned Dutheil into an inexorable seller, cashing in gaily on all the legends, making capital out of the tensions and anxieties, whereas Laure wondered secretly whether, if the books sold less, they might not be...less smooth. Mention such a notion to god and he became very irritable with no delay at all. Mention it to Marcus and you got a lot of blah. Voice and manner of someone sweetening home truths were assumed.

'My very dearest Laure. The total public for the printed word is perhaps four hundred thousand souls. Jostling to attain it is a stupefying quantity of what are loosely termed men of letters. Meaning doctors, physicists, architects, chemists, all horribly articulate, all burning to immortalise their table conversation over the last year, sponsored naturally, by a reputable publisher. Does this explain the terrible urge to be known, the psychotic juggling and manoeuvring, the anguish over every tiny notice? There are too many writers chasing too few readers.'

'Yes.' Impatiently. 'You're not in the Palais Bourbon – don't orate.'

'But grasp it, my dear – hundreds of good books selling three hundred copies. The publisher expected to show a loss and love it, on account of Art. When the poor devil of a publisher attempts to promote a novelist who has the fortune to be widely known – why, then you abuse him for being commercial.'

'Pooh,' said Laure crossly, 'promotion among Paris dinner-tables – two thousand nobodies pretending to be arbiters of taste.'

'But who buys books.'

'At the risk of seeming conceited, when one sells all round the world one is not awfully concerned about the sixteenth arrondissement.'

'Oh my poor Laure. Have you forgotten our total inability to admit that anyone outside our frontiers has passed the caveman stage? The rest of the world – anthropoid apes who have learned to manipulate machinery. Tell us that Shakespeare never blotted a word and we chorus in unison that if he had blotted a hundred thousand he might have been on the way to becoming a writer.'

Hopeless. One had to laugh at the jokes and agree to change the subject. But Marcus was not a good influence. Dutheil was too much of an anarchist, fatally warm of heart and weak of head, spontaneous, and vulnerable. Still, she was fond of Marcus.

He was still holding her by the shoulders, taking her in with the famous eagle glance with which he transpierced manuscripts in ten minutes without sitting down.

'Very nice...pretty, that... I rather like the ending, myself...sags somewhat in the middle.'

'So young! So young and so pretty... I never see anything like that in Paris! Startlingly good frock – Balenciaga? – how right you are. But I forget myself – allow me to present Mr Robert Thomassen, my excellent friend from New York.' So this was the American. A bit earnest? Something stodgy? Laure was quite prepared not to love this fellow terribly.

'You now, my dear Dutheil, will find him a most civilised companion. He's been telling me admirable Jewish stories – never did that awful road pass quicker, never have I driven so dangerously, shaken with ribaldry. We are here in one piece, we had a good lunch, and will shortly in this superb air have a splendid appetite for dinner.'

'Happy to see you here, Mr Thomassen – can one tell Jewish stories in French?'

'Happy to be here, Madame – alas, only in the purest of New York accents – but Marcus! I quite forgot to tell about the shepherd.'

'Tell us about him, so that we can hear for ourselves.' Had he noticed that her manner was a bit cool?

'The shepherd,' in a hesitant, apologetic way, 'sorry, my accent's not that good – well, he stubbed his toe, see, on a rock you know – going into the cave?...and it hurt his toe so bad, it was so painful he just couldn't stop himself. Oh Jesus, he says, rather loud too, so that he was pretty ashamed, but Mary looks up, she's real nice and doesn't frown or anything but she says to Joseph, did you hear that? – that's a real pretty name – shall we call him that?'

Laure laughed and Nora smiled politely; Marcus beamed upon his protégé and Dutheil looked appreciative – not bad, the technique. Thomassen was looking downwards at the floor, modestly.

'But tell,' began Dutheil silkily, 'how it is that a New York Jew dare skulk under a name like Thomassen?'

'Well, that way he can always fill in as a Santa Claus if they don't love him any more on the paper. It's tough being a Norwegian in New York, but just think for a moment about being a Jew out in the plains – why, to avoid getting found out I had to circumcise damn near the whole of Nebraska.'

'And my darling Nora,' Marcus was saying with his warmth that sounded so professional but that startlingly was real. 'Delighted to see you – looking marvellous. You're keeping an eye on him? – not letting him get too slack?'

Dutheil had to get away from all the welcoming togetherness, and tow the American along. He seemed reasonable enough, but it was all very well, this having people in one's bosom just because they came sailing in under Marcus' wing. A wangle, that; one couldn't just let them stroll about writing things down in little books.

# SEVEN

Thomassen was amused. Be on your best behaviour! The careful looks he got from everyone, and Marcus lecturing him since before leaving Paris...just don't show any signs of feeling in your pocket for a notebook! What was coming now? – writer-man, with phony-philosophical monologue? He got drawn into the hall – his briefcase had vanished already; were they going through it upstairs? Spare suit but no tape-recorder – all right, pass!

'Figaro!' Fellow startled him, bawling like that. Hm, snazzily appointed library.

'Come and sit down – like some gin and something, would you?' Too smoothly said – another test.

'Wine of the country if I might – grow your own, don't you?'

'That's right – bring a bottle, Figaro.'

'Why Figaro?'

'He runs the household by intrigue. By the way – did Marcus mention it? – we don't have journalists here; we have guests. You're here for pleasure; make some business out of it but don't write any biographies – my wife wouldn't like it.' Door opened; Spaniard bringing bottle, followed by Madame. Losing no time!

'Yes, Marcus mentioned that you didn't go much for interviews.'

'All right, Figaro, I'll pour it out.' Taking up her cue.

'I better be careful,' said Thomassen mildly, 'seeing I'm here surrounded on two sides already.'

'Has my husband been on at you so quickly? – a cigarette, Mr Thomassen?'

'Good drink, this.' He wasn't going to go pretentious about the vino…

'It's only fair to tell you – any sort of celebrity, even little ones, get nervous after they've caught a few photographers hidden in trees.'

'You won't allow any photographs – fair enough. I'm clean; wouldn't know which way up to hold the thing anyway. This drink – gets better as you go along.' Dutheil seemed pleased. Why was she so tense?

'People have in the past misquoted things.'

He felt like being naughty.

'If we have a little talk we can put it on tape. You keep a copy.'

'He's very fond of tapes,' said Laure, smiling brightly. 'You have to do the job you came for, of course. Quite simple – you write what you please, and we ask only that details of our private life be left out and no quotes in direct speech be used – not very dreadful is it? Mademoiselle Noël will ask you to sign a little undertaking. Of course if you don't want to – well, we lose a friendship, which would be a pity.'

'No quotes – tough. The public just loves that sensation of eavesdropping.'

'You take my point. It's such a lovely undertaking too; no holes, as guaranteed by Swiss lawyers.'

She had humour, anyway. He wasn't going to find words for her yet: plenty of time.

'Sure I'll sign it. Expected it. I haven't any tiny concealed mikes – I was just kidding.' She looked happier, going to the door.

'Nora dear.'

Dutheil grinned. She was transparent with her little ways – very human. Nora dear! You are the invaluable secretary and if I do know you go to bed with him occasionally don't worry, dear: servants' gossip! Nora dear had come in with her little form, and the American was smiling over it, appreciating the Swiss legal mind. Fellow had been studying Laure, looking for a slant on this charming and intelligent woman who had something unsympathetic about her. People were often content with a superficial shot, calling her 'hard' as though she were a chocolate. Banality; the slick blonde with the thin lips, cheapest cliché in the business. Laure! Softened, rounded woman who has grown a shell, but it's an eggshell. The opposite to me, a soft choc with a hard pebble in the middle.

Thomassen was signing his name – damn thing in duplicate like a literary contract! Not bad like that, the woman, sitting upright on a stiff chair: gravity, poise. Pretty too. Lot of tension. That silky skin was stretched thin and would bleed, he guessed, at a scratch.

'I'll leave you together. Any allergies, Mr Thomassen, or things you can't bear to eat? No? Americans often feel the cold and we're near the mountains. I've given you an extra blanket but just tell me if you find you need something. I'll have the pleasure of seeing you at dinner.'

'I'll be fine, thank you though.'

Dutheil was absent, thinking of the right word. Tensile, elastic – there wasn't any right word. She was well-tempered; that was it perhaps. He had such a shrinking from rubbing himself on the sandpaper of other people, which in the old days caused her to sigh a little as she paid the rent, bargained in an auction room, got on to workmen about a mislaid key or a burst pipe.

'We might as well talk about books,' Thomassen was saying plaintively. 'I've got to fill three thousand dirty great words.'

'Three thousand dirty great words!' repeated Dutheil with admiration. 'Yes, that is a lot, isn't it?'

A nice chat! All the usual questions about one's youth, one's early ambitions, one's time in the army. Thomassen duly admired the library, expressed polite interest in the leather editions, and the nice chat turned to one's favourite authors. They went for a walk in the garden, where the bastard refused to play croquet – been tipped off by that miserable Marcus! Fellow was rather bland, with traps for authors, saying smoothly the house reminded him of Tara, perhaps how he had imagined Tara when he was a boy reading *Gone With the Wind.* Dreamhouse, what! One made a few classic remarks on the usual subjects.

'I'll be most interested to study my grandchildren – I hope I live a long time. One of my boys is studying biology: literature – pah.'

'Of course I like Maugham. Writer's writer – always liked the special pen and the armbrace. Go to your desk and write, nine to one, especially on Sundays and birthdays: good, that.'

'I like vulgar pedestrian pleasures; striptease and television wrestling. Must be English blood – the English have these perversions, like eating over-ripe camembert.'

'Don't go on at me about starving humanity. Suffering is a universal experience. It's sent us; we get it. We're all in the same bath – don't go all Jewish on me.'

'Israel – being hemmed in, exercising the youth with martial prowess and marching along with spades singing songs – where have I heard this song before?'

'Air Force – radio-telephones. Peculiar schoolboy jargon.

Flash your weapon. My weapon is bent, my cock is strangled – tallyho, bandit. Filling in bomb craters with a shovel.'

'I enjoy getting cheated, and I enjoy watching all these bastards working out ways of cheating me. Just one of the differences between me and the bourgeois.'

'You like being rich?'

'I love it.'

Cocktails, as Figaro put it, would be at seven. Dutheil was in his dressing-room, tired, not unpleasantly. Fellow had his interview – would be amusing to see what he made of it. Waste of time, but did no harm and pleased Marcus. Not a bad fellow; one could tease him, and he saw it, and didn't get mad about it. One could make a joke without his flying into a panic.

It had been a lovely day – be a splendid sunset. Perhaps they would have drinks on the terrace; the green and lilac afterglow, vivid as any polar aurora, would make the salon look marvellous. Dinner would not be a bore. Last week there had been his tax inspector, delightful man who wrote lyrics for pop singers. Was there anyone tonight? Gilbert, perhaps. He rather thought he was in form, himself; one could see, after a couple of drinks. Meanwhile, have a little rest, empty the mind of preoccupations, put your feet up, and close your eyes.

Thomassen, not tired but feeling a bit baffled, climbed stairs slowly, looking at pictures he found pretty mediocre but watch it, he didn't know all that much. Which room was his? He found a little card with 'Mr Thomassen' typed on it tied to the handle – efficient secretary hereabouts! He flopped in a chintzy armchair and looked about. Efficient hostess too, and the lordly Spanish service Marcus had promised. All his clothes had been hung, and his shoes brushed. He took off a sweaty shirt and washed splashily, with a pleasant certainty that next time he passed the shirt would have vanished and the bathroom would be spotless again. By his bed stood a bunch of grapes, three apples and a bottle of Vittel; on the other side was a reading lamp which worked, Jane Austen in pocket edition, a large comfortable ashtray and a box of matches – mother, it was like a Sheraton. In the bathroom was Kleenex and a tiny notice saying 'Sorry – hundred-and-ten volts.'

He went in search of Marcus, whom he found lying in dignified ease on a day-bed like Madame Récamier, glancing at a novel belonging to someone's inferior publishing house.

'Hallo my boy; I've had a rest while you've been running round the countryside – nice game of croquet?'

Thomassen made a face, sitting down heavily with his hands in his pockets.

'I thought I'll be real earnest, get to grips straight away. What do I get? – fistfuls of nothing.'

'Ha – I warned you; not the type one can walk in and interview.

'No – too goddam tangential. Takes me for a walk and looks at birds the whole time.' Marcus yelped with laughter.

'He loathes birds!'

'Looking at them through binoculars,' gloomily. 'I haven't a damn thing but background – technicolour crap off a postcard.'

'Now don't be a clown, Robert. Be Jewish, subtle – Dutheil is background. You've plenty of time. The castle, the croquet, the food we'll eat shortly – make up your own dialogue; he expects you to.'

'I need a few keys.'

'I see that – he's like Linear B. What's your impression?'

'Trivial, nearly.'

'Oh dear.'

'Yes, oh dear, I know, I'm being earnest and perplexed – well I am perplexed. He's being foxy? – I see self-satisfied frivolity. Must be far from stupid – a stupid man can't write like that. Got a good eye, sensitive and all, but how does a good writer come to be buried here surrounded by this tripe? – this castle stuff. He seems pleased with it like some goddam mortician who's sold up and gone to live in Florida.'

Marcus laughed some more, enjoying this.

'You don't like the country squire act? – watching birds through binoculars – always amuses me intensely.'

'I don't find it terribly funny – I must sound unusually stiff and priggish but I'm almost tempted to use the word shocking.'

Sabatier took his glasses off and swung his legs off the sofa, evidently perturbed.

'Can't have this. Let's see whether I have understood you – you meet a writer with a high level of technical brilliance and you expect to find a high quality of thought, call it what you like. When you do meet him you are bothered at not quite distinguishing how much is concealed light and how much is bushel. What d'you want him to do – political journalism? If you find him insufficiently dynamic, forgive me but you seem to have been meeting the wrong writers.'

'I'm not exactly the student any more,' said Thomassen mildly, 'writing a composition about how Jane Austen is not much of a writer really because there are no symbols in her work.'

'No,' blandly, putting his glasses back on and looked politely attentive.

'Because I used the word tangential you assume I meant superficial. Perhaps peripheral is better? I get a feeling of someone being swung round and round on the end of a string, and lacking the force to combat it. Force meaning courage, or moral purpose, or anything – hell, I don't know. Being controlled by circumstances, or perhaps pushed about by a lot of objects – I told you, I don't have any definitions.'

'Being peripheral…slung out on the edge and skidding off at tangents – not bad at all – you mean this figure rather literally, don't you?'

'Yes, I rather think I do.'

'Perhaps you've been remarkably quick and unusually acute,' said Sabatier half to himself. 'A disc, revolving fast because there's a lot of motor – I'm able to see this because, you know, I've been a friend of his for some years, after all. I've heard him talk along somewhat similar lines. Writers like to construct these elaborate metaphors and follow them to see where they lead.'

'Turning a metaphor into metaphysics.'

'That's a cocktail-party remark, but yes.'

'All right; you tell me.'

'Some journalist – was it Koestler? – said he came to Israel pro-Jew and anti-Zionist, and left anti-Jew – but pro-Zionist…same sort of thing… Forgive a personal remark? You're a bit inclined to think people have the idea of Norwegians as very dull. Dour, introspective, puritanical or whatnot – you don't want people to think of you like that so you put on this Jewish comedian's act. Isn't Dutheil like that, perhaps? Lazy, frivolous, self-pitying, a weak character tangled up in neurosis – but he's a good writer. You see him idling around the house – but ask the wife. Comes a day, pretty soon now, when he starts work. Sits down in that damn silly library and bats out five thousand words. Day's work. But he does't sit there then all pleased with it. Nor does he chuck it away. He keeps it. When the time for imagination is past you'd find a serious, skilful, extremely conscientious craftsman taking over. Cutting a word here, transposing a line there, tightening. One sees these people when they're off-duty, playing the clown. I have a notion that his foolery that worries and upsets you is necessary counterpoise – an antidote maybe? – to a high level of concentration. We don't see the other side to people like this. I don't suppose even the wife does. She knows it's there, though. She goes all out to cuddle her genius, protect him against everything that might upset or worry him. She overdoes the maternal stuff – but he needs it, perhaps.'

'The frivolity is a defence against diffidence, timidity?'

'More than that, perhaps. Fear, possibly. Fear of having talent and fear of not having any – manic depressive, isn't it? – depends whether the swing of the moment is up or down. He knows that, of course. Fear of being capable of he doesn't quite know what – a bloody good book, maybe, or a violent maniac crime. Or fear he's not capable of keeping going, of bringing off the act on the high trapeze each time he sits down and starts hitting the typewriter. The books vary in quality – I don't need to tell you that, huh – but every damn one is a seller. He's scared of a moment when the public might turn its back to him. Not critics – he hasn't given a thought to a critic in twenty years. But why have us here at all? Because you're a journalist, a witchdoctor with the public, and I'm a publisher, the godforgotten imbecile who slogs out to put the stuff on the public's plate. And he knows that's important, that without us he'd starve. Whereas if we were literary critics he'd have us both horsewhipped by the servants, most likely.' The thought amused Sabatier, at his own wit.

'You might ask the doctor,' serious again. 'Whether he'd tell you is something else, but to my knowledge he's the fellow who knows Big Chief as well as anyone. It's my guess he'd agree that at work the man achieves detachment. Exteriorises everything, sees it with a peculiar clarity. Once released from work, there isn't only a nervous reaction, but a psychological regression.

'There's an overactive imagination – runs riot at times. There's a line from Shakespeare, is it? he's fond of quoting. Is it the Fool in *Lear*? – "With a heart of furious fancies and a burning spear I wander" – something like that. Might give you a key, that: rather good, I think,' with vanity.

'Frivolous, but very intense – and extremely secretive. Tells lies all the time, and if he mentions his mother he's apt to describe her as "a woman I used to know" – some significance in that, I think. Holy cow, it's seven o'clock.' Sabatier rushed to the looking-glass and began to tie an outrageous bow – butterfly of bright yellow, with cream-coloured spots. Thomassen watched with some amusement. Pretty good publisher, he thought, and slips frivolity on and off like a silk dressing-gown. How much of what you're telling me here is Dutheil – and how much you yourself?

'Anguished, huh?' looking out of the window.

'Terribly anguished,' said the reflection in the glass, grimacing horribly, half at the anguish and half at the tie. 'Always has been, always will be – knows no other human condition. Writing those books is a means of relieving that anguish – that's the clinical view, the way the Court Doctor sees it – he gave me that definition of a writer and why he writes. Maybe that's why old Dutheil's such a prolific scribbler. Let's get down; if we're late for cocktails there'll be hell to pay.'

# Part Three

# One

Laure was changing in her dressing-room; Dutheil had a way of dropping in at this time, to tie his bow or simply to have a gossip. If he liked best the time before lunch, when still suffused by the glow of good conscience from his morning's work, she liked best the time before dinner, when at last she could shed the dragging load that was the Castle of Fountainblue. Now it no longer existed, and she was back in Perpignan, in Aix, or even in Brighton, before there had been any Kieffer, any Figaro, any Nora. When journalists had been rare and exciting happenings – think of it, she thought wryly; an excitement!

With the bravado of a small boy he had put his feet up on the little table which she had brought in here till it should be mended, and the fragile chair he sat in was tilted back, which was a way no doubt of telling everyone to go jump in the lake. She was standing by the window to catch the light, in her underclothes, stitching an inch or so of petticoat-seam that had given way, and he was enjoying her, the old Turk, with a big gleam in the eye as though all set to rip the seam again the moment she had finished. He frequently became amorous around twilight; medicine, in her opinion, for an inner skin bruised and rasped by the day that was ending. A need for comfort?

There was a cloud today, certainly, not very menacing-looking, perhaps, but thundery, charged with electric tension. Just the American? She did hope he was not in a stew about Véronique. She did not know why it was suddenly impossible to let the electricity discharge harmlessly into a nice comfortable earth-mother, and when she was painting her eyelids and discovered a large possessive paw descending upon her brassière she found herself saying, 'Your guests will be kept waiting' in a more severe tone than she had meant. He was disconcerted.

'Figaro will guess, you mean. Has that really any importance? Susanna writes it all in her diary every time she changes sheets.'

'I was thinking more of the visitors.'

'Publishers – journalists – who cares about them?' A good noisy rejoinder, but he had understood, and began to tie his tie, signal that she was now allowed to put her frock on.

'That American,' she said indulgently, 'running about everywhere with his eyes popping out.' And next month there was an English Sunday paper, she thought: he didn't know about that one yet. Interviews…

'Get the stupid bastard out of here, and then take me to bed any time.' It sounded feeble. She wanted to say something about Véronique too. He certainly had it on his mind, and once freed of one tension he would talk about the other. Somehow she was not able to. Almost she wanted to reverse things, say 'Go on; make love' but she could not. One's plans never went the way they were intended – but she was too uncomfortably aware of all those people hanging about downstairs.

Marcus – always the professional – was reading a book. The American, loose and comfortable in a corner, was scrutinising a commode – forty per cent restored but one hoped a literary journalist had no eye for such things. Dutheil was sure a few pep-talks awaited him from both quarters; Marcus had that not-quite-so-happy-about-the-last-manuscript look in his eye, and all New Yorkers, neurotic about Vietnam, would confidently expect him to be so too.

'Figaro, I want a large glass of Evian. And open two bottles of champagne.'

The door opened and the boys appeared, with Nora, sharing some joke apparently, at his expense no doubt. Trust her – glittery beads of some sort stitched to the bodice of her frock. He drank his Evian, not really listening to various things being said to him. Gilbert Royan arrived last – family party, thought Dutheil. Publisher, critic, doctor, wife, secretary-mistress; absolutely classic. Gilbert looked gross and scruffy as always. Since his suits were expensive why did they always look rumpled, as though just out of a fast clutch with Strapping Steffi? Is rumpled a better word than crumpled? wondered the writer automatically. Gilbert had the great merit of looking stupid; looking brighter than one was would be the worst of evils – he didn't think it applied to him but it was a thing one had to watch. There he went, complimenting Laure on her frock; bravo. Jean-Luc, nice well-mannered boy, was being polite to the American, whose name he had forgotten, damn it. He would have some champagne; he felt lots better and the court was present.

No it wasn't. Where was Véronique? Twilight, twisting country road, the careless and unlit pottering bicycle, the sudden forced swerve, the stunned bleeding, the dozen tired and snappy drivers who hit and felt the bump and just carried on their way home to light and supper and television: doubtless it had been a cat. Just as he reached the farm tractor coming home late, and the peasant wondering what that bundle was, half in the ditch, his daughter appeared, very much alive. Not at all disfigured-in-the-ditch. Cool, with the thick layer of sophistication aimed at by the modern sixteen-year-old, and a cigarette, by god, in the corner of its mouth… Dutheil, stunned in his ditch, tried out and rejected various phrases. Pert little chit – his mother's Edwardian vocabulary. Demi-virgin – what a pre-war sound it had. A delinquent. Banal, somehow…

How had she achieved it? Calculated to enrage him, no doubt of that, but a lot of effort had been put into it. He shut his eyes, veins swelling. Trousers at his dinner-table – now if it had been those tight après-ski things it would not have been so bad, however unsuited to the solid behind of the female adolescent, but this… Véronique was wearing a thing he had bought for Laure to amuse both of them, a sort of one-piece pyjama with floppy wide legs, bare shoulders, a big bow in front, in swirling violent colours with a zip starting provocatively in the middle of one's bottom. Known to copywriters, doubtless, as a television frock, or a hostess gown, or a lounging robe: known to the vulgar populace – him – as a rape-me-quick. So suitable for one's wife, on one's daughter merely indecent.

'For whom, may I ask, is the clown role? My guests?'

'Good evening, Father.' Quiet, polite. 'It looks nice, doesn't it? Mother thought so too.'

'Did she now?'

'Don't start making a scene now, will you, please?'

'I'm sorry if I appear unappreciative. I can't have this at dinner. As you very well know.' She looked stricken, and he searched clumsily for a way of changing his mind, of saying oh well… What harm was there in it, after all? Thomassen's voice, penetrating, came from somewhere behind.

'Why, she looks fine.'

'She'll never look any better than she does now.' Jean-Luc, words and music carefully suited to the big brother part.

'But she's lovely. This is your young sister now, that right?' Véronique was doing her best to surmount the snub.

'Look, I'm sorry, but I've been working like a fool all day. I've got more work tonight. I tried not to look too much the inky schoolgirl at dinner, but if you make a fuss very well, I'll ask Leonarda to give me a boiled egg in my room. Suits me, because I can do some work instead of having to be social. That all right with you?'

Doubtless it would have passed over with that. Only the very greenest passengers in the liner's smoking-room would feel sick at the little swell. What happened was Marcus' fault. He was sitting in a straight-backed chair, holding his book in a period way, up level with his shoulders and slightly sideways. Was it from good manners that he had paid no attention to the muttering? Had he not even noticed? Now as Dutheil stood undecided he glanced up for a bare second and squinnied sideways at the harlequin trousers. Oh! He did a take, poking a narrow polished fingernail at his spectacles, hitching them up long enough for an eyeful. The lenses dropped again like a firecurtain and he went back to print. Probably he was waiting, courteously, for a better moment to say good evening. Had the curtain dropped too hurriedly? But the rayed lines round his eyesocket had neither bunched in distaste nor opened in even the least lecherous of appreciations. There was nothing to justify an outburst. Why did he say nothing, thought Dutheil in a rage. Stupid things, rages. One used terrible clichés like 'Thrash you within an inch of your life' – but the fact that it is such a cliché shows how easy it is to be enraged with a child. What frightened Dutheil was his detachment. He stood there viewing his own rage, calm and reposed, raising his glasses like Marcus, the better, one might say, to view the absurd performance he was now going to give. Voyeurism – how was it possible to get in a bone-breaking rage and be reminded of watching a striptease?

'Go up to your room, Véronique.' His voice was soft and sounded to him perfectly normal.

She looked at him, shrugged contemptuously, turned with no further ado and drifted out, wiggling her hips slightly to show she was not caring. A rather lovable gesture – young girl's interpretation of dignity: to Dutheil it was an insolent defiance, which showed he could be on occasion a bad writer. Very good; he would teach that girl her four truths and not much later than now.

He glanced around. Life was going quietly on, nothing to show anybody had noticed. A log slid and blazed in the fireplace, Figaro stood bland by the door waiting to refill glasses, the American was asking Danny about universities and laughing heartily at answers. Gilbert Royan seemed to be choosing whether to flirt with Laure or Nora and Marcus turned the page of his book. Without meaning to, Laure put the lid on disaster. Her eye, very bright, was trying to catch his, saying 'It's my fault – I suggested to the girl that she wear it. Do her good and cheer her up maybe. She had a bad day and was all distraught – boyfriend trouble!' He refused, arbitrarily, to catch the eye. He lit a cigarette and drank his half-glass of champagne, that had not even had time to go flat. A crisis. He was so deliberate about it that he was quite sure he was doing the right thing. He walked out slowly and shut the door behind him. Figaro would not announce dinner till Laure gave the sign. They could all wait four more minutes.

Véronique was standing looking out of her bedroom window. There was not a lot to see; sunset long over, dusk fading swiftly, a band of paler sky along the horizon giving an anaemic souvenir of daylight. The outlines of the lawn and borders, the summerhouse where the deckchairs and the croquet things had been put away. She was still smoking the bravado cigarette, which must have been lit to help her with her entrance downstairs. She turned and they stood looking at each other, each with the stupid cigarette wobbling about in the mouth, neither knowing quite how to say it. Both of them were sorry, both wanted to say so, both realised that they had humiliated the other unnecessarily; both in absurd *amour-propre* waited for the other to speak. He cleared his throat.

'Really, you know, after this morning I determined to give you a good beating.' And that was why I was disagreeable, he meant to go on, but her nostril started to twitch at once, and she ran for her hard scornful look to protect against fresh humiliation.

'Like a Polish railwayman. Take a strap to the girl. Aren't you supposed to be a writer? The mentality seems more like a Czech overseer in a shoe factory.' He walked lumpishly towards her, and she withdrew as though from contagion, as though at no cost might his arm touch hers.

'Take that off and put on a frock and come downstairs.'

'What do you want? – to see me undress?' Gratuitous, shocking, frightening remark; he felt blood surge again in his head.

'Very well – then I will beat you – you seem to think by god I'd be scared to.' Abruptly, he left the room.

Outside he became aware of a slight technical problem. All very well – what was he going to beat her with? He didn't have any whips or anything. He wasn't even wearing a belt. What was he to do – go down to the kitchen for a wooden spoon? – that would really please all the Spaniards no end. He found the solution in a floppy palm-like green plant in an alcove on the landing, held up by a bamboo stolen by some Spaniard from Kieffer's precious chrysanthemums. He wiped earth off and held it self-consciously down his leg, alarmed somebody would notice. Véronique looked taken aback at seeing him, but sneered at the awkward way he was holding the stick.

Stiffly he drew the curtains across the window.

'I'm not going to draw attention to your antics by sending you from the table. You will change, and you will behave normally.'

'Do you think you're behaving normally?'

'Rude this morning, sullen tonight, insolent now – do you think I'm putting up with it? Take that thing off. Since something is needed to impress elementary manners on you I'll give it you.'

He did not know why, but he had expected her to look frightened. She looked taken aback, still, but she did not seem to take him seriously. She jerked her head in a graceless way. She's not pretty like that, he thought impatiently. She has a certain splendour, and destroys it with that sullen look. Why can she not look like her mother? Why like me, plain and clownish? Why is she so sharp?

Was this how I looked, at my Hamilton-Smith stage? asked the writer, suddenly.

'The great dictator,' said Véronique. 'With a little stick. He already has the room where you walk a hundred steps, the bureau where god gets inspired. Why haven't you a globe you can play balloons with?' He gave her an angry, childish push back on to her bed.

'Now get those trousers off, and look sharp.'

She looked at him, not even jeeringly. More knowingly. He could not contain himself, caught her shoulder and jerked her to her feet, so angry he wanted to wrench the silly thing off her, feel the material tear. The stick encumbered and mortified him, and she saw this.

'You want to struggle with me now, I see. Don't you? I'm sixteen; you'll get a kick out of pulling my pants down and beating me. You can go tearing down then to rape Nora in the west room – or would you rather rape me?'

He was so flabbergasted at this remark that it tore a hole in the blindness of anger. Never could he remember being so shocked. He let go. She was now so angry herself that she noticed nothing. Furious, she reached awkwardly behind her, tore the zip open, wrenched the frock off – and threw herself down across the bed, a childish bottom sticking up pathetically.

'There,' her voice muffled by her hands, 'now beat me and I hope you enjoy it and I'll never speak to you again.'

The idiocy of it calmed him. What! Insolent little misses, so knowing, full of fake Freudian rubbish, so pertly sex-conscious at fourteen, thinking Pa was showing barely concealed incestuous desires every time he kissed them. He wasn't having that! Yes he was an artisan, a manual worker. Yes he was a Polish railwayman, yes he was a Czech shoe-factory overseer, a Hungarian fruit-farmer, any peasant they cared to name, bourgeois sluts, snotty brats; he gave her a tremendous bang with the little stick and realised at once that he had hit her far too hard and hurt her abominably.

Véronique gave a hoarse shriek, forced from her with such brutality that it appalled him, not recognisably a human sound, so that he stood terrified at causing her this injury. Then she did a dreadful thing; in an instinctive effort to protect herself and dull the burn upon the cool silkiness of the counterpane she rolled over. His daughter! – yes he knew how the tiniest girl has the same delicately gross femininity which he had last noticed when she was a baby. Her face was screwed shut by intense pain, blinding her, of which he was glad, engulfed as he was. He felt ashamed, confused, as he had not been since Hamilton-Smith – why did he see himself standing stupefied in his pyjamas, damp splashes of boyhood on her starched overall – and that vague smile on her face, the empty, seeing-nothing eyes?

This most unpleasant memory was replaced of a sudden by another, so unimportant, so meaningless, so banal that he wondered where on earth he had seen the striptease girl who put her thumb in her mouth, greasy threadbare gesture the poor cow had learned to hit the customer as she took the last rag off. Innocence, no, in that pretence of innocence? So shocking a gesture, far more shocking than any obscenity she could have thought of in the crude light between the huddled, stiffened little group of men leaning forward without knowing, wanting it without love, without desire, without any real interest at all – just wanting it through stupid implanted instinct. Was not that poor draggle-tail one and the same as Hamilton-Smith? And now, more shockingly still, it was Véronique with her immature sun-browned thighs and her appallingly mature triangle of black hair upon indecent white skin – which he desired. Was that a man, then? Head swimming with nausea he walked out, closing the door softly, very softly, and with the same patient meaningless concentration walking down the stairs, step by step, glad too of the effort needed to push the little stick back through its loop of raffia and slot it home into the sharp tiny hole drilled in the moist firm earth.

Getting one's head back inside one's skull is no easy job sometimes, thought Dutheil. It was like pulling out the metres and metres of bedded cotton-wool enclosing some delicate and elaborate glass instrument: the familiar problem of getting it all back in the box, aghast at there being enough packing to fill three such boxes. Still…a handful of eau-de-cologne on his face in the little lavatory off the hall, and within five minutes of leaving the salon he was back, holding his glass for more champagne, which Laure was pouring in without meeting his eyes. Lighting a cigarette – what had he done with the other? Dropped it? Would Véronique notice a burning smell, and pick it up off the rug and chuck it out of the window? What was she thinking, up there?

Whatever it was it no longer mattered; she was down inside two minutes, her pride quite as useful a turn-screw as his, washed and combed, all youth and resilience, her round face showing nothing but polite obedient gaiety, and everyone who had thought her rather harshly snubbed made much of her. People were nice!

Marcus complimented her on her hair, so alive, so deeply blue-black, so unlike the blunt rusty scrubbing brush that was his hair. Thomassen, Norwegian pig, Jewish swine, complimented her on her frock, which deserved it; nice simple linen thing. She looked surprisingly pretty – even the boys noticed. 'You'd better beat her every day' they would say, laughing heartily, if they knew. Stockings, plain leather shoes, a crystal necklace: she stood sipping champagne, every inch a lady, exactly the image of his castle that Dutheil liked to present to guests. Such a pity, wasn't it, that he had to know about the secret shameful stripe under the bright lozenge-patterned linen, know how white the skin was and how much woman there was concealed by a silly scrap of childish beach cotton.

'Señora' – Figaro was bowing urbanely in the doorway.

'Aha,' said Laure, collecting people.

Dinner did not go too badly, not badly at all. Dutheil could see Thomassen taking everything in, well reined in by the furniture, which was indeed the most formal, intimidating in the house; one might almost think oneself in a real chateau. Rigidity of Louis Seize. Hideous stuff, mahogany, and useful at least to corset journalists into their best behaviour. Fellow was examining marble tops, little bronze galleries and door-handles, a lot of bituminous pictures, with an impressed but disrespectful eye; he glanced once or twice at Dutheil as much as to say 'Really – do you need all that?' And there were The Servants – whereas at lunch things got forgotten, people went back for second helpings, the table had a cloth on it, on which he frequently dropped spoons or spilt food.

'I'm inexpert but I'm only a poor ex-barman – if you want a head waiter you'll find plenty of writers who are good ones, bowing people in and out of their lousy books…'

And nobody was ashamed of being greedy with the mayonnaise. Whereas at dinner dishes were presented portentously, at an awkward elbow height, by Figaro, with Leonarda (who inclined to heavy breathing) crowding in upon one after him with a glassy religiosity as though in a Holy Week procession in Seville.

Dutheil was quiet, so that Laure, who liked to think of her housekeeping at meals and leave the verbal ping-pong to the literary set, had to chat.

'Is your job perhaps easier at home?' Thomassen, as the new boy, was sitting next to den-mother. 'Of course I don't mean foreign countries – there's no such thing really, now, is there? But aren't Americans perhaps more frank – more spontaneous?' Everybody listened but Thomassen was not going to put his foot in his mouth.

'Frank? – or afraid of giving the wrong answer?'

'Questionnaire-conscious.' One of the boys – Daniel, not missing a chance to tease…

'Earnestly reading the *Digest* to Improve one's Word Rating.' It had been seized on gleefully.

'Questionnaires – so old-fashioned somehow – associated with Marcel Proust.'

'Terrible Immigration officers, granite-faced.'

'The Census – the sixty-four-page booklet.'

'Do shut up, boys, and let Mr Thomassen speak.'

'You can't get out of Census alas – it's been tried. The others you tear up, or send to Civil Liberties – but isn't it unfair to associate a poor Nebraska farm-boy with the Census? I don't ask those sort of personal questions.' It got the right kind of laugh.

'It's appearing here too – even in France starry-eyed characters charging about asking schoolgirls whether their parents tell them about sex – hey, Nique, do your parents talk to you about sex?'

'I imagine,' drawled Véronique, 'that most of my class would agree that every now and then they felt obliged to talk to their parents.'

Dutheil woke up suddenly and switched on like electric light.

'Today I experienced a phenomenon that seems well established and that nobody questions – the neurological memory: you know, feeling pain in an amputated member.'

'Have you an amputated member?' much interested.

'A wasp stung me about six weeks ago, on the back of my hand. It continued unusually painful for some time. Today I felt the pain again. Only then did I notice a wasp buzzing around. I am forced to conclude that the buzzing noise was enough to awaken the memory.' The children, Thomassen noticed with amusement, were sceptical about this tale.

'Was stung, and thought it was the time before.'

'False analogy anyway – association of ideas, that's all. Like smelling coffee and imagining it's breakfast time.'

Thomassen put his fork down carefully.

'Then if the buzz alone produced physical pain it might also produce mental pain from an occasion long ago.'

'Hell yes, that's a truism. What else is writing about – the *coup de la madeleine* – who mentioned Proust? It was the physical pain that interested me.'

'But it's uncertain,' said Laure. 'I mean the wasp produces a sensation of being stung because that's about all it's capable of – but if it was an occasion where the wasp was just a bystander it might be anything. Mental associations are much more complex.'

'I'm sure psychiatrists have some dope – send one back to infancy.'

'Yes but to recover a specific memory – only writers can do that.'

'I always did wonder what it was Proust's mama really did do,' said Thomassen amid hilarity.

They were off, thought Dutheil who had lapsed again into silence. All talking, and none of them knowing a thing about it. Writers spent a lot of time with the problem, thinking up new tricks to make it more reliable, more exact. To put it on paper knowing you had it right, exact...not so easy. Spirits will come all right from the vasty deep when I do call for them, but one never knows quite what may come.

'Have you enjoyed your dinner?' asked Laure. She was unhappy at Dutheil sitting so long upon his little cloud, wishing she knew some way of getting him down.

'Very much,' said Thomassen. 'Chateau food.'

'Good heavens, this isn't chateau food. We wouldn't know how.'

Food was a subject that rarely failed to interest god, and perhaps he would react. To her great relief he did.

'It's a trap,' he said with deep seriousness. 'People who got exiled from Versailles went back to the country and died off, fostering a delightful legend that, deprived of the light of the Sun King, one could do nothing else. The more prosaic truth is that they burst from overeating. No mental resources, you see.'

'You mean writers have mental resources so it's all right for them to overeat?'

'You perhaps don't die – not if you watch your liver pretty near as close as you watch journalists.'

'Ah – then the French liver is not altogether a legend?'

'No it's not – why d'you think God filled France up with springs of mineral water everywhere? Now if only Moses had had the sense to come here he wouldn't have had to strike any rock.'

'Oh yes he would,' said Thomassen spitefully, 'the old show-off.'

'Coffee in the other room, Figaro, please,' said Laure, much reassured. Heaven knew what he'd said to Véronique but both of them seemed to be behaving quite sensibly.

# Two

The two boys, having done their duty, disappeared. Véronique went politely the round of the guests to say sorry but she had lessons to learn. Marcus, who had no intention of getting mixed up in anything, settled down to be charming and to be cuddled by the women, and Royan, curious to know how an American journalist went about interviewing tiresome old Dutheil, went over to join them.

'We are discussing the effect of food on the mentality.'

'Brutish,' said the doctor happily, 'Country food should only be allowed to those who work in the fields.'

'Quite right,' said Dutheil. 'Writers should be kept in English teashops and fed on baked beans and vinegar.'

'I'm more interested right now in country drinks.'

'You notice, Gilbert,' virtuously, 'I ate hardly any cheese and had no cream on my tart. Have something with your coffee,' he added, to Thomassen. 'That one's made from greengages; it's rather nice.

'Yes but I've eaten everything; what will it do to my liver?'

The doctor had a soft teasing laugh.

'It's a corrective,' helping himself from the bottle the American was eyeing with suspicion. 'Home-made – we're all illicit distillers round here. I get it from farmers, who would rather pay me in drinks made by their grandfathers than in money, an idea I indulge them in occasionally.'

'Go on,' said Dutheil. 'Eat too much, drink too much – a corrective like he says. Good for your proud-stomached intellect. He thinks I ought to be more ascetic,' to Royan.

'When we eat so much, instead of having a bowl of rice, you don't think we're on that account luckier, do you? Alcohol, showered by God with such embarrassing over-generosity upon France, is our greatest blight – go on, it's certainly over thirty years old.'

Thomassen, to stop being laughed at, took a small drink, found it delicious and helped himself to more, to the audience's amusement. He decided to have a try at least at getting a few grievances off his chest.

'Lot of everything here. Architecture, furniture, beautiful objects – vines, fruit, drinks – outward marks of civilisation, such as we import from France at home with such startling naiveté, in great profusion. Astonishing to find you here in the middle of all this – embalmed, I'd almost be inclined to say, only that it sounds rude – as though you were dead or something.'

Dutheil smiled instead of getting cross.

'I'm not quite dead – don't embalm me yet. Who said civilisation was the creation of its outlaws?'

'You're an outlaw?'

'Living in a castle like a robber-baron – ask Royan there.'

'He only means,' said the doctor's high soft voice, 'that I'm a friend of some years' standing, that I'm his doctor, and that I understand him pretty well because, you see, I don't read his horrible books; I'm quite literally the man who didn't have time: prefer music anyway. I can make his point clearer than he can. He feels out of place and out of time in the world – feels outlawed if you wish; this alarms and irritates him. He takes refuge in the castle, where he pretends to be a robber-baron, reacting in an aggressive and hostile manner to his own cowardice.'

'Now write that,' said Dutheil pleasantly, 'and I'll take a rusty two-handed broadsword to you.'

'Perfect,' said Royan. 'Mention robber-barons and he starts to play the part at once. You wouldn't even feel safe in Israel – he'd be launching huge stones from a catapult on the wall of Krak les Chevaliers.'

'It's not bad at all, this technique,' drawled Thomassen. 'You make me your guest, smother me in creature comforts, and now you're wanting me to get mad and lose my mild suffering Yiddish resignation. Must be the reason State Department told me not to trust the French.'

'Better,' said Dutheil. 'Much better. Thought he'd come storming in like something out of the *New Yorker* and sew us up. Three thousand words of deep intuitive understanding. Now quieten down and enjoy yourself; you've been jumping about like a squirrel, screaming with joy at detecting peanuts. When you get home you can add up all your sneaking furtive lisping cringing money-lending thoughts, but stop being all sensitive and deceptive.'

'I'm speechless – do you know what the prophet Isaias said when New York gave him a tickertape reception?'

'No,' said Dutheil crossly, 'but do you know what Jesus said when Satan lifted him up in the desert and he beheld forty cities?'

'No.'

'That's just a mirage and I told you all along we should have shot the scene home in the studio.'

Laure's voice floated across. 'Some more coffee, Mr Thomassen? Come over and talk to me; they sound to me as though they're getting thoroughly beastly over there.'

As he walked across carrying his coffee-cup he heard Royan say in a jeering tone, 'You and your little Versailles. What next – the Venetian ambassador?'

'I'm not having any more drink,' said Dutheil in penitential tones. 'That's how you see him? The Venetian ambassador?' He sniggered in a self-satisfied way.

'Isn't it? Going to make a cunning diplomatic report for the literary circles, no? Deflate Dutheil, who is a spurious bastard in a spurious setting.'

'Doesn't worry me,' indifferently. 'Nothing alters my reputation. First-chop second-rate, over-prolific. Critics hate my guts. But the place to be in the papers, my boy, is on the monthly seller list and not in any poxy critics column.'

Marcus had been looking on at the teasing and enjoying it; do the lad good! Had the idea that Dutheil was a manuscript worth deciphering taken root? The old boy was a phenomenon after all, perhaps not a very interesting person but a wonderful writing mechanism. Hopelessly imprisoned in the writers' opal – who was it that had made a book of the opal metaphor? One of those admirable English pre-war writers now unjustly forgotten. Dutheil saw life in an optic of strange fires and milky obscurities: distorted faces and movements peopling a sinister inferno. He needed his Laure and his Nora to reassure him, or he would go round the bend; if he had lived in Paris he would have been taken off to Sainte-Anne long ago. Lucky he had the gift of being readable. Public liked him, chose him off the shelf, bought him. Each book turned into a marvellous little barrel of real *louis d'or,* and Dutheil could live in a castle surrounded by adoring women who encouraged him to be Voltaire and go to bed with litres of tisane the moment he felt ill.

Marcus liked both the women and was sincerely fond of them. Laure was a treasure; intelligent, delicious, generous, free of all petty jealousies, never worrying lest another one scored an extra point, thought of something first – got ahead... A far wider reader than Dutheil, a much better critic, she liked hearing the Paris gossip – she hankered after tastes of her lost world of intellectual endeavour. He had sometimes proposed her working for him, bothered lest she slide into the cow-trodden clay of a housewife's rut, but she had always refused. 'I have my job,' she said. It was her choice. He recalled hearing Royan once, pressed on the subject of not reading books, say smilingly, 'Happiness is the deliberate sacrifice of something prized.' Laure would agree, from her heart.

He had complimented her on her frock.

'I like a designer to be a designer,' she had said, 'not a prinking perruquier.' Laure had a Balenciaga mind, which he was not sure Dutheil altogether deserved.

Nora was provincial if you like; dowdy, plain – but she had lots of character. Said oddly convincing things sometimes in a way showing she had thought things out. An enigma, of course, a bottomless pit, marvellous complement to Dutheil; the one drove out the other's demons, they neutralised each other's acids and neither, in his opinion, would support life at all equably without the other. Laure, he guessed, knew that. Where would Dutheil be without those two women? Hanging in an alley like Gérard de Nerval, most likely.

No, one couldn't tell, ever, with writers. Worry about their books, but leave them alone. Give them small sums of money from time to time – writers were like blackmailers – but do not try to fix them up with lives, houses, or women. Writers of course always thought they needed people, were fond of gushing dedications saying they owed all to dearest so-and-so, but that was all cock. A person had come along: at the moment a writer starts to write there will always be someone coming along. Even without Laure Dutheil would be a saleable, publishable writer. Perhaps with no Laure, no Nora, no Castle, he might have been a much better writer. But would not have made a tenth of the money! No, be grateful to Laure, grateful to Nora. Monsieur Sabatier was!

Good food, pleasant company, shortage of women – there always was in this house. But the daughter is growing up. He had noticed the little brush with Dutheil – no importance, that. One's teenage daughters were always rude, and needed a very light touch. This one was going to be a bit of a beauty, just realising it herself, too. It would be collecting its first cavaliers, causing upheavals. Stupid Dutheil saw nothing, of course – to him she should still be romping with Papa, and he got indignant, the old fool, because she was wanting to stretch, spread her wings. Laure saw it, but she spent so much energy and effort on her tiresome husband that she could be oddly obtuse at times.

He was full of good digestion, would sleep well. Damn it, he had been up that morning at six.

Thomassen was not getting much out of Laure. His own fault, he thought. Eaten too much, drunk too much? He knew where he stood with whisky, but this fruit vodka stuff was slaughterous. Everybody had reunited into one group and was telling Provençal stories. Somebody called Raphael – Corsican? – at first he thought this was like Marius, or Ike Isaacs the pawnbroker, but it seemed to be a real person, something to do with that odd French world of bicycle racing.

'So the boy was all of a sudden in the lead, looking even perhaps capable of winning in Paris, and the journalists race off to ask Raphael whether he's happy with that, and he says "You'll see in Paris in three days' time – I'll either have my hands up in the air like You-Know-Who or stretched out like Our Lord on the Cross." '

They were all laughing but his face must have shown signs of creaking because Dutheil pounced on him.

'No use making eyes at my wife; she's allergic. Get on to Mademoiselle Noël to write it for you – we've got to do a good job on these critics, tell them I'm a very very important writer – count on you for that.' He turned to Marcus. 'Read a beauty the other day in London – that one who has a literary dove descend upon him at Pentecost every year. Talking about some unheard-of miracle boy he says in that inimitable manner, "One of the five novelists of genius at present working in our language." Pretty good hey – jammy for the four but they're all eyeing each other. So I sent him a greetings telegram saying "Captain Queeg, edition such, page so, line this". That way he can't resist looking it up, you see.'

'What does it say?' asked Thomassen, amused.

'Well, you remember Captain Queeg, wonderful character – someone comes belting up saying the ship is sinking or whatnot, and he yaps out in his best style, "Tell that man not to be so goddam positive with his goddam surmises." ' Thomassen was pleased to be able to laugh, genuinely this time. Dutheil wagged an admonishing finger at him.

'Don't let me catch myself saying it to you forgetting I've used the joke once already.'

'I'm off,' said Royan yawning.

'Bed everybody,' answered Laure. Marcus, infected by the yawn, was delighted. 'What time would you like breakfast, Mr Thomassen? – we have ours early.'

'You do? – I thought he wasn't working.'

'I'm always working,' said Dutheil. 'I'm a peasant boy, up at six come what may.'

'About eight,' said Marcus, 'country-house breakfast – American breakfast, with maple syrup.'

'Figaro will love that,' said Laure. 'He looks forward immensely to your coming; prides himself on American breakfast.'

'Yes,' added Dutheil, 'starts using phrases like "sunny side up". Buying him a ticket to New York might be my only chance of ever getting rid of him,' already making for the stairs. 'Good night.'

'What is the quotation from *King Lear?*' asked Thomassen suddenly. 'The Tom-o'-Bedlam song.'

'Aha,' leaning over the banisters. 'Who told you that?'

'Marcus.

'Bright of him. It's not in *Lear.* It's in Aubrey or something.

With a heart of furious fancies
Whereof I am commander
With a burning spear and a horse of air
To the wilderness I wander.
With a knight of ghosts and shadows
I summoned am to tourney
Ten leagues beyond the wide world's end
Methinks it is no journey.

Put that in your pipe and smoke it.'

'Good night,' said Thomassen politely.

# Three

The very end of the day belonged to Laure, tradition from the early years when the barman came home from a night's work, and it was two hours before he had unwound enough to go to sleep. The habit had developed, become more sophisticated, but remained the same. A shower first to get the stink of cheap smoke and bad drink off his hair and skin: he did this still, though nowadays the bathroom was grander. Laure's was modern, with a pattern of nasturtiums giving a black bidet an agreeably oriental cockeyed look. But his was nineteenth-century grandiose, pride of the Castle: florid Victorian peonies, bronze cherubs blowing trumpets, a great slab of mahogany to sit on and pull-and-let-go like a stirrup pump producing cavernous Wagnerian rumblings, Nibelungen-music down in the sunless sea. The walls were faded cracked Delft tiles, with seascapes, eighteen-seventy Dutch railway systems, canal barges, and a wealth of rococo cloud.

In the old days Laure had made cocoa in draughty kitchens while he unwrapped the parcels bribed from late-duty cooks. Nowadays she had a little fridge built into a corner cupboard that had been gutted without remorse, not being genuine. Here he kept water biscuits and mineral water, caviare and cognac, brown sugar, and marzipan petits-fours – a weakness of Laure's. And in her dressing-room there was an electric heater. Aladdin's cave – thus armoured against insomnia, boredom, and midnight terrors Dutheil could disregard the world when too much with him.

For it was. Visitors wondered what he did for raw material, for the sense of swimming in the human soup a writer surely needed. 'Why not live in Paris?' – or New York, or Rome – 'somewhere life beats in a strong rhythm?' Rhythm indeed – ten minutes on a pavement terrace was soup enough to last six weeks, but they never grasped that.

Journalists were fond of 'recluse' clichés: he wasn't going to tell them. Of course he went out, once a week at least, Laure driving him in the little Lancia, to eat in a restaurant. (Laure cooked when he was working, on Il Cuocco's day off, because he could not stand Susanna's cooking. 'One finds her hair in everything.')

And very often he went away for days, weeks, Figaro driving the thirty-year-old Rolls-Royce (he had had to be sent to Derby to learn how to look after it) – for it was most important to have an old one, wheels a yard in front of the bonnet. The day they put the wheels back of the radiator, said Dutheil, a Rolls ceased to be a Rolls and he'd as soon the tiny Simca.

Like this he visited towns he was fond of; Prague, Leningrad, Venice, or Istanbul. One could even go to Paris and sit bang on the Saint Germain crossroads without anyone noticing – advantage of being neither academician nor pop singer, and never getting your picture in the paper. Nice to be rich. He wasn't beastly rich: he didn't have a yacht or a plane. A Black Sea beach and Laure to rub his back – he liked phrases and would tell people straight-faced that he refreshed his tired soul with the bucking beam-sea roll of a Black Bilbao Tramp, and watch them rear up in horror. Boats he loved, and trains.

Laure, who loathed boats, sometimes took planes to meet him in Innsbruck or Montevideo or Santiago de Chile – for the places Dutheil visited had to have pretty names. Not for the world would Dutheil go to Hamburg, Moscow, Vancouver. The system meant disillusion sometimes; neither Philadelphia nor San Antonio had lived up to promise: nor, alas, had Vladivostok. But generally the system worked well enough, and he had no regret at missing Djakarta, Ottawa, and Bangkok.

When asked why he preferred New York to London he replied primly, 'Purely a question of nomenclature.' How could one resist Manhattan Island (even if one could and did resist Macy, Gimbel, Bloomingdale, and Grant's Tomb)? There must be a good reason for detesting ice cream – Schraft and Howard Johnson. One visited the Plaza, but not the Guggenheim; one loved Duke Ellington, but not, to one's regret, Count Basie.

Laure came to rub his back.

'Good day?'

'No.'

Even now he could not tell her about Véronique.

He never could; he had to wait some days before feeling able to tell Laure about whatever was eating him; for the metabolism was slow, often painful. It made her unhappy for she could not follow the complex process of worry; she thought it showed a lack of confidence in her.

'But I am here for that,' she said. Childishly unable to explain, he feigned a principle of 'carrying his own suitcase'.

'My wife is not just a little bag to be sick into.'

She had learned that if she guessed the source of irritation, and spoke of it openly in an offhand manner, he would sometimes respond. She thought now that it was the American who had given his tongue a taste of gall.

'I am cross with Marcus, really. He should have given us more notice; we might have discussed it then, perhaps.'

'No no, he doesn't bother me at all. In fact I rather like him.'

A don't-want-to-talk voice; very well, she would not insist. It was the favourite segment of her life; she liked nothing better than to go to bed at nine, as they often did when there were no guests, after a meal of soup, salad, cheese – and read in contented silence. Or read bits aloud. Or talk. Or play one of the old-fashioned games he enjoyed, like cribbage or backgammon. If he was dour and silent, it was generally a literary pregnancy. Both would fall asleep around eleven, and if one stayed reading with the light on the other would mumble crossly every five minutes until the light was put out.

When there was a grim silence on he was unpredictable. It might end suddenly in an abrupt command to take her night-dress off – not lovemaking in any real sense; a clinical obliteration of whatever skull happened to be grinning at him. Laure was aware that this happened with Nora, but was surprised to find it agreeable that it should happen to her too sometimes…

It was nearly eleven and she was dropping with sleep, yawning fearfully, which would irritate him.

'I think I'm going to sleep.'

'Why, certainly. You need it.'

'Will you sleep?'

'I hope so.'

It was all the answer she would get.

An astonishingly warm night, for autumn in the hills. Later, before dawn, Laure – always a chilly thing – would, without really waking, come to the surface long enough to switch her blanket on. She was already nine-tenths unconscious, he saw, winding herself into her cocoon: three pillows in a special pattern and coverlets up over her ears. When asleep nothing of her showed but a fragment of nose: comic woman.

He himself lay flat and quiet, waiting for her to go well under. He knew perfectly that he was not going to sleep, but noise would wake her. Movement would not, for he was always a restless sleeper himself, and she was used to a heaving twitcher next door. After a quarter of an hour he slid out, went into the dressing-room, drank some water, and fetched a deckchair out on to the balcony. He did not feel irritable and made no awkward movements, for he knew what his symptom was. It happened two or three times a year and he called it his 'examination of conscience'. It took three or four hours, after which he could go to sleep as though nothing had happened, and have a siesta the following afternoon.

What was it? A need to get back down to bedrock, to rethink his whole mentality, perhaps. Not just a simple overhaul of the machine, quickly resolved into the need for a trip, a notion of having got into a rut, or being stuck inside a book. A good long walk sufficed for that: just a question of priming the pump, turning the motor over by hand till it warmed sufficiently to stop spluttering and rev up. But these times were different, critical. The whole machine seized up, and there was nothing for it but to dismantle the whole absurd structure. For one could not call it a machine. The English talked about things being 'Heath-Robinson' to this day, quite rightly – he recalled the man from his own childhood, a caricaturist who filled his drawings with wonderful complicated mechanisms made out of every kind of rubbish-tip junk held together with knotted bits of string. It was him, it was everyone, it was the human mind.

Examination of conscience… A technical term associated with Going-to-church: the results of his dismantling labours were not always along these lines. Indeed the results had only one thing in common: a ludicrous quality, and it was a temptation to jeer at them for that reason. Once the machine had been reassembled on the basis of getting up at five instead of six, taking the 'utility' station wagon and going to Mass at five thirty in the town, in that same church with the spire whose accusing needle made it impossible to look east, from up on the Whaleback…

He had kept it up for six weeks, despite fatigue. Finally he had been taken bad with a book, a condition that gave him morning-sickness, and just hadn't been able to manage it any longer.

Another time he had had a vision (succumbing to the need to jeer, that sad little proof of vanity) like something out of Somerset Maugham! He really had gone abruptly to Cambodia to find out about Buddhism. And yet another time he had made a secret trip to South America – Marcus, for instance, never would believe he had really gone – haunted by gigantic ornate Spanish churches built by Jesuits whose mentality he felt he understood, in which sixteenth-century Virgins have become inextricably confused with earth-mother Inca divinities, in which Indian women repeat the Angelus as a strong charm towards bearing a healthy boy baby. Peru and Chile: it had left a deep mark. Crossing the Andes was a watershed in his life; he had been within a sheet of paper's thickness of abandoning Europe altogether, so sure he had been at that time.

These amiably pathetic notions of self-renewal had not always a religious mechanism at the base. Once he had made the Tour de France by bicycle, following the coastline and coming back down the Ardennes-Vosges-Jura line; starting from Briançon, the highest town in Europe. He had carried an oilskin, a sweater, one spare set of underclothes, a set of Michelin maps, and a pair of binoculars which he later lost, as well as four pairs of sunglasses, and two handy first-aid kits. He bought, on the way, eight ballpoint pens – he had lost count of pencils. He brought back (and had bound in leather, the snob) twenty-one school exercise books of a hundred and eighty pages. He had started on April the First and got back in November with the most incredible callouses on his hands and behind.

They were painful, these occasions. How poor one was, how little one knew. How few resources one had, and how many layers of self-pity protected the worm from the cold. Fortitude, justice, and temperance – how hard it was to learn anything about these, and how easy to forget. He had tried, following these nights, endless experiments in 'an evening once a week'. In hospitals, prisons, mental asylums, slums, art schools, university extension courses. He had never managed more than a month. He didn't know, sometimes he might have managed more; always a book got between him and the light: damn books.

Once he had only gone one evening. Once two. Second-chop boy, second-chop writer. He didn't need any journalists or critics to diagnose him! Yet somehow he still hoped that there might be a good book in him somewhere. He would tame imagination, learn to think... How boring it did sound.

He got up and fetched a cigar from the dressing-room, an enormous Cuban thing, only tolerable here in the night air, between cloud, wood, and river. Fire, said scientists, was not an element but only a chemical change or something – nonsense they talked. Fire was an element – on the balcony at night, anyway, when it was the fire of a Cuban cigar. The church clock struck eleven-thirty: Laure's breathing, soft as rainwater, sounded even in the room behind him. He had a lot to do. Not only read Pascal. But learn all the different stars and study Easter Island, collect stones, and understand Florentine painting – what, all that put off till the cottage with the pump in the back? Why did he think, suddenly, of the man in Austria who went about stubbornly defying ridicule and planting edelweiss everywhere? He had a lot of admiration for that man. Was it not possible that at the end of his life he would have done more than Dutheil?

What a stupid notion. His job is to plant edelweiss. Mine is to write books. And never mind anything else – you don't weigh out 'how-much-done' by the kilo like split peas. Smoke your cigar and enjoy it.

Véronique – she had never known him other than rich, assured, cigar-smoking. The boys could remember the slummy life of Perpignan and Aix, but she had known him first as the trained and poised professional. She saw him as a bourgeois bastard, which he was, embedded in satisfaction like goose in a little faience pot.

That's me – goose! Cuddled and clucked at by a big fat mama, stuffed and stuffed and stuffed with lovely golden maize so that the public may buy and daintily devour my liver by and by.

It is not riches that is the enemy; it is comfort. One of the chief sins of this our lousy century has been to abolish luxury and replace it by comfort. I am a man pushed like the goose into a life of supreme comfort and I sit here smoking a cigar wanting a bit of grit. '*Un homme comblé...*'

One sought in such circumstances to propitiate the gods. A sacrifice was a nobler notion – but it must be a sacrifice of oneself. A sheep or a dove was in a bourgeois society replaced by a cheque for the Earthquake Relief Fund. How one envies Jew Süss, who atoned for a vulgar, luxurious life full of sinister corruption by becoming a Jewish scapegoat, and introduced so exquisite an irony by doing so at the precise moment of learning that he was not a Jew at all but the son of a distinguished and soldierly German nobleman. So handy for him. Such piquancy it added to the sweaty bourgeois ruffians all holding their Teutonic noses and complaining of the frightful stink of Jew. Dutheil wished he could make a nice dramatic sacrifice like that. One that made good reading, said the craftsman with a complacent cynicism. He had been over all this ground a dozen times. A lot of good it did running around into jungles. Going up a mountain in the Andes where one's nose bled from the altitude was no different from going up the Whaleback at home. One still sat in a padded cane chair, drawing gently on a cigar tasting of paradise and looking out at the milk-and-honey night. Suddenly Dutheil got an abominable fright.

He sat perfectly still, hardly daring to breathe, cigar drooping from a mouth at once stiff and limp, finding the man who sat in such comfort on the balcony of a sudden appallingly loud and conspicuous. He felt all the classic physical symptoms of a man in fear. The cause of this fear was a man, who had appeared soundlessly on the edge of the lawn and was standing quietly, watching the house. In the shadow of the dark box trees one saw no detail – even Dutheil's eyes, accustomed to the starlit dimness, could make little out. A young man – a slim light figure whose youthful movement was constrained now by watchfulness. Darkish shirt and trousers, darkish hair – it was all he could make out. It was the face that had caught his eye against the blackness of box, and that was no more than a whitish blotch. What was so alarming was the furtive, cautious movement, sidling along the line of box, plainly not happy about the naked lawn, so brilliantly lit and painfully bare after the overgrown shrubberies. Whatever this young man was up to it could be nothing good. Very gently Dutheil put the cigar down on the floor, where it would go out by itself, and hoped that behind the creeper-grown balcony he was invisible from the ground. The trouble was that the shutter of the French window behind him stood invitingly open, and a robber could hardly fail to miss that invitation. Climbing up that balcony would present no problem to an eight-year-old – much more of a problem to get off the bloody balcony himself, where he was pinned like a hen on an egg. Alarm grew to panic proportion when the young man appeared to make his mind up and stepped forward on to the croquet field. He's as frightened as I am, thought Dutheil.

Not a reassuring thought; a frightened young gangster was the type who would hit out.

Mind made up, the stranger advanced with a stealthy tiptoe action. Wearing rubber sand-shoes, it was absurd that he should seem worried about noise on the dew-laden grass. He left footprints, but they would fade quickly. Dutheil's fear changed to a point of astonishment; instead of making for the house the boy moved towards the little Astérix-hut, paused to look at the house, and opened the door with precaution, exactly as though he knew it was inclined to creak. There was nothing there, as Dutheil knew well, except the croquet things, deckchairs, a couple of old rugs, bits of broken bamboo, two or three parasols, and some stained mouldy cushions. He had made himself as thin as possible to slip in sideways – it made no sense. Come to bore little holes in the red ball and pour in melted lead to nobble Dutheil's next game? The surroundings were as ridiculous as the action – that absurd hut with a flavour of lubricating oil where someone who had been oiling the mowing machine had kicked the tin over. Draughty walls full of chinks, a ragged straw-thatch roof and a wrought-iron weathercock in the shape of a squirrel, corny as hell. However, a small window overlooked the house, and though smeary, cobwebby, and obscure, who knew what could be seen out of it?

Dutheil had now to attempt the difficult feat of getting out of the cane chair without being seen or heard, which he finally did, proud as Harry Houdini. Preposterous it might be but the fact was there: in his summerhouse at midnight lurked a young man with decidedly sinister ways. He gained the shelter of the bedroom, breathing heavily, having made, he felt sure, a hell of a racket, but he had got away with it, since no gangster came leaping pantherishly out of the hut. He melted back into darkness and thought. What he needed, he decided, was a gun, for with a gun one could keep bandits from swarming up the balcony, and the shutters elsewhere were reassuringly solid. The only thing was, who might not come whizzing up the wistaria while Dutheil was fumbling about in the dark? – gun-room was simply miles away. With an immense sense of being very very very clever he thought that the last time he had the Mauser out he had left it in his dressing-room. Now had that do-nothing Figaro put it back where it belonged? – he would make a little bet the bugger had done no such thing. In the dark Dutheil crept, and touched and grasped the door of his big cupboard, trying the while to keep the balcony in sight across the bedroom – it took some time before he realised this was impossible. Brilliant fellow – miserable cowardy custard. He opened the cupboard, felt in the far corner and with sweet joy grasped cold steel tube: rifle barrel. He pulled cautiously and cradled it in his arms.

It was not like the little Walther; this was a seven sixty-four, a great thing that would stop a lion with a shattering din. He had had it out a few weeks before to shoot a crow in the cedar. The Walther would have made a neater job (nothing was left of the crow at all) but the Mauser had a telescopic sight, an aid to the middle-aged sniper who takes his glasses off twice to polish them while deciding whether that is really a cat there a hundred metres off, or only a dead tree stump…

Hell and hell and hell, what a lot of time he was wasting; where were the goddam cartridges? He scrabbled in a dressing-gown pocket, found nothing, and remembered he had put them back among his woolly socks. He opened the breech, paddled among socks with fingers and palm, found three and pressed them in one after another: now, friend, we will see what we will see. Dutheil tucked the rifle under his arm and crept out like a flatfooted Duke Mantee – in fact he was Duke Mantee, beard, lisp, twitches and all.

There was no nasty rustle in the wistaria; there was nothing at all. The hut did not look in the least sinister, and he wondered fearfully whether the bandit could still be in it. Stealing about trying ground-floor shutters? You do that, my lad; you lay a nail-file on that little lot and bells will ring from here to Grenoble.

The church clock chimed for the hour and began to count monotonously to twelve. Nothing happened. He could hear Laure's breathing in the stillness, unusually noisy and rustic; crossly, he realised it was his own breathing: you awful stupe. Despite this lapse he felt confident. I know he's there, but he doesn't know I'm here. Still less that I'm holding a thing which hasn't come out of a toyshop.

Very amusing – but not to Dutheil – how suddenly the languid sense of superiority could disappear! His hair bristled. There had been a metallic snap followed by a thudding clank – unmistakably the noise of a ground-floor shutter opening. He nearly screamed. He looked first in agony across at the switch by Laure's bed, but could not make out whether it was on or off. He stood paralysed, not daring to budge. Of course it was on – just closing the shutters put it on. The bandits had bribed Figaro, and it was an inside job! For it was the heart and centre of Figaro's life, the ritual promenade with the torch. If any catch failed to snap right in and close the electrical circuit a red light went on – this could only mean that the system had been tampered with. Trembling and sweaty Dutheil waited. What else could he do, with enemies behind him and before him, all about him? The big rifle seemed sadly impotent – who knew how many of them were creeping about the darkened house? Was the one in the hut there to receive a signal, or to give it? Since the shutter had been unlocked, he would now come out of hiding; Dutheil leaned over a tiny scrap to cover more of the lawn.

He saw, indeed, a figure. It was not the greasy and supple burglar he had expected; it was a young female who had just reached the bottom of the steps from the terrace. Wearing a beach-pyjama outfit that had given him trouble that evening already. Véronique – the brazen slut. Now he understood the whole thing at once – far simpler than his heated welter of bribes and bandits. Mademoiselle had not quite summoned the cheek to receive her follower in her room – up two flights and a passage whose ancient oak boards creaked. But the follower can be met in the garden at midnight, and since there is a heavy dew the fornicators arrange to keep their bottoms dry in the helpful summerhouse.

'Relief,' Dutheil would be saying two hours later. 'You are tense with fear, and the source of that fear is removed in an abrupt and bizarre fashion. Relief from fear is itself painful, and to neutralise pain anger is a simple frequent remedy.' Stabbing a cigarette out and noticing how steady his hand was, despite shock, thanks perhaps to that injection Gilbert had insisted on giving him.

He did not know what he thought. But he was lucid; he recalled bracing himself against the heavy varnished shutter. He moved efficiently, economically. He had not bothered wondering who was sacrificing what, nor to what. He thought he had yelled, but was told, later, that he had spoken in a level tone. What conclusion would a judge, for instance, draw from that? Insane, not insane, or neither, but simply suspended…between heaven and Charing Cross. To untangle these little details would not be simple, though to him it was perfectly simple. He brought the rifle up easily, tucked it into his shoulder and without sighting – the hut was twenty-five metres away – he fired three cartridges, unhurried, pulling the bolt back and sliding it firmly, with a slow double click, back into place. Into the dark grimy little window of the hut.

# Four

Véronique screamed, a hoarse shriek that shunted Dutheil abruptly back, a few hours now, in time. Raucous, harsh – for a moment it seemed to him as though it had never stopped, and was still the same tearing noise of pure pain that had gone on in his head till now. Whatever he had been before he was clear now in his mind. He stepped out on to the balcony, as Véronique recovered her ability to move and ran towards the hut. His voice came out quietly but sharp.

'Stop.'

He was still holding the rifle when Laure behind him wrenched it out of his unprotesting hands, and threw it over on to the paved terrace. It fell with a dull clank, and the stock broke across. It would never be good for anything again, he thought regretfully, but it had done its work; of that he felt oddly, calmly certain. Laure was shaking, beside herself, face distorted, unable to speak, looking at Véronique – they both seemed pinned against the balcony as though by a strong wind – not looking at him. The strong wind had taken her breath away; her chest heaved as though there were no air at all instead of too much. It can easily happen, said Dutheil wisely to himself, that when there is a strong wind your breath is literally blown back down your throat. It must be a real hurricane, he concluded pedantically, to give one that impression of the wind attacking the fortress from all sides at once.

Everything stood stone-still, and then began to move again in a jerky badly-timed way, like a Mack Sennett picture. It all reminded Dutheil of a pie-in-the-face and a merry chase; he wanted vaguely to laugh. Véronique on the lawn made faces with her mouth open grotesquely, but the wind stopped him hearing what she said. Laure fumbled at his arms and he pushed her crossly away. Another figure appeared on the terrace below – his son Daniel, improbably wearing nothing but bright yellow nylon shorts.

Daniel said nothing, but walked fairly rapidly along the terrace and down the steps. When he reached his sister he took her by the arm, turned her towards the house, and gave her a gentle push as though to say 'Now girl, don't get in the way of the firearm'. Dutheil, still on the balcony, was struck by his methodical calm. Was this the modern generation? Let's see, how old exactly was Daniel? Twenty-two? Three? He stopped and studied the shattered window, of which remained nothing but a half-rotted frame and a few hanging splinters. He nodded as though this was no more nor less than he had expected, opened the door, looked carefully around at the interior, came out, shut it, leaned against it, stood a moment in thought, lifted his eyes, saw Dutheil, and said calmly, 'Better come down, Father, I think.' Dutheil turned and came downstairs without thinking a second of challenging this unexpected authority.

On his way he met Thomassen, who presumably had been taking everything in as usual, out of his window on the floor above. The American was wearing virulent poison-green pyjamas with a yellow snake – or was it a dragon? – winding around the jacket. Looked at him with the usual expression of benignant curiosity. 'What will he get up to next, pray?' Nobody was saying anything downstairs. Jean-Luc, in the open window, was leaning against the shutter, smoking a cigarette, seemingly waiting for his brother.

Dutheil was visited by a sense of…irritation? Helplessness came closest, allied to a frustrating dependence. Really he might have been a small child that has wet its trousers, now to be scolded without real conviction, slapped in a routine way without its hurting, and changed with a brusque but affectionate roughness, to be finally reassured that it is of no great consequence but that really one must take the trouble to ask in future. All the members of his family were being so damned cool and competent. Laure in that high-handed maternal way, taking his gun and throwing it away – there you saw the schoolmarm blood coming out. Overprotective, he thought indignantly: second Carrie Kipling. And Daniel – one would almost think that he was Pa and oneself merely tiresome teenager Son. What did that boy Jean-Luc think he was doing? – last straw that – smoking a cigarette with his air of negligent woodcraft, all patient and tolerant of Father's latest temper-tantrum. He had a wish to knock the cigarette off the child's supercilious lip and tell him to go and study his quadratic equations. Somehow the wish appeared unable to translate itself into performance, and he just stood there, exactly like the little boy who was unable to get the lavatory door open.

Around the corner of the house now appeared a whole group of Spaniards, led by Figaro in his striped pyjamas, blue-chinned and majestic as a brigadier of gendarmerie, carrying a shotgun and fully prepared to repel boarders. This seemed to undo the knot of impotence that had formed within him. He stepped forward past Véronique and Laure, who were in one another's arms behaving like stone figures – Rodin design for the Burghers of Calais, he thought crossly. He repelled the armada with large impatient arm movements, and was surprised to hear his own voice, coming out exactly as it always did, grating, with a querulous, faintly whining note that made him refuse ever to be registered on tape.

'Nothing any of you can do here – go back to bed and stay out of my sight; I'm handling this.' Nora advanced tranquilly in a cotton housecoat, paying no attention. Daniel in his bare feet and the outrageous yellow shorts joined the group at the same moment; the two of them with that air of kindergarten teachers supervising break in the playground, indifferent: whatever the catastrophe they know how to handle it. Daniel looked at Nora, then at Dutheil.

'You've made a very thorough job,' in so natural a tone that Dutheil thought it sounded exceedingly unnatural. 'Whoever the fellow is he's very dead.'

Nora drew her breath in, but did not budge.

'Are you sure?' she said.

'Yes.'

'I mean – I'd better get Doctor Royan.'

'He's got no back left to his head,' brusquely, as though she were being obtuse. Nora said nothing but looked at the group still formed by Laure and Véronique. The whole party was now complete. Thomassen had joined Jean-Luc and was standing there in exactly the same attitude. Behind, in the doorway of the salon, Marcus had his hands in the pockets of a flowery robe and his glasses on. It was time for Dutheil to stop being a bit-player and become stage director.

'Yes, Nora, phone Gilbert if you please and tell him we need him – and then, please, the gendarmerie.'

'Very well,' in a flat secretary's voice. 'And what d'you wish me to tell them? That we've had burglars?'

'That I shot at a nocturnal loiterer – a thing I'm well aware I should not have done. According to Daniel, who appears to speak with indisputable authority, he is dead. That is their concern, I think.'

'Very well,' she said again, walking away rather slowly.

Figaro appeared behind Marcus, still brandishing the artillery.

'All the doors are shut,' important. 'I got in through the kitchen with my special key. If there are any more of them they've cleared off.'

'There are no more of them,' said Dutheil patiently. 'You have no need to stand guard with that great gun.' Figaro appeared less deflated than he should have done. 'Danny, you'd better open the courtyard gates – Gilbert will want to drive in and so will the police. You might see that that crowd of chatterers gets back indoors – if I see any more of them I'll shoot them, too.' Sounded a bit hollow. Daniel in his primrose shorts looked absurd, no doubt, but he had just realised that he himself was wearing jockeyshort underpants and a silk pyjama-top, and must have a downright vaudeville appearance.

Jean-Luc had opened the drinks cupboard and was pouring whisky into glasses, which seemed a sensible move.

'Is there anything I can do for anybody?' said Thomassen in an overloud voice. Laure and Véronique had disappeared.

'Sit down,' said Daniel hospitably, 'have a drink and please forgive me. This is not a show we put on for visitors as a rule.'

'You had a prowler, mm? And he's come to an abrupt end to his career – well, you were perfectly within your rights, seems to me.'

'Unfortunate that it should happen while you were here. Sorry,' again. Stupidity. He must be making a bad impression.

'My dear Dutheil,' began Marcus in a pompous voice, like Figaro announcing dinner.

'Shut up, Marcus, do you mind? Forgive me, I don't mean to be rude. Not used to shooting people.'

'Frightened Véronique, poor girl.'

'Yes. I'm afraid it's more complicated than it looks.' A silence, which was just becoming embarrassing when the door opened abruptly on Gilbert Royan, exactly as usual in his crumpled suit and even wearing a tie, making everybody else not only dishevelled but frivolous, as though out of a Feydeau farce.

He walked up to Dutheil and shook hands as though they had not seen each other for a week.

'From what Daniel tells me I'm superfluous to requirement – or is there anything for me here? Where are the girls?' His eye fell on the whisky glasses. 'I don't want you to drink,' he said to Dutheil bluntly.

'I'm not going to drink. The girls are next door, perhaps.'

Nora appeared by magic, fully dressed, and said 'Yes.' She held the door open, shut it after him, and said 'Give me a drink, Jean-Luc, will you? – The police will be here in a minute,' she added to nobody in particular.

'I'm going to get my trousers,' said Dutheil. Now why did he have to sound so defiant about that? Small boy again. Yes I have wet my pants and I don't care, and if Nora wants to play nanny then let her wash them.

When he reappeared they were all sitting in the same attitudes, and he felt curious whether any of them had had anything to say, during his absence. On the terrace a pair of official boots sounded. Daniel's voice came clearly.

'I'd better show you this, first. Doctor Royan's here but he hasn't bothered looking yet – you'll understand why.' The boots went down the steps; another pair, more hesitant, approaching vaguely; Nora put her glass down and went to cope.

'Nobody hanging about, Miss, definitely. We found a scooter outside – might have been what he came on. Don't know yet where he could have got over the wall. Probably be marks – we'll find them.' The first boots came back and stopped on the terrace outside.

'The rifle there?'

'Is my father's,' said Daniel coolly.

'How'd it get broken?'

'I think my mother was frightened and threw it over the balcony.'

'Oh.'

Two bulky uniformed figures; the local brigadier and a younger, more diffident dogberry. Two hands saluted, and the first one poked out for the handshake of politeness. Dutheil knew him well.

'Well. Sorry to disturb – but there, you've been disturbed. We'll need the ambulance – Johnny, Mademoiselle Noël will show you where to phone. Better see Doctor Royan first, I suppose – he's here, isn't he? Next door? – right. Thanks son,' largely to Jean-Luc who had poured him a large whisky. 'Cheers. Seems straightforward – bad luck on him; walked into a bullet, bump. Bad luck all round. Your bad luck – his bad judgement. You've a lot to protect here, after all. Alarm went off, did it, and woke you?'

'No, the alarm didn't go off,' said Dutheil. 'That's just the point, unfortunately.' The brigadier looked puzzled, drank some whisky to cover the fact, cleared his throat, and was saved by Royan coming back from the library.

'Don't talk,' said Gilbert abruptly. 'I want a little look at you first. *Salut*, brigadier. Dead, I hear.'

'Past your help, doctor. Sorry, sorry, am I in the way?' Royan felt Dutheil's pulse, sat him down firmly on the nearest chair, and dumped his bag on the table. He took the glass of whisky handed him by Jean-Luc, just tasted it out of politeness, and said, 'I don't need it, thanks,' without irony.

'I think I'll give you a tiny prick – quicker than a pill. If I know you you're talking nonsense already.'

'If you don't mind, Gilbert, we'll skip the tiny prick. I am perfectly well and totally totally calm.'

'I'll do the shouting,' unfairly – he hadn't been shouting.

'I was NOT shouting.'

'Arm, please. Don't jiggle. Thank you. All right brig, let's just look at your customer, even if he is past my help.' It seemed painfully obvious to Dutheil that Royan, damn him, was steering the police away till whatever dope it was hit him. Surely the police weren't having that? But the brigadier paid no attention.

'Got to sign the form.'

Nora went through to the other room. 'It's all straightened out, Laure. Nothing to worry about, believe me,' before the door shut again behind her. Nobody spoke and Dutheil, in the gesture of someone who does not know what else to do, lit a cigarette. He wished they would all clear out, but felt diffident about throwing them out. They weren't just irresolute; they were curious. Curious about what had happened; they were none of them, surely, under any illusion about the night-prowler. Thomassen would think – he couldn't blame him – that the whole show had been put on for his own benefit. It was so nearly the exact truth!

Oddly enough, Thomassen was thinking something of the sort. What the devil was going on? A night owl with evil designs upon the safe or the Rubens or anything you pleased transformed itself into a teenage love-in on the summerhouse cushions. Fair enough, and altogether within the Dutheil pattern of dramatising small incidents into leitmotivs fraught with plangent dooms. What he now didn't get was why three bullets? Letting a gun off to impress the children was one thing, but he and everybody else in the house had heard three careful, leisurely-spaced shots. He was curious to know how the police would react.

To tell the truth he was shocked. The whole thing had so staged and phony a smell that he had difficulty taking it seriously at all! The whole court rallied round with a smooth greased ease born, very likely, of long practice! He would almost place a small bet that they had learned their lines…

Yet something had gone wrong. Maybe the star had been smoking pot before making his entry – that might account for the three bullets? There was no smell of pot, but there was a strong pungent smell of calamity. The boy had died, and that was not in the script. The doctor had acted in a hurried way, moving in fast before writer-man got any higher and started saying things he shouldn't. The 'tiny prick' had been smoothly administered and covered by slick professional patter. Just what was it?

What was Sabatier thinking? That he was badly worried was evident. Anyone with half an eye could see that everyone had been caught off balance and greatly upset, but in front of me, good old stupid Robert who is going to write us a swingeing good piece for the jolly old *New Yorker*, ranks are closed with praiseworthy speed.

Laure was fighting to overcome the horrible numbness that followed inevitably upon shock.

'Give me something to make me lucid,' she had said with a stupid desperation to Gilbert. He had shaken his head, smiling.

'A knockout drop for the girl is one thing. We don't want her mixed up in this. Sleep is what she needs anyhow, and I've given her a king-sized nembutal. I can tell any policemen that she has nothing material to say and that even if they insisted on questioning her she'd make no sense at all. But if I give you something you might be tempted into saying things you might regret later. Just take it easy and don't talk till you have to.'

'And what about him?'

'Him? Ah, that's more complex – or maybe not: maybe it's more simple. He'll say plenty of things that may well appear unbalanced – and that's very likely no bad idea. Anybody else would predict with utter confidence that some defence mechanism would take over at once – vanity, chiefly. "I didn't do it but if I did then I was right and justified in doing so" – classic. Whereas the one really engaging thing about him as we both know is his ability to shed all vanity at a given moment and say "Lord, thou seest a worm". How is she doing now?'

He moved over to the daybed where Véronique was in a nembutal haze, felt her pulse, and took a quick glance under her eyelid.

'She'll do nicely. Between us, what has he been saying or doing to her – did she gabble anything out?'

'I can't make out,' said Laure. 'There was some scene between them at dinner, as you saw, but she has a natural recklessness. This idea of – of this business in the garden – it might have been planned earlier and it might have been spontaneous. Either way I can't believe he knew anything about it. He wouldn't have laid any cruel traps, you know. But what was he doing on the balcony?'

'Did he go to sleep as usual?'

'I don't know,' ruefully, 'because I fell asleep myself like a log of wood. He seemed quiet enough. He certainly hadn't drunk much, and he didn't complain of any miseries. Whatever it was with her he wouldn't tell me straight away – he never does; he's incapable of doing so, I think... What I most regret is my own hysterical foolishness. I snatched that horrible gun away from him – I've always been frightened of his guns – and threw it away. They're going to think I knew what he was about – that I guessed or at least had some suspicion.'

'That is exactly the kind of notion you must guard against. On the contrary, what you did is perfectly natural and so they will think. You were startled out of deep sleep, hazy, and in a sudden panic, and you're frightened of guns – that's all. He's never been a type, thank heaven, either to contemplate a genuine suicide or to stage a fake – he has too much lucidity. I think myself we stand a good chance of keeping it all in the family – the police know him, and know me. I'm a little worried about the three shots. Why three? It almost seems as though he were enjoying himself – rehearsing a scene in a book to see whether it came off…'

'In the family,' said Laure bitterly. 'Marcus I don't mind – he's a loyal friend – but what about that American?'

'To tell the truth – a thing I shouldn't, probably, be doing at this moment,' said Royan slowly, 'but it may help you – I did ask myself whether this may not be a drama improvised for that journalist's benefit. He was worried about him – afraid he wasn't getting over, afraid of making no impact, and being written off as a conceited hound thinking of nothing but money and wrapping himself in castles out of pure psychosis.'

'But that's absurd.'

'I am relieved to think that Thingummy is quite bright enough to see it as absurd. That our poor old Dutheil is intensely humble, vulnerable, and self-effacing is obvious even to a fool – and he's not a fool.'

'You're making me feel better, Gilbert.'

'I only hope he's not going to give us a bravura encore.'

When the brigadier came back, a minute or so later, there had come a change in his appearance. He seemed fatter, redder, sweatier. He looked faintly unhappy and his uniform subtly ill-fitting. He looks, in fact, thought Thomassen, like an amateur actor frightened of forgetting his lines. Dutheil, whose professional habits had been undisturbed by whatever Gilbert Royan had shot him with, noticed it too. Poor old Simon, he thought; looks as though suddenly interrupted while making love to the waitress in the café cellar… He felt remarkably well-balanced, himself. Presumably that was Gilbert's idea.

The brigadier now had the centre of the stage, with everyone hanging on his words. He was accustomed to this, and wasn't going to let it worry him. Just that in this house full of eccentric characters he didn't know exactly what sort of a tone to take.

'Uh – yes, like I said, seems quite straightforward. Very bad luck on the boy – but like we often see such things happen, mean to say, an auto skids and goes right across the road, kills maybe someone twenty metres off. Well, this boy – asking for trouble, uh? Loitering with intent – and infraction of domicile. Can't quite make out what he thought he'd find in the hut; still it's beside the point. Mean to say, breaking into the hut is just as much infraction as entering a bedroom. Puzzling though, because if he was looking for loot the hut holds what you'd expect it to hold; garden furniture and that – nothing of value. Likeliest we can suppose is the ground-floor shutters put him off and he suspected alarms. We might assume that perhaps he was looking in the hut for some tool – maybe to force the shutter?' Pause. The brigadier had been all jam so far. He now seemed to be considering how best to slip some nastier medicine into the jam spoon.

'There's one slightly puzzling aspect.' Everybody breathed out more or less abruptly – the three shots… The brigadier bumbled on without seeming worried.

'The Spanish man of yours, Monsieur Dutheil – he seemed a bit confused. Went on about the alarms. It's part of his job to see that the shutters are all closed at night and that the alarms function properly. That right?'

'Yes.'

'He reliable?'

'Perfectly.'

'Only that he claims there was a shutter open and was at great pains to tell me it couldn't have been his fault. I didn't make much sense of all he said, but I take it that he's just worried at it being thought, maybe, he had not made a proper job of an important kind of duty, right? Wanting to justify himself to me. So I just mentioned it to see whether there's some comment you wish to make on that.'

'We were all – at first – under a misapprehension,' said Dutheil in a placid, faintly sarcastic tone. 'I mustn't leave you imagining that he really was a burglar. He'd have needed to be very incompetent to find nothing better than the summerhouse.'

'You'd be surprised, if I may say so,' said the brigadier a bit defensively, 'how many of them are very incompetent, downright cretinous, the things they get up to.'

'I thought that too at first. I realised then I was mistaken. Not a burglar. He seems to have been an admirer of my daughter.'

Everybody reacted without wishing to. The two boys had stiff, half-embarrassed smiles and looked cretinous, thought Dutheil – petulantly. Thomassen had his look of benevolent detachment, fake as hell, like a man in front of a television camera while the announcer is prating about 'the well-known expert here with us tonight'. Marcus looked uneasy. Laure, who had put on a peignoir, wrapped it in a nervous gesture tighter around her body. Gilbert Royan looked deeply bored – much too deeply bored. I am the only person here behaving normally, he thought querulously.

The brigadier appeared relieved, as though this solved everything.

'Aha. The one explains the other. Hanging about after Mademoiselle Véronique – no wonder she was so upset. Sniffled about trying a few doors – is there any truth in this Spaniard's allegation that there was a shutter open? I think not. He goes into the summerhouse – looking maybe for a ladder? Every bit as serious an infraction as though he intended to steal. He'll know better in future, the tomcat.' He remembered suddenly the boy was dead, composed his face hastily, and rubbed his jaw to efface the gaffe; it made a scrubby noise in the stillness.

'Now let's just get this straight. You were disturbed by a prowler – you were asleep, Monsieur Dutheil?'

'No, I was awake. Sitting on the balcony having a cigar.'

'Just so. Naturally a small sound would disturb you. You were alerted by what?'

'I saw him – standing at the edge of the grass, by the box trees. I thought it was a burglar.'

'So you went for your gun?'

'Yes.'

'Perfectly legitimate – defence of domicile in nocturnal hours. Did you see him approach the house?'

'No – he went in the summerhouse. I was puzzled, so I waited to see what would happen. I then heard the shutter downstairs being opened, and thought there were more burglars – I was most alarmed.'

'Oh – you heard the shutter. You mean Mademoiselle Véronique... Well, that's neither here nor there. You thought it was a burglar – a whole gang for all you knew – and justifiably you fired – at the figure visible?'

'No, I fired at the window.'

The brigadier heaved an audible sigh of relief. This removed the last possible loophole to a charge of criminal negligence.

'Oh – you couldn't see him, behind the window.'

'No – there wasn't much light and anyway you'd only see the gleam of reflections on the glass. Anyway the glass is filthy – was I should say.'

'Fired at the window – warning shot, quite classic. And unhappily he was standing behind it. That's consistent with all the facts – the position of the body, the angle of the wound – Doctor Royan's confirmed all that already and we get the ambulance and take him away. And that's everything, I think.'

With a sour smile, Thomassen understood – and with relief Royan understood – that the brigadier had blandly decided to say nothing about the three shots. The moment there was more than one burglar, well, more than one warning shot, what?

He had put his képi back on, to indicate that he was quite satisfied and was now prepared to take off.

'I'll just see what the hell's keeping that ambulance,' muttered Royan, wanting to hurry things up.

'Oh yes – one thing,' suggested the brigadier, almost diffidently. 'Mademoiselle Véronique had a nasty shock. Of course I wouldn't think of asking her to look – but I wonder does she know who this boy is – make the identification easier, you know.'

'She's asleep,' said Laure. 'Doctor Royan gave her a sleeping pill – the less she recalls about this the better. You could ask him of course – but I'm sure he'll agree.'

'I won't bother for now – likely carrying some papers or letters. Well – about all, I reckon. Everybody better go back to bed and get some rest. Sorry to have to trouble you with it, Monsieur Dutheil, and upsetting for your guests. Uh – I make a written report and pass it along, and we'll pass by today some time to ask your signature on it. Just the usual legal formalities, you know.'

'As little to it as that?' Dutheil appeared startled. The brigadier smiled vaguely. He seemed to be casting about for a way of explaining that this was all very bread-and-butter from his point of view. He looked immensely reassuring; massive and weather-hardened, his face leather-tanned to the white line where his képi sat, comfortably hairy with his thick moustache and the bunches of unexpectedly fine silky hair on the backs of his dirty, competent fingers.

'You have an auto accident,' he suggested. 'Skid on wet leaves, say – can happen to anybody. And just there by the roadside is a young man hitching a lift. You are very disturbed and unhappy at your front wing having pulped him – but there are far more deaths like that than gunshot accidents, even in the shooting season. He knew, or ought to, the risks he takes standing at a road verge, huh? All I'm called on to do is to satisfy myself with measurements and so on that it happened in such and such a way. And of course that there was not grave negligence – amounting to criminal negligence – on the part of the driver.' The solid oracle, speaking in so heavy a common-sense tone, was guaranteed to convince the thinnest-skinned moralist.

'Suppose I was drunk?' said Dutheil with an irritable eye on Thomassen, so damned bright-eyed and alert.

'Why then I'd have to arrest you,' with a shrug. 'It'd be a thing I'd have in mind of course – I'd look for it.'

'What would you do then?'

'I'd have you medically examined, take a blood test, and if you contested the findings, or if it seemed obscure, or if other people were involved, the prosecutor might open an instruction, convoke witnesses – that'd have nothing to do with me.' He was humouring Dutheil, being patient – nobody thought that he too had been dragged out in the middle of the night because an imbecile had killed another imbecile.

'I see,' said Dutheil wisely. 'Of course if I had an auto accident and you were there – you know me. Nervous character, you'd say, easily alarmed, given to abrupt impulsive movements.' A large smile spread behind the moustache; small blackish eyes vanished behind the bars left by forty years of wind and sun.

'Don't torment yourself now, Monsieur Dutheil. I know you. You're an artist. You made a hasty movement in a moment of alarm, and you're upset because a boy lost his life.'

'I didn't act impulsively. I fired after I realised who the boy was and what he was doing here.'

The brigadier took his képi off again, looked at it for help, worked the huge hard hand over his face, stopped his moustache getting all bristly and aggressive, and made his voice even more patient and reasonable.

'Doesn't alter the facts. Intruder in your house during the hours of night. Householder entitled to possess firearms – it's all laid out in the code.'

'I fired three times, rather slowly.' Marcus, who was chewing his glasses, dropped them on the floor.

'Sorry,' he said stupidly.

'I know that, Monsieur Dutheil,' slowly. 'I could see there was more than one. Doctor Royan told me he was here last night, all evening, and that you had drunk very little. I belong here in the village – I know you. I observed that from that balcony nobody could see through that window. You could not have known he was in your line of fire.'

'Where does a lover stand?' rhetorically. 'He has an assignation, he looks to see if his mistress is coming. Where does he stand? At the back of the bloody hut or by the window?'

'I suppose,' said Thomassen in a vague drawl to nobody in particular, 'that it's the same as at home and a prosecutor would have to prove intent.'

'That's right, Mister Clever,' snapped Dutheil, wheeling on him. 'A prosecutor considering three carefully spaced rifle shots fired by a practised marksman might reasonably conclude that this fact carried a strong suggestion of criminal intent.'

The silence was thick as fruit-cake. Everybody looked at the gendarme, who seemed to grow thicker and redder, and observed Thomassen slowly as though along the sights of a rifle-barrel. He might have been about to say 'Papers' when the door opened and Gilbert Royan blew in briskly.

'That's all right at last.' He stopped after a look at Laure's face.

'Quite,' said Marcus loudly. Nobody said 'Quite what?' He advanced with decision, addressing the wall between Royan and the gendarme.

'He's much more upset than he realises. I'm glad you're here, Gilbert – he's saying all sorts of nonsensical things – delayed shock one supposes but that's your province. Typically he blames himself and we're having a desperate-honesty type of dramatisation, though fortunately our friend here is intelligent and experienced and has the advantage of knowing him.'

The brigadier, unused to being accused of intelligence by the public, was pleased with this glowing tribute, however much stitched with white thread it might be.

'That's his job,' solidly. 'Making up stories, I mean. Huh? But nobody tells a straight tale after a thing of this kind, and I've known people accuse themselves of the unlikeliest things.'

'I see,' said Royan gaily, reaching for Dutheil's wrist. 'Probably the shot I gave him – unexpected side-effects these things often have.'

Dutheil took a step back, and spoke in a friendly tone, that had a sarcastic note, so that he might have been congratulating an opponent upon a good shot at croquet.

'Gilbert, kindly keep your hands away from me. I was never healthier in my life and need no doctors to make me feel ill. Marcus, you are an old friend, I am obliged to you for many kindnesses, and it is with regret that I must tell you in my own house kindly to keep your mouth shut.'

There was a scurry of voices from all directions.

'Quixotic as usual…'

'We've read Truman Capote and we know all about cold blood…'

'Anybody will dramatise this kind of happening…'

'You're being irresponsible and now I am talking as an old friend and I feel bound…'

Dutheil suddenly became angry, quite impressively.

'Out of here,' to his sons, with a slap of his hand on the table. 'Obey me at once, do you hear?' It was exactly as when they were ten and behaved badly at table. 'Now,' to the adults. 'Whose house is this? Very well, let's have less infernal chat.'

'Do not raise your voice, please,' said Royan coldly. 'I'm not interested in this being your house; I'm called on to do my work anywhere. Apart from that you may act as you please – in half an hour you'll give an account of yourself that does you more justice.'

Marcus looked at the policeman and shrugged exaggeratedly. The policeman kept quiet.

Dutheil, expected by everyone to make a scene, did the opposite.

'All right,' good-humouredly. 'Give me a few pills, another prick, anything you like. When you're all quite persuaded I'm not hysterical I will give you the facts you don't know, which is why you're talking such nonsense. Véronique will confirm them – I gave her a thrashing for insolence earlier this evening – I wonder whether she asked the boy to come and rescue her, or some equally romantic notion. It has no great importance – she may have telephoned after dinner while Nora was here – I only mention it to demonstrate that I know what I'm talking about, whereas you do not.'

The door to the hall opened and Figaro appeared, dressed. 'The ambulance men are asking for Doctor Royan.' There was a momentary hesitation. Royan looked at the gendarme.

'I administered a sedative, not a soporific. There's often a flare-up of tension and excitability before it properly takes hold – nothing to it.' It sounded apologetic.

The brigadier cleared his throat.

'Yes. Well – I've seen it, you've seen it, there's no dispute about how it happened. Tell them to take it away.' He addressed Dutheil bluntly. 'If you're not satisfied with the way I handle this, you've a right to say so. If you want me to I'll ring the PJ. I'd better make clear that I'm neither asking for the responsibility of deciding this nor trying to back out of it.'

'Whatever you like,' spitefully. 'Tell them to take the corpse away, Gilbert. Figaro, out of my sight. You two boys, go and look after your mother.'

'What's the PJ?' asked Thomassen with interest.

'I'd forgotten about you,' pleasantly. 'Police Judiciaire – the detective branch.'

'Would you like me to go too? None of my business.'

'By no means. Have some more whisky. On the contrary – the law and medicine are represented, but we need the press.'

The door to the library opened, and Laure came in, under control of herself.

'She's fallen asleep but please don't make a noise.'

'You'll excuse me,' said the brigadier. 'I want to see if we can find anything to establish this identity.'

'Go with him, please, Nora, and show him where to use the phone.'

The brigadier stepped out first on to the terrace, and said a word to his subordinate, who nodded, propped his back against the balustrade, and lit a cigarette.

'Aren't you causing everyone rather a lot of trouble?' asked Royan mildly. 'You know, the best thing you could do would be to lie down here for a bit and see if you can have a little sleep. It would do you good, and the injection I gave you will make it easier.

'A good idea,' said Dutheil meekly.

'Why don't you go to bed too?, said Royan to Sabatier, at the door.

'Nothing would please me better,' mournfully, 'but I'm worried about Laure.' He looked back at Dutheil, who had put his feet up on the daybed and placidly closed his eyes. 'Is that normal or is that more acting?'

'Quite normal – like a child falling asleep after a temper tantrum.'

'What is that gendarme going to do now?'

'Wrestle with his conscience, I suppose – like the rest of us.'

They went out. Nobody stayed behind but Thomassen, who poured himself some more whisky, settled comfortably in a Voltaire armchair, and stared at Dutheil. After a minute he got up, chose himself a cigar from the box on the table, and lit it with a flourish before leaning back in a comfortable way like a Red Indian at a peace conference. Dutheil was sleeping unselfconsciously, just as though he had eaten too much lunch and decided upon a little siesta.

Five minutes later there was a conference going on in Nora's office. The ambulance had gone, and there was a little heap of objects on the table: the contents of the dead boy's pockets. The brigadier was sitting writing in his notebook. Laure, Nora, and Marcus were grouped opposite. Royan had gone home.

'Don't hesitate, Laure, to call me if you feel you need me. But I'll come round anyway before my consulting hour.'

'Forgive me,' said the gendarme suddenly to Sabatier. 'I don't know quite who you are.'

'Mr Sabatier is our publisher,' Laure answered. 'And an old friend, who knows us both well. I am happy to have him with me.

'Of course,' vaguely. He went on writing, muttering.

'Height one seventy-seven. Weight about sixty-five. Hair dark, eyes – well, we'll skip that. No artificial teeth. Now. First name Antoine. No identity card.' The others stared at the little heap. Chrome sport wristwatch. Three personal letters in one envelope in girl's handwriting, all beginning darling Tony. Dirty handkerchief. Clean handkerchief. Ring with miscellaneous keys – the policeman was turning each item into officialese as he wrote carefully in his notebook.

Everybody was quiet and patient. Identity – and once somebody was dead, it became important that there were exactly twenty-three francs fifty-one centimes in his pocket.

Comb. Cigarettes, and enamel lighter initialled AR Tin box containing contraceptives. Red plastic ballpoint pen. Laure looked bleakly at the tin box and Véronique's handwriting.

'Have you such a thing as a paper bag?' apologetic.

Nora produced a large manila envelope. The five minutes of pure administrative routine had helped him.

'There is something here I don't properly understand. I think everyone here will agree… It's all clear – and it all becomes unclear. Don't think now that I take what Monsieur Dutheil says all too literally. I've been out shooting with him a couple of times after duck – I know he's a safe shot and careful with a gun. I know too that he's always been nervous of bandits breaking in. Now somebody opened the shutters from inside – that can only have been Mademoiselle Véronique. Did he see her before he fired the shots? How is he so sure that this was her, uh, boyfriend?'

Véronique has not said a word yet, thought Laure listlessly Nora didn't know what she was thinking of, but her mind was full of the Convent of the Visitation, and damp hankies, and little lists of sins written out on bits of paper before going to confession in the over-ornate chapel.

'You see,' said the brigadier, 'this boy's family will want to know exactly how he came by this accident. If there's doubt about the circumstances they will likely ask for an inquiry. If Monsieur Dutheil took him for a burglar that's one thing – and if he knew or saw he was there just to meet a girl in the summerhouse… I have the responsibility for this. I'm sorry, but I've got to call the PJ, and have the magistrate here. If these parents make trouble he's the one to answer them. There's another thing… I don't want to wake Mademoiselle Véronique up to ask her a lot of questions – but it looks as though her account of events is going to decide this – one way or another. Thing is – it'll take the Parquet an hour to get here. I'm afraid I've got to ask you all to go back in the house and wait.'

'I will make coffee,' said Laure sensibly, and the brigadier brightened up at once. Minutes later they were all in the kitchen. The clock struck one and Laure thought they were only five hours out of reckoning. Now if we were only in New York – Dutheil would be here making the breakfast and nothing would have happened at all.

The boys reappeared, washed and dressed. The brigadier sat at the kitchen table and wrote carefully in his notebook. Laure confirmed that she had woken upon hearing shots, that soon afterwards – she didn't know if it was immediately – she had heard Véronique scream. She had run out on to the balcony. She didn't know why she had snatched the gun – it had been pure instinct and she had been in a fright. She knew nothing about the boyfriend – except that he existed. No, she didn't think that Dutheil knew either. Yes, he had had words with his daughter. He might have punished her – he hadn't mentioned it. There had been guests. Nobody had made a scene.

Daniel confirmed that he had looked out directly the shots woke him. There had been a scream – he had thought it was his mother, perhaps… He hadn't noticed Véronique. Yes, she was there when he came on to the terrace. He had supposed she had come down ahead of him. She had seemed frightened – well, that was pretty natural, wasn't it?

Quite.

Everybody had forgotten Thomassen, or supposed he had gone tactfully back to his room. He was still sitting in his chair, looking at Dutheil, who, he decided was not asleep at all. Rehearsing his story, very likely – he must realise that the cops would arrive any minute. He stood up, took his glass which still had some ice-cubes in it, and went ting-a-ling-a-ling by Dutheil's ear.

'Wakey-wakey,' he said pleasantly. Dutheil opened an eye, studied this figure for a moment, decided this was a hostile manifestation and opened the other eye. He got up, poured out some water, sipped it, and said, 'What do you want – an interview?'

'If you like – I'd be interested, sure enough, to know what the hell you've been getting up to.'

'What you been doing – sitting here wondering about it?'

'Yes.'

'Damned if I know,' vaguely.

'You saw a boy hanging round. You went and got your gun. You then realised that he was there after your daughter. I get the impression you couldn't stand the idea of that, so you took a pot at him. To your surprise you hit him. Spread him all over the landscape by all accounts. You had to think up something then, so you adopt quite a dainty attitude of being a sinner and working up for a grand sacrificial third-act curtain. Sort of getting the accounts straight – book-keeping with your success. To whom much has been given much shall be asked – crummy kind of attitude. Only how it strikes me,' politely. 'Maybe I'm all wrong. Just thinking it over was all. Can't hardly say you staged it for my benefit. Have you realised, though, that this boy had a family, a life, a career, or are you just a psychopath, who can let nothing stand in the way of fulfilling his own desires? – that wouldn't look too good, would it?'

'No,' agreed Dutheil seriously. 'It wouldn't.'

Thomassen was walking about with his hands in his pockets, turning constantly to look at his target with an odd kind of respect.

What's he got to be respectful about, wondered Dutheil crossly.

'Yes – the hell is you're quite sharp enough to realise it. You're a pretty good writer – high-fidelity, built-in stereo, all the little transistors you could wish for and classy Japanese optics stuck on in front. So you're not a psychopath, and it wasn't an accident, and this is not just a pose – the cops will have to take this seriously. What are you going to do? Everybody around here is used to you firing guns off into the landscape to relieve your frustrations, but this time you've killed a human being. You got it worked out?'

'No. And I don't care. Get the message? I don't care. Go and analyse some other clown's sensations.'

'Doubtless you'll be able to talk your way out of it.' Dutheil shrugged.

Hell, thought Thomassen, he really means it. He really doesn't care. It's not just vanity, not just a self-pitying dramatisation.

He looked out of the window and was startled to see a gendarme still there, chewing gum, looking as though he had not moved at all from the spot on the balustrade where he had propped his backside half an hour ago. He doesn't hear our voices, but he doesn't ask himself what is going on, what we're talking about. He doesn't care either. He's just there to see that nobody else goes mataglap and grabs a gun, that everybody stays put, that nobody runs away or commits hara-kiri. And is that just what Dutheil wants? For everyone round him to stop poking at him all day and treat him with total, uncaring, uncomprehending indifference? Maybe at that I wouldn't blame him.

Thomassen suddenly saw the castle as an intolerable burden. Bloody awful house – and those two women – and that crowd of servants – and all the wearisome reputation of being a 'writer' – a thing the fellow thought of no worth at all. What was a writer – a more or less bad telephone line? Damn it, maybe the fellow's dead right.

'I'm not so bright,' he said, realising afterwards he had spoken aloud. And Dutheil winked at him, in a thoroughly friendly way, as though guessing his thoughts.

'Neither am I,' he said.

Laure came in, followed by Nora, both carrying coffee things on trays. She was surprised to see Thomassen.

'Oh – you're here.'

'We're keeping one another company,' said Dutheil.

'And you're awake?'

'I didn't sleep – just had a little rest. Breakfast time?'

'Breakfast time in New York.' Dutheil laughed.

'Wrong way round, honey – in New York it's yesterday evening.'

'I never get it straight,' apologetic.

'If this was breakfast time in New York the coffee wouldn't be this good,' said Thomassen in the most relaxed way he could think of.

'I won't pour Nora's out yet.'

Nora had decided that her presence was an embarrassment. It wasn't that she had seen nothing, understood nothing. But this was a family affair. And she did not belong. There was work to be done and she had gone to do it. Policemen were going to arrive, perhaps several sets of policemen. Had anybody in the village noticed the comings and goings? Would anyone have notified the press? – horrid thought. An American literary journalist is all the press we need. Chattering idiot servants – nosy villagers – Nora was going to be on her guard. At least that gendarme had had the tact to take himself off – but had Figaro?

It was like a party before the guest of honour arrives: people a bit stiff, with nothing useful to say.

'This is not my spoon,' said Dutheil in quite the old querulous manner, stirring his coffee. He drank some.

'Good,' he said, sounding surprised. Laure smiled faintly.

Sabatier had decided that he couldn't do any earthly good, but at least his presence might keep the police from doing anything too silly. Thomassen looked oddly contented – anybody'd think he was getting copy or something. And Dutheil looked more relaxed and happy than he had ever seen him. Was that just the effect of the dope Royan had shot him with? Did he not realise just how extremely serious this was. God-in-heaven, could they not guess that everything – everything – now depended on what sort of a policeman this was?

When he appeared it was disconcerting – one could not tell at all. Didn't look stupid, didn't look bright, neither nice nor nasty, neither peasant nor bourgeois. He might be a farmyard mentality or he might be intensely sophisticated but one couldn't tell from looking at him. The usual figure of an ex-shotput athlete slightly gone to seed from eating too much spaghetti. Adjunct Officer of Police Thomas who came with him was taller and thinner, with pale bank-teller's hands and a silver pencil. He kept his mouth shut so you couldn't tell anything about him either.

'Petitjean, commissaire of police. Who is everybody? You're the householder? Monsieur Dutheil, right? Spell it please.'

It brought a chill commercial note into the affair. Just when everybody was sitting comfortably installed in the orangery snow started coming through the roof. The brigadier of gendarmerie had been too friendly, too accommodating.

'Madame Dutheil? – yes, thanks, I'd like a cup of coffee. Sabatier? Publisher? Paris? – friend of the family – staying, I see. Thomassen – spell it please. American – journalist – staying likewise. Right, we take first what we already know. A so far unidentified young man was noticed hanging about the house, and in a series of so far unexplained movements got himself shot. Right. You call the doctor and the gendarmerie – doctor certifies death, the brigadier has made the usual inquiries, taken the usual measures. Nobody queries the shooting, Monsieur Dutheil admits full responsibility, permission is given for the ambulance to come and take the dead person away, all as simple as could be wished. Right? I'm not under any misapprehension? Very good. Till suddenly you, Monsieur Dutheil, inject a note of doubt and talk about a criminal action. Everyone says pooh-pooh, shock and so on, and you persist, until the brigadier tells you that in that case his responsibility is to call me. Any query about that?'

'No,' said Dutheil.

'Very well. I will put some questions – to you, to everyone else as the need arises. Question and answer are written down. No need on that account to worry about being consequent or consistent. Just be brief. Later, probably, Mr Thomas and myself will ask further questions separately. We start with you, Monsieur Dutheil, since by your own account you fired these shots. You saw a burglar? – call him that. You were on the balcony? Where is this balcony?' When shown he said nothing, then turned to Sabatier.

'You were woken – by shots or screams or whatnot. You sleep where? The floor above – you looked, first, out of the window, right? Now what I wish to know is whether the light is the same as it is now? Much the same…yes yes man, your impression – you're not a photographer.' He turned back to Dutheil. 'You sat here on this balcony in this position. What were you doing?'

'I couldn't sleep and I was sitting in that chair there, doing nothing – or meditating, if you want. I was smoking a cigar – look, you can still see the ash.'

'I like evidence not at all,' said the commissaire, dry, 'and explanations even less. When I want you to support a statement I'll ask you.' And it's been a long long time, thought Sabatier piously, since anybody spoke to Dutheil that way.

'You went and got a gun – which was where? In the wardrobe in the dressing-room – good. Was it loaded?'

'No. They never are.' Mindful of the snub he did not embroider.

'The cartridges?'

'Last time I unloaded it I put them with my socks. I put in three.'

'And three were fired, I believe. Has the gun a bolt action?'

'Yes.'

'This boy went into the summerhouse – would that not show that whatever he was he was no bandit?'

'I couldn't tell what he was up to – I did nothing. Then the shutter opened. And the alarm didn't go off – that frightened me.'

'So you fired.'

Dutheil thought and the commissaire showed no sign of impatience. 'I waited. My daughter came out on the terrace. Then I understood – I was very angry – and very upset. I shouted something at her, I don't remember what, and almost at once I think I fired at the window.'

'Why?'

'I don't know why.'

'Make an effort.'

'Perhaps to head her off? Draw a line? – so far but no further… Take vengeance on her for the fright I'd had by frightening her.'

'You were concentrating on her.' This struck Dutheil for the first time.

'Now that I think of it, yes. I wasn't thinking about the boy, it's true. But why fire at the window?'

'You're not going to tell me you fired at your daughter – without quite meaning to, but blinded by your rage?'

'No,' said Dutheil seriously. 'That's out of the question. She was still a good way off – and I was above. And I'm used to handling guns. I fired well ahead of her.'

'Good. Go on from there.'

'She gave a frightful scream, and I did nothing, I think, till my wife came out on the balcony. She…'

'Stop there. Madame if you please. I would like to know exactly what you saw from the balcony.'

'I hardly know,' said Laure. 'I saw my husband first, with the gun – he had it under his arm, not pointing it… I didn't see the broken window. I saw my daughter, still on the steps of the terrace. She had her hands up to her face – she didn't move, I think. I – as you know I snatched the gun and threw it away. I don't know why.'

'A brutal question and I want an unqualified answer. Did you think he had shot – or shot at – your daughter?'

'No,' without hesitating. 'He would never do that – he would be incapable of such a thing. He has rages, yes, and with her, but not…'

'Thank you, Why did you snatch the gun?'

'I was frightened,' simply.

'You knew nothing about the assignation?… You'd never seen this boy?… I am to conclude you knew he existed?'

'I knew he existed – but I knew nothing of a meeting, and I did not know he was there. I don't think I looked at the hut at all – I looked at her. I went downstairs to look after her. I saw my son out on the terrace – I know now that he saw the broken window of the hut and went to look. It was only then…'

'Very well. You two gentlemen. What have you to add?'

'I went downstairs,' said Sabatier. 'I looked first – I saw the girl on the terrace, just standing there. I had a vague idea of being of some use or help. I had no idea of what might have happened. When I got down I saw Madame with her daughter – and her son Daniel by the hut.'

'You, Mr Thomassen?'

'I don't think I've anything to add. I met Monsieur Sabatier in the passage, and said "What happened?" or something equally stupid, and he said, "I don't know but we must look" – I don't pretend to have his exact words – and I saw the scene downstairs as described.'

'What kind of light was there?'

'A light in here – it seemed quite dark outside. When I looked out I saw nothing except the young lady – she was wearing some palish dress – and that dimly. I agree that one didn't even notice the hut.'

'Until one's eyes got accustomed to the dimness? Any comment on that, Monsieur Dutheil?'

'No – you've understood that my eyes were accustomed to dimness. I could see this young man, before. Well enough to see it was a man, I mean – not enough to distinguish features.'

The character of this policeman was beginning to take shape. Total concentration. He drinks his coffee without looking at it. He takes out cigarettes and puts them in his mouth, but does not light them. Sometimes he throws them away, and sometimes he puts them absently in his breast pocket – and then forgets, and takes a new one from the packet. He would make a good research technician. Used to observing minute fluctuations in temperature and rhythm, writing them all down, not drawing any conclusions. He had looked at the bolts on the salon shutters, and the alarm above Laure's bed, at the spent cartridge-cases, and the cigar-ash. He had seen that a splinter of glass hanging in the window frame of the hut still gave a reflection. You would notice that window, but only if you looked for it. He didn't ask to see Daniel, nor, apparently, was he in any hurry to talk to Véronique. This sobriety fascinated Dutheil.

'The doctor came,' went on the commissaire leisurely; he had got round at last to lighting one of his cigarettes. 'Local doctor? Knows you well? Maybe even a friend?'

'Certainly. Close friend. Spent the evening here.'

'What did he have to say about all this?'

'I think he thought I was dramatising the situation.'

'Of course you were. What one would expect. He gives you something to slow you down a little? Pill or so?'

'Yes.'

'And do you think that, now, a bad idea? You think you're presenting a fairly coherent statement of events? Sufficiently to do yourself justice? Mm?'

'I suppose so,' vaguely.

'Do you think of yourself as a neurotic personage?'

'Fairly frequently.'

'Moments of excitement alternating with patches of depression?'

'Yes.'

'Are you an intelligent man, Monsieur Dutheil?'

'Sometimes.'

'You weren't on this occasion, were you?' dryly, and paid no further attention to him.

'What happens now?' asked Laure, nervously.

'We wait for the magistrate, Madame. He is the person who decides whether or not justice is interested in what happened here this morning. Thomas, go and phone, would you?'

The clerkly man got up and went out. His notebook and the silver pencil stayed where they were. The commissaire smoked and appeared to meditate.

'You are a writer, isn't that so?' suddenly. 'And, plainly, a successful one.' He glanced about the room. There seemed no comment Dutheil could usefully make. 'I would like to go back to something said by you earlier, apparently, when the brigadier was here. This evening, you said, you had words with your daughter. Let's talk about these words.'

Dutheil was at his worst, batteries flat, lacking all juice, and now feeling a tremendous wish to go to sleep. Asked for words, his stock in trade, he was disconcerted to find himself out of stock.

Laure noticed at once, knowing that nothing humiliated him more than to be helpless in front of a situation.

He tried to pull himself together.

'I had words with my daughter, as I admitted openly. I'm not obliged to offer any explanation. There isn't any. It would be idiotic to look for one.'

'A bit late in the day for discretion,' in a sour way. 'Look, Monsieur Dutheil, this is all very banal, practically without importance. Householder shoots at intruder – it's as flat as a road accident.'

'But the boy's dead.'

'Ach what?' irritated. 'Shut up – what's that to do with it? I mean all this – were you nervous, tired, drunk, had words with your wife – the police gets all that for dinner as often as sausage and sour cabbage. You might get charged with unlawful wounding or even unintended homicide and who cares? Not me – I run a criminal brigade. Now you chose to worry the gendarmerie. As though you had stated after a road accident that you saw a man and ran him over deliberately because you didn't like his face. You chose here to hint that you shot this boy deliberately and that your quarrels with your daughter gave you a pretext for doing so. Against my inclination I get dragged into this. Much good may it do you. A word of advice – if you commit a crime make it a big one. It expedites justice. Don't imagine crimes and think you're giving everybody entertainment.'

Dutheil could contain himself no longer.

'If you're not satisfied then arrest me. I don't ask you to keep yourself out of bed. I'd like to go to bed myself.' Sounding petulant again, he thought sadly. The commissaire had written something down, and sat calmly tapping his biscuit-coloured teeth with the silver pencil.

'I don't know why I shot that boy. I was badly upset by my daughter – by her behaviour and by words she said to me this evening. I was moved by resentment or by jealousy, or by humiliation – how should I know?' Mr Thomas came back in and stood waiting.

'Well?' said the commissaire.

'On their way – be about an hour I should think.'

'Gives us time to set the stage,' without irony. 'I'll have to talk to your daughter, Madame. She's asleep, I take it.'

'Doctor Royan gave her a nembutal.'

'That's all right,' tranquilly. 'She'll feel a bit foggy, but she'll make sense.'

'Very well, I'll wake her up.'

'I prefer to see her alone. Don't be concerned, Madame, I won't be nasty to her.' He followed Laure's look to the library door, and shut it behind him firmly. The group stayed with Mr Thomas, who said mildly, 'We'd like Monsieur Dutheil to stay handy till the magistrate comes, but you don't all have to sit here.' They none of them budged.

'Rather like a dentist's waiting-room,' said Marcus, 'where one reads things one would never dream of looking at anywhere else.'

'Or the Department of Immigration,' murmured Thomassen. 'An academic interest is the line to take. One has committed an enormity, without being in the least aware of the fact. None of the habitual norms apply.'

Dutheil felt touched. They are showing a kind of solidarity that is admirable, he thought. It is not just a vulgar curiosity to see what is done to me. They are showing that they feel my burns, that they taste with my tongue, that their skin cringes with mine. Mr Thomas paid no attention. He read over his shorthand carefully, rewriting the more illegible bits in red ballpoint while his memory was still fresh.

Véronique was asleep, looking natural and peaceful. The commissaire did not bother thinking about this, but woke her up by pressing gently behind her ear till she opened her eyes, which looked at him in surprise. It was typical of him that he did not use any polite formulas like 'How do you feel now?' but spoke to her with the brisk indifference of her maths professor at school, whom indeed he rather resembled, so that the girl had a sensation at first of having fallen asleep over the binomial theorem.

'We have to have a little talk,' he said equably. 'I'm the commissaire of police. Tony got shot, and we need to know his name.' The realisation that it had really happened confused her; she sat up and opened her mouth, but nothing came out.

'Name and address – we have to see his parents. Exactly like a road accident.' He took out a cigarette and put it in his mouth. 'Make you feel sick if I smoke this?'

Véronique looked without enthusiasm at the gaudy frock she was still wearing, frowned, ran her hands through her hair, and said, 'No. Give me one too, would you?' He lit both, leisurely.

'He's dead, I'm afraid – you know that?'

She nodded.

'I guessed at once.'

'Were you very fond of him?'

'No – not really. He was a very nice boy, and I'm very…it was through me…'

'No it wasn't.'

'I wasn't in love with him. I thought I was, once.'

'You had told him to come?' Nod. 'It was you undid the shutters? After fixing the alarms? And you had no idea your father was still awake.'

'I wanted… I wanted…'

'No, don't try to explain.' Quite right. It was a theorem. One didn't explain it. It got demonstrated and that was all there was to it. Simply knowing the logical sequence.

'You wanted to do something defiant, am I right? You were going to let him make love to you?'

'I phoned him. He'd never have dared on his own. I told him I'd fix the shutter. I thought of the hut, uh – if I tell you you'll laugh.'

'Why? Time was I went out in the country with girls myself. Too much dew? I guessed as much.' He sighed; it was such bad luck.

'And your father had to choose that night to sit on the balcony.' Her answer had a simplicity that was comic.

'I couldn't bring him in the house – that wouldn't have been fair, you see. Poor father.' Her affection was so natural that it appeared nonchalant. 'Trust him to fuck it all up.' He could not stop the slow smile working through his face muscles.

'He was the wrong man in the wrong place there, all right.'

'I'll tell you,' impulsively. 'I was furious – oh, I was furious. With him – he's always interfering, making rows, making remarks to put one down, hold one down, because – oh – discipline – it's part of his precious dignity, don't you see?'

'Yes, I think I do see.'

'He's jealous and possessive and all that.'

'Most parents are.'

'He's a writer, you know. He worries. Worries worries worries, all the time. Playing psychiatrist with his own emotions, my brother says.'

'He told me that he didn't know why he let the gun off but that if I wanted an opinion he'd let me have one.'

To his satisfaction she laughed.

'That's so typically father. Oh, he's an old woman. My mother – no, I can't tell you that, it's not fair.'

'Yes, but now and then it's important not to be fair.'

'How true that is! Mother always calls him panicpot.'

'Do you think that's the explanation – panic? That he was very frightened at the noise of the shutter opening, and then seeing you – furious at you, or furious at being frightened?'

'It would be like him.'

'Then tell me why he says he fired deliberately. Everybody would accept the panic theory. It can't be a stupid wish to draw attention. Mm?'

Véronique was becoming agitated, fidgeting nervously with unravelled threads on the binding of the blanket that she had been covered with.

'He certainly wouldn't. He goes to any lengths to avoid publicity.'

'Must be another reason, then, mustn't there?'

Tears started coming out of the corners of her eyes.

'It was my own fault. I wanted to hurt him, really wound him, be savage to him.' She wanted so much to cry like an adult, and was furious with the adolescent hiccup that insisted on coming out.

'Today?'

'This evening, at dinner. I did a lot of things on purpose that I knew would get his goat. He sent me out of the room.'

'Yes?' helpfully, lighting another cigarette and giving it her. 'He came upstairs after me, very stiff and pompous, and said he'd beat me.'

'Beat you?' blandly. So this was what Dutheil had been blurting about, with the brigadier – doubtless a bit over-relaxed by the stuff the doctor had shot him with.

'Yes with a stick. He had a little stick. He must have screwed his courage up a good deal,' with a touch of the sneering tone, the adolescent sarcasm that must, he reflected, have sent poor old Dutheil raving.

'You've a remarkably developed observation.'

'I know him, you see,' she said with simplicity.

'Go on.'

'Well…I said something to him.'

'You'll have to tell me what, I'm afraid.'

'I said – I said – maybe he'd like to go to bed with me, sneaking into my room like that.'

'Wasn't very nice, was it?'

'No,' and she started to cry in earnest. He let her cry.

'Did he hit you?'

'Yes, once. He was so mad at me. He hurt me dreadfully – I screamed like hell. He was frightened then, I think – he ran away.'

There was no need to ask her for evidence!

'All right. You see? – just a stupid accident. Run off now. Go upstairs and get into bed. I'll ask your mother to come up for a few minutes.'

'No,' she said fervently. 'I – I – please ask my father. You see – I…'

'Don't explain. If you like – now skip.' She scrambled off the bed staring at him. 'Take your blanket.' She scuttled off through the hall. Left alone, the commissaire picked up the half-smoked cigarette she had left and pulled at it without noticing that it was not his. Tomorrow she will remember the boy is dead, and spend the whole day crying. Shock is an odd thing – and so are teenage girls…

He had all he needed. One could – nowadays, in court, one did! – call it temporary insanity. An emotional trigger-point. The commissaire shrugged. He had two daughters of his own – grown up now, thank heaven. One married.

'The poor bugger. He couldn't sleep with the girl himself, so he was damned if anybody else would, either. Prepared to shoot anyone who tried. One can see him, picturing the boy standing there behind the window, crunched up with excitement when he actually saw the barricades opening, and a girl coming out, in that sexy pyjama thing… He certainly does not lack brains. Has he worked it out? Wouldn't be altogether surprised to know he has – but he doesn't know it yet, and of course he can't say it. Rather go to prison – rather be torn in bits.' He got up and opened the door into the salon. There they all were, sitting stiff and glum. Now how was he going to tell the magistrate?

'Madame Dutheil – a moment if you please, in here… Just for the record, Madame. During the evening, your husband sent, as I hear, your daughter out of the room.'

'Yes – while we were having drinks before dinner. I knew that must be the root of it somehow. She came down in that frock you've seen – with the flappy pyjama-legs – that upset him, but she'd been rude to him that morning at breakfast already – it upset him all day. He was very nervous anyway – he always is when he's not working.' And there, he thought, is the thing in a nutshell,

'Did he go out of the room after her?'

'Yes,' said Laure, realising that though she still did not know, he did.

'How long was he away?'

'About ten minutes.'

'That's all, Madame, thank you. And give yourself no further anxiety – this will all blow over.' Would it, he wondered. Would the magistrate insist on an unlawful wounding charge?

Sabatier and Thomassen, called separately, confirmed the tale in different pieces. Total confirmation – without hesitations or sudden losses of memory – what model witnesses! They won't be asked to this house again in a hurry, he thought dryly.

Now – the chief villain has had long enough to cook.

'Monsieur Dutheil, if you please.' The fellow looked like death warmed up.

'Sit down. That's all right, we don't need Mr Thomas and his little book – this is just a private chat. You insist on baring your behind – it's an open invitation to kick it. What did you hit her with?'

'She told you?'

'Rather fortunately for you, she did.' If anything, he looked relieved.

'With a little stick that holds a plant up, on the staircase – on the first landing.' He didn't need to go and look – he knew it was there.

'Very well, Monsieur Dutheil. The magistrate will be here any minute, and he will have to decide whether you come under the unlawful wounding article of the code.'

'You mean – what have you decided?'

'I decide nothing. You did something exceptionally stupid, so stupid that it must be the work of an exceptionally stupid person. The weekly papers – you know the kind I'm talking about – would have a fine time with this if it came into court, wouldn't they?'

'God.'

'You're a bit late with your god. Go and think about it.'

Rather a severe punishment I've given him there, thought the commissaire, smiling to himself in a nasty way. The door opened and the secretary appeared. A bright woman. The few words he'd had with her at the start had put him on the right rails.

'Sorry Monsieur le Commissaire,' said Nora politely. 'The Parquet… This way, please, Monsieur le Substitut…'

There now, he had forgotten to send Dutheil upstairs to the girl. All they needed really was a good cry together!

'Bonjour, Monsieur.'

'Morning, Commissaire. What kind of nonsense is this?'

'You've picked the exact word,' said the commissaire gratefully.

He was a youngish forty, with fair hair and a full, handsome face. He was very spick and span, looking indeed as though laved in lavender water, and had a beautiful pair of trousers. At present he was in a slightly evil frame of mind.

'Damn it, Petitjean – the one night this week I'd promised myself some proper sleep. Why do these things always happen at two in the morning?'

'Night hours, Monsieur, old criminal habit – primitive beliefs, elemental attachment to the dark…'

'Yes yes, to you it's funny. Now what's going on? Isn't this Dutheil's house – the novelist's?'

'Quite right. Our criminal.'

'Good God! I've never been here myself – but the Procureur has dined here – by way of a friend of his. Now let me get to the bottom of this.'

'Shooting.'

'Passions?'

'Just a young man's – student of sorts. Came to have a behind-the-bushes meeting with the daughter. Was taken for an intruder in the dark.'

'Ah,' relieved that there were no passions. 'But that is pure accident. Why call on me? Come to that, what are you doing here?'

Yes, thought the commissaire, we do make a comic pair. Just look at him! – the magistrate had the kind of pale skin that reddens exposed to sun, and at two in the morning he had a snowy shirt and a greyish silk tie, and raw amethyst cuff-links, and he kept on looking at his gold wristwatch. Whereas his greffier, poor old sod, whom I've known for twenty years, is decidedly scruffy, with a shoelace broken and yes, tied in a granny-knot. These young magistrates – that awful Thomas was the same type, always washing his blasted white hands and filing his nails. Thomas looked in mirrors as he passed, and slid combs out surreptitiously – a magistrate was too well-bred to do such things but the pattern was the same. One couldn't show such people Véronique's behind! Or even Dutheil's…

'Monsieur le Substitut…' He would be very formal.

'I am all attention,' sitting down and putting his briefcase carefully on another chair. What did he want with a briefcase! To show it off – present from his mama, no doubt.

'Not altogether – an accident.'

'Not? Dutheil?' Horrified.

'An artist slipping if you like. A failed book, or a bad picture.'

'Commissaire – less metaphor, I beg.'

'Stupidity – banality – fatality.' In a few phrases the mechanics of Dutheil's three rifle-shots were exposed.

'And he fires – but what could be simpler?'

'The moment he sees the girl the burglar theory collapses. However – we have all the motivation: painfully simple. He had words with the girl, on some such point of conflict as staying out late. She was disrespectful, disobedient, mm? He sent her from the dinner-table last night.' (He was amused to see the magistrate, married one year, nodding in approval – bastard had one baby and an English nanny…) 'He is overwhelmed at the new defiance – breach of trust in opening his house to a stranger, assignation at night – the girl was in pyjamas.' By gum yes – the appeal for maintenance of parental authority was the safest gambit there was. 'I had better begin by inspecting the scene. No no, after you, Commissaire.'

The door opened upon a dulled and fatigued group.

'Madame… Monsieur. Honoured albeit distressed – we meet in ambiguous circumstances.' A good word that, thought the commissaire; I must remember to use that.

'Monsieur Sabatier – the publisher of course – delighted. And Monsieur Thomassen – an American guest? – well well, we must see what we can do to make your stay a pleasure… Is this the garden? *Je vous en prie*… Aha, I see, I see. Yes, we can certainly conclude that these shots were not aimed at any person. The gendarmerie was called? – splendid, no unlawful concealment. Well, Commissaire? No prohibited or concealed weapon, clear infraction of domicile and consequently no unlawful wounding. Aid brought immediately, neither denial, concealment, nor falsification – what are we left with?'

'Unintentional homicide,' in as flat a voice as he knew.

The magistrate was irritated.

'Come come, man, where are your wits? I'm not saying the grounds don't exist, since indeed it's the obvious one, but you can't bring a charge like that into court. The Procureur – good heavens, man, do you think I want to earn a reprimand? What d'you think the defence would be likely to consist of – something chosen off a free aid list? The cream, the tenors – you fancy yourself in the witness box? Now come man, don't sulk. Look at the facts. This girl – plainly harbouring resentful, revengeful – lets this boy into the house, wreak their immature moods and whims upon – I know these delinquents – see that in court: girl handing out flowers and kissing you – yes you – telling the President she believes in Loving the Fuzz. No no. Isolated district, no Police Secours within ten kilometres, householder entitled to a reasonable show of the armed hand – all laid down in the jurisprudence.' Let him talk, thought the commissaire, doing himself violence to keep his face thoughtful and respectful – he'll be giving me flowers next.

'Chilly out here,' muttered the magistrate suddenly. 'Don't be concerned. I'll speak severely to Monsieur Dutheil. I'll pull his ears for him.'

What shall we do with the drunken sailor early in the morning? Dutheil had been left alone. The uniformed policemen had all disappeared, quite likely been gathered up by Nora and drinking whisky in her office. Laure had gathered up a litter of glasses and coffee-cups and been escorted down to the kitchen by Marcus. And where the devil had Thomassen gone? Writing up his notes, no doubt – well let him, much good may it do him. Everybody writing up their notes – he was even denied access to his own library because that drip of a young police officer was writing up notes, with the magistrate's greffier on the other side of the table writing up – good grief, the entire household was scribbling busily away, his working room had been converted into an unsavoury annexe to the Palace of Justice, and he, whose business it was to write, who knew how, was left here to kick his heels and examine his conscience. I am just a nasty boy again, waiting to be called up by the Prefect of Discipline and expelled from school a second time.

What would that magistrate decide? That publicity in this instance was undesirable? One certainly cannot count on the Procureur having had his knees under my dining-room table! It will hang on a small thing: is this bland cream-faced young man a lawyer, or is he a wielder of legal doubletalk?

Nora had been desperately tactful, not letting herself be seen at all, bless her. And the boys – he was sure that they realised how every minute that passed did nothing but add to his humiliation, and did not wish to degrade him further. Marcus on the other hand – standing by to be sure of safeguarding a valuable piece of property – and that American; what does he want, what is he after? There isn't any 'understanding' involved.

Of course the boys might have gone off like two indifferent young bulls, thinking it a fuss about nothing. Véronique's beau had gone out tomcatting – a risk of leaving whiskers behind; they knew about that. So he was dead? At that age, thought Dutheil, one is not concerned. Vietnam or a traffic accident – kill a few more off; every blow against over-population is a good blow. There is now nothing dramatic or heroic about death – death is gravely out of fashion.

There wasn't even a policeman hanging about to see that he did nothing stupid. Why should they? He wasn't going to commit suicide or anything. He had never contemplated suicide in his life, though one was almost tempted to, now – just to show them... But one couldn't kill oneself just because reality slipped in for a second, touching one with a cold and sticky wing. Like Mr Jones, in the Conrad book, arriving on the desert island and saying 'I am the world, come to pay you a visit...' Well no, I am not going to play at being the neurotic popular novelist. I am just an ordinary working man, doing the job to earn a living like any other and grumbling about it. It is hard, hard, very hard, hard as any coal-miner's job. Do they think I should never be tired, never be frightened, never be sickened by hope deferred and thirst unsatisfied? I am a small man and here is the proof; I am not a murderer pleading insanity. Nobody is saner than Papa Dutheil.

The French window opened briskly with a draught of clean air, and the magistrate appeared, rubbing his hands, followed by the commissaire with a stone face and a cigarette in his mouth, unlit as usual – perhaps a stone cigarette? The air smelt of dew, trees, starlight. The door to the library whisked open at once and the subordinates came tumbling in with their paperwork. Nora – and Thomassen; what had they been plotting? – appeared like magic from the hall. Damn it, had all these people been listening at the door or what?

The magistrate's social manner was flawless. With the gentlest of emphasis on his position as arbiter of fate he took station in front of the chimneypiece, smiling agreeably at a portrait across the room. (Is it somebody one knows? – one has a vague feeling of having been introduced at someone's party? Or is it the Empress Maria Theresa?) The room had filled up again – Dutheil noticed, suddenly, that the two boys had reappeared, and Laure, and Marcus. Nora…of the evening party only Gilbert Royan was missing – but they had a Substitut for a substitute.

'Ah. Everyone is here – all the witnesses to an unhappy incident. That is what it is. I have read the depositions, I have examined the ground, I have benefited from the conclusions and experience of Monsieur le Commissaire. I find, I may say, nothing to support the laying of informations. The Court need take no cognisance of this occurrence and we may safely say,' with a little elegant bow towards Dutheil, slumped in a chair and beginning to look scruffy and unshaved, 'that the Republic is not threatened. However. There has been grave imprudence, negligence, haste, a failure to weigh the possible consequences of dangerous and careless manipulation of a loaded firearm. An unfortunate young man, with his career before him, has himself suffered the consequences of his own imprudence; it could – could it not, Monsieur Dutheil? – have been a member of your own family. A family mourns. It is neither my purpose nor function to speculate upon the likelihood – still less the success – of a possible civil action for damages. In the event of such my report will be placed before the court, as will the deposition of Monsieur le Commissaire containing the statements given him. While repeating that the office of the Procureur has in the immediately foreseeable future no voice in this matter I must urge upon you, Monsieur Dutheil, to think carefully about the consequences that this deplorable contretemps might well have had. Monsieur le Greffier, have you a full and exact account?'

'Yes, Monsieur.'

'Very well then, we will trouble you no further. Monsieur Dutheil, my thanks for your sympathetic understanding of my disagreeable duties. I shall greatly hope for the pleasure of meeting you in circumstances more advantageous to both of us. Madame, my most respectful homages. Ladies, gentlemen, good morning.'

Petitjean, his eyes malicious, stopped for a word with Dutheil. 'I need your signature on two or three papers – I'll send an inspector in the course of the morning. Seeing as how – I won't say you've got away with murder since that would clearly be usurping the functions of the magistrate – but seeing as how, I take the liberty to suggest that you make a little call upon the family of this boy – we'll have his identity very shortly. You say whatever comes into your head, hm?'

'Why did the magistrate make that decision?' asked Dutheil, very well aware of how stupid a question it was.

'Why,' casually, 'that's an American journalist you have there, right? I guess he just wished to give the press a favourable view of justice back here in the woods. Mm? I'll say goodbye now.'

Laure was conducting the magistrate to his car, since her husband was doing a rooted-to-the-spot act not unfamiliar to her. Marcus, Nora, the boys they had all vanished as quick as a flash leaving a heavy smell of tact behind. None of them would ever by the slightest word or sign allude to the last three hours – was it really only three hours? Yes – time to get some sleep still, before a splendidly normal breakfast. Even Véronique would get up, and go to class, very likely, to make sure that nothing had happened at all.

Only Thomassen was left: fellow had no tact and Dutheil felt a certain sympathy for him – not for the first time. Was not this fellow, perhaps, the one person who at moments looked like understanding? He found a crumpled pack of cigarettes, and held them out to the American as a clumsy way of showing there was no hostility, and that he badly wanted – what was it he wanted? Not sympathy. Could one talk about friendship, still?

Thomassen took one.

'Well…if I had wanted to give you an impression of life in the castle I'd have done better to stick to croquet, huh?'

The American smiled faintly. Why say faintly, wondered Dutheil; a weak, fainting word, meaning without conviction. It was a silver-point smile. Faint, but the line is not easy to rub out.

'Any of us has passages out of which he comes no better. Any of us. You don't need to be a court reporter to appreciate Judge Jeffreys.'

'You need to be Christ, though, to appreciate Pontius Pilate.'

Thomassen's laugh was genuine.

'If Pontius Pilate's court reporter had realised he was on to a best-seller, don't you think he'd have altered the script?'

'I gave you a lecture,' said Dutheil. 'Forget it. And you were asked to sign a lot of warranties – tear them up. I'll talk to Nora. Get some sleep – leave a note on your door for the servants, telling them what time you want breakfast. I have to get up at six and write a book, but you enjoy some comfort. Remember we're both guests in a high-class hotel.' He walked over to the window.

'One unbolted window and the castle was stormed,' said Thomassen with no irony.

'Not bad,' answered Dutheil seriously. 'You've got a theme. Better than that Shakespearean crap I gave you last night.'

He walked out on to the terrace. The starlight was paler, but the cloud had broken and it was clear. Was it perhaps turning silvery already over the mountains? – no, false dawn. Last night's sunset had been a bouquet of sweet peas. Nile green, and lilac. Lime, lemon, lavender. Vermilion, carmine, crimson lake. Can one have sweet peas of that particular burnt-orange shade, Dutheil asked himself anxiously. It would be a silver-point dawn, on Chinese-white washed paper. Another splendid day for the vintage. If this year's wine were not a good one then he was Edgar Wallace. He would like to have a good serious bossy talk with Kieffer: a pity that he had to go and start a book. No time like the present, he thought, heading for the library.

# Five

He held the rifle cuddled into his shoulder, looking over the sight, breathing shallowly through his mouth. A nerve screamed at him and the barrel wobbled; he made an effort and loosened his arm and shoulder. Véronique's feet pattered swift and noiseless across the terrace. On the steps she turned and glanced fearfully up at his balcony, and his arm became tense again. Fire now and hit a star…

She seemed to have lost courage. Was he visible? Could one see anything? – the blue steel of the barrel would not reflect, and the hooded lens of the telescopic sight would catch no light unless she was almost in line with it, and mercifully, she wasn't – it was pointing ahead, at the door of that awful little hut. She went on down the steps. Now he could only see her head. He stood in the shadow of the tall wooden shutter and looked through the sight. The graduated T of the pointers fell exactly on the small of her back, and vertigo almost pressed the trigger. They had a terribly light action, these rifles, and a double trigger. Release the back one and the faintest touch on the front sent a copper-jacket seven-six-four into the small of a girl's back. He felt as though he were standing on top of the church spire, and shut his eyes.

When he next looked there was nothing. He put the sight on the window, wiped the sweat out of his sighting eye, and smeared the middle of his trigger hand against his pants; it was white and bloodless. The cold metal felt wet and slippery, and burned his cheek. One could see nothing. A cobweb. He longed to send shots smashing into that windowpane, sighted into the centre of the cobweb, his finger pressed the back trigger. Anything would now suffice – the faintest twitch of a nerve in the cold cramped hand…

Slowly the rifle traversed, across rough creosoted boards, full of knots and chinks, while he breathed in the smell of musty cushions, rotted grass, and lubricating oil. The 'thatch' – was it bamboo? Reed of some kind, bound in bundles with some kind of withe; he had never looked closely. For a moment of pain he wondered whether to fire at the skyline or the trees, explaining innocently later that he had seen a nightjar. It would get the mice out of the mouse-hole, and he could see them already, floundering in a sticky bog of embarrassment under his sardonic eye.

It was not a thought of much dignity, he told himself regretfully, and lowered the rifle with a kind of sadness. What is lacking – courage? Why do I not walk downstairs, out through the opened shutter, following that slut's footsteps through the dew, with the gun in my armpit. And kick the door in… Shotgun wedding, boys. And would that not be even more ignoble than to put a bullet through the thatch from here? I could try for that goddam iron squirrel – why have I never thought of that? Instead he found himself on one knee, holding the rifle on his thigh, working the bolt and catching the three cartridges in the air as they popped up. He turned his back resolutely, went to get a drink of water, put the big rifle regretfully back in the cupboard. Remember to tell Figaro tomorrow to take it back to the gun-room. Can't have rifles in the bedroom. Shoot a burglar and you were more outside the law than he was.

He stood by his bed, reminded – amusing, that – of an elderly neighbour in his childhood, an immensely polished elderly gentleman with a pretty little manor house and a small farm. What had been the old boy's name? He had been something in the École de Chartres, spoke in a literary, elegant, elaborate style that somehow in him had not been in the least unnatural or affected. Very tall, dry, with a tweed Norfolk jacket and knickerbockers, and the manners of a duke.

He had been kind to the boy, and sometimes let him come along on a little walk around the domain – sometimes the Swann way, sometimes the Guermantes way. He did not carry a gun, being far too distinguished – he had a silver-mounted stick with a pear-shaped knob of chased silver, which he carried under his arm as though it were a gun. And an antique labrador with a faded elegance walked slowly after him. One day they had come to a gap in the hedge, and a deeply hollowed nest in the ripe corn of the field beyond. The old gentleman. had stopped to look at it in as near a thing to indignation as he allowed himself to reach.

'Fornicators,' he had said in his exquisite old voice. 'Effing fornicators.' A long pause, while he twirled the stick, before adding, in a tone of elegiac regret, 'Lucky, lucky, lucky fornicators.'

What are you going to do? The strange thing was that he knew perfectly well. He had to get into bed and go peacefully to sleep, deliberately oblivious of his daughter. That was easy enough, it seemed at first sight. Could he not tell himself that however appalling a thing it was that Véronique had chosen to do it was now too late to interfere? The time for 'training' a girl was – well, whenever it was, it wasn't now.

He became suddenly so angry that his whole body clenched in a nervous spasm that shook the whole bed, so that Laure rolled over, seemed about to wake up, and even lifted her head off the pillow. He managed to stay very still, and she flopped again. Everything tickled, and he wanted to give the blankets a horrible great kick, but he held it down. Like holding out against seasickness out of sheer pride, or not letting Kieffer see how fed up you were with grapes at vintage time.

Would that not be the most difficult? – to persevere… Not only must he allow Véronique to do whatever she was doing – he writhed and snatched a cigarette, and bit it deliberately to get a nasty taste on his tongue. He must not let her see that he knew. He could beat her, yell at her, sneer at her – but he must not act like the Prefect of Discipline with Rosemary Hamilton-Smith. He must be quite clear

– he might have a whore for a daughter but he was not having any fallen women.

What would have happened if he had fired? It would have been worse; much worse. To take his mind off the pain he started to think about it. After five minutes he realised he was not going to sleep. That was of no consequence now. He could sleep at any time. He would have to talk to that American though. He had made a gross idiot of himself there. The extraordinary mania that all writers have for seeing everything that happens to them as a scene in a book… Well, this time he would make it serve.

He went down to the library and turned the desk light on. That would give Véronique an abominable fright – she would wonder whether he had noticed the shutter in the salon. Not to speak of tiptoeing past! Do her good. Nothing like a few added risks to lend flavour to the experience.

Rather sadly, thinking of what a hopeless father he was, but happy as he always was when starting a book, he chose a new exercise book and threw a handful of ballpoints on the table. It would give his opening pages an unusual colour knowing of Véronique out there, and nobody would ever know but him. It didn't matter how much one told American journalists, how public one's life became – there would always be plenty of secrets over.

# Nicolas Freeling

## Castang's City

An intriguing case presents itself to Castang where assassination and terrorism are the order of the day. A deputy mayor is murdered and his family, friends and colleagues are all suspects. In this pulsing mystery, Freeling lets loose a quirky, inventive crime fiction that should taunt and tease.

## The Dresden Green

The placid freedom of whiling away the hours on holiday seems like a dream. But there's no rest for the wicked. At least, not where Louis Schweitzer is concerned. After a day in the countryside, Schweitzer is back home, having murdered two victims and now in possession of a most amazing gem. Follow the twists and turns of an incredible story of love, betrayal, a Communist crime ring, a naked girl at gunpoint and four more murders by a master of storytelling.

# NICOLAS FREELING

## A LONG SILENCE

For Piet van der Valk it was just another ordinary case. No crime had been committed. It was just a matter of following a lead on a wealthy Amsterdam jeweller. But two bullets put paid to curiosity. For Piet van der Valk, this ordinary case turns out to be his last.

## LOVE IN AMSTERDAM

Elsa de Charmoy is found shot with a Mauser 765; a gun bought by her lover Martin who swears he hasn't seen her for five years. But Inspector van der Valk, the unorthodox hero of Freeling's crime blockbusters, has misgivings and applies a subtle, insidious pressure in a masterly performance of police interrogation. Martin is driven to examine his past culminating in an edgy and ultra-hypnotic reprise for van der Valk amidst the streets and cafes of Amsterdam.

'Unusual, absorbing, and altogether not to be missed'
*The Sunday Times*

# NICOLAS FREELING

## VALPARAISO

The peaceful bay of Porquerolles looks out over the waters to Toulon and to Kapitan, an extraordinary drifter who lives for his beloved boat, *Olivia*, bobbing among the bustling blue of the shores. Kapitan is an enigma; a man who has sailed the Mediterranean for years. When Kapitan is given a chance to raise money for his boat he swoops at the chance, but this seemingly unassailable plan leads to big trouble in a little harbour.

## WOLFNIGHT

Replete with the volatile tensions of a political thriller, Freeling introduces the reader to the nebulous, frightening world of conspiracy. Henri Castang, renowned police inspector, is called in to investigate a car accident involving a French politician and his mistress. When Castang uncovers a top-level plot linking industrial and political leaders, he takes the law into his own hands with what turns out to be incredible consequences.

'Wolfnight has it all – politics, sex, metaphysics'
*The New York Times*

'Exhilaratingly rich in wit and humanity, indignant at the right things' *Detroit News*

## OTHER TITLES BY NICOLAS FREELING AVAILABLE DIRECT FROM HOUSE OF STRATUS

| Quantity | | £ | $(US) | $(CAN) | € |
|---|---|---|---|---|---|
| ☐ | The Back of the North Wind | 6.99 | 11.50 | 16.95 | 11.50 |
| ☐ | Castang's City | 6.99 | 11.50 | 16.95 | 11.50 |
| ☐ | A City Solitary | 6.99 | 11.50 | 16.95 | 11.50 |
| ☐ | Cold Iron | 6.99 | 11.50 | 16.95 | 11.50 |
| ☐ | Criminal Conversation | 6.99 | 11.50 | 16.95 | 11.50 |
| ☐ | Double-Barrel | 6.99 | 11.50 | 16.95 | 11.50 |
| ☐ | The Dresden Green | 6.99 | 11.50 | 16.95 | 11.50 |
| ☐ | A Dressing of Diamond | 6.99 | 11.50 | 16.95 | 11.50 |
| ☐ | A Dwarf Kingdom | 6.99 | 11.50 | 16.95 | 11.50 |
| ☐ | Gadget | 6.99 | 11.50 | 16.95 | 11.50 |
| ☐ | Gun Before Butter | 6.99 | 11.50 | 16.95 | 11.50 |
| ☐ | The King of the Rainy Country | 6.99 | 11.50 | 16.95 | 11.50 |
| ☐ | Lady Macbeth | 6.99 | 11.50 | 16.95 | 11.50 |
| ☐ | Lake Isle | 6.99 | 11.50 | 16.95 | 11.50 |
| ☐ | A Long Silence | 6.99 | 11.50 | 16.95 | 11.50 |
| ☐ | Love in Amsterdam | 6.99 | 11.50 | 16.95 | 11.50 |
| ☐ | The Night Lords | 6.99 | 11.50 | 16.95 | 11.50 |

ALL HOUSE OF STRATUS BOOKS ARE AVAILABLE FROM GOOD BOOKSHOPS OR DIRECT FROM THE PUBLISHER:

**Internet:** **www.houseofstratus.com** including author interviews, reviews, features.

**Email:** **sales@houseofstratus.com** please quote author, title and credit card details.

## OTHER TITLES BY NICOLAS FREELING AVAILABLE DIRECT FROM HOUSE OF STRATUS

| Quantity | | £ | $(US) | $(CAN) | € |
|---|---|---|---|---|---|
| ☐ | No Part in Your Death | 6.99 | 11.50 | 16.95 | 11.50 |
| ☐ | Not as Far as Velma | 6.99 | 11.50 | 16.95 | 11.50 |
| ☐ | One Damn Thing After Another | 6.99 | 11.50 | 16.95 | 11.50 |
| ☐ | Over the High Side | 6.99 | 11.50 | 16.95 | 11.50 |
| ☐ | The Pretty How Town | 6.99 | 11.50 | 16.95 | 11.50 |
| ☐ | Sandcastles | 6.99 | 11.50 | 16.95 | 11.50 |
| ☐ | The Seacoast of Bohemia | 6.99 | 11.50 | 16.95 | 11.50 |
| ☐ | Strike Out Where Not Applicable | 6.99 | 11.50 | 16.95 | 11.50 |
| ☐ | Those in Peril | 6.99 | 11.50 | 16.95 | 11.50 |
| ☐ | Tsing Boum | 6.99 | 11.50 | 16.95 | 11.50 |
| ☐ | Valparaiso | 6.99 | 11.50 | 16.95 | 11.50 |
| ☐ | What Are the Bugles Blowing For? | 6.99 | 11.50 | 16.95 | 11.50 |
| ☐ | The Widow | 6.99 | 11.50 | 16.95 | 11.50 |
| ☐ | Wolfnight | 6.99 | 11.50 | 16.95 | 11.50 |
| ☐ | You Who Know | 6.99 | 11.50 | 16.95 | 11.50 |

ALL HOUSE OF STRATUS BOOKS ARE AVAILABLE FROM GOOD BOOKSHOPS OR DIRECT FROM THE PUBLISHER:

**Hotline:** UK ONLY: 0800 169 1780, please quote author, title and credit card details.
INTERNATIONAL: +44 (0) 20 7494 6400, please quote author, title, and credit card details.

**Send to:** **House of Stratus Sales Department**
**24c Old Burlington Street**
**London**
**W1X 1RL**
**UK**

Please allow for postage costs charged per order plus an amount per book as set out in the tables below:

| | £(Sterling) | $(US) | $(CAN) | €(Euros) |
|---|---|---|---|---|
| **Cost per order** | | | | |
| UK | 2.00 | 3.00 | 4.50 | 3.30 |
| Europe | 3.00 | 4.50 | 6.75 | 5.00 |
| North America | 3.00 | 4.50 | 6.75 | 5.00 |
| Rest of World | 3.00 | 4.50 | 6.75 | 5.00 |
| **Additional cost per book** | | | | |
| UK | 0.50 | 0.75 | 1.15 | 0.85 |
| Europe | 1.00 | 1.50 | 2.30 | 1.70 |
| North America | 2.00 | 3.00 | 4.60 | 3.40 |
| Rest of World | 2.50 | 3.75 | 5.75 | 4.25 |

PLEASE SEND CHEQUE, POSTAL ORDER (STERLING ONLY), EUROCHEQUE, OR INTERNATIONAL MONEY ORDER (PLEASE CIRCLE METHOD OF PAYMENT YOU WISH TO USE)
MAKE PAYABLE TO: STRATUS HOLDINGS plc

**Cost of book(s):** ______________ Example: 3 x books at £6.99 each: £20.97
**Cost of order:** ______________ Example: £2.00 (Delivery to UK address)
**Additional cost per book:** ______________ Example: 3 x £0.50: £1.50
**Order total including postage:** ______________ Example: £24.47

Please tick currency you wish to use and add total amount of order:

☐ £ (Sterling) ☐ $ (US) ☐ $ (CAN) ☐ € (EUROS)

VISA, MASTERCARD, SWITCH, AMEX, SOLO, JCB:

☐☐☐☐☐☐☐☐☐☐☐☐☐☐☐☐☐☐☐☐

**Issue number (Switch only):**

☐☐☐

**Start Date:** ☐☐/☐☐ **Expiry Date:** ☐☐/☐☐

**Signature:** ______________

NAME: ______________

ADDRESS: ______________

______________

POSTCODE: ______________

Please allow 28 days for delivery.

Prices subject to change without notice.
Please tick box if you do not wish to receive any additional information. ☐